A DANCE with DARKNESS

OTHERWORLD ACADEMY
book 1

JENNA WOLFHART

A Dance with Darkness

Book One of the Otherworld Academy Series

Cover Design by Covers by Juan

Original Copyright © 2018 by Jenna Wolfhart

Second Edition Copyright © 2020 by Jenna Wolfhart

All rights reserved.

No part of this book may be reproduced in any form or by any electronic or mechanical means, including information storage and retrieval systems, without written permission from the author, except for the use of brief quotations in a book review.

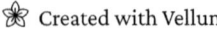 Created with Vellum

CHAPTER ONE

It all started with bright lights and pulsing music. Bass reverberated through my body as I moved my arms and legs to the beat. My best and oldest friend, Bree, spun in circles by my side, basking in the neon glow of the club. Hot pink and emerald lights bounced off the walls. It was my eighteenth birthday, and I'd only had one request. I wanted to go somewhere I could dance.

Out of the corner of my eye, a tall hooded figure caught my attention. The guy was staring right at me with eyes the color of midnight. A spark of heat burst into my cheeks as I cast a sideways glance his way. He stood away from the crowd, leaning against the neon-lit wall with his arms crossed over his muscular chest. His gaze was dark and hooded and strangely intense.

With a slight shiver, I frowned and glanced away.

The upbeat song spiralled away, replaced by a more melancholy tune that chased away my feverish dance energy. I loved dancing, more than I loved most anything else, to any beat, to any song, but there was nothing quite like a fast tempo to get my feet moving. Now that the rhythm had slowed, I finally realized just how long we'd spent on the dance floor. My breath was ragged, my mouth parched.

Bree leaned forward and grabbed my arm. "Come on. Let's try to buy a drink."

I opened my mouth to argue, but it was no use. Bree was a force of nature, and once she got an idea into her head, there was no talking her out of it.

When we stepped foot off the dance floor, my eyes were instinctively drawn to where the strange hooded guy had been watching me. He was gone, replaced by nothing but the swirling neon lights. A twinge of disappointment went through me, even though that was completely ridiculous. It had been a long time since a guy had given me even the most fleeting of glances. All the guys from school knew me, well enough to know to stay as far away from me as they could. I was the weird girl who kept to herself, the one who nobody liked. No one except for Bree.

It had been nice to feel like maybe I wasn't the pariah everyone at school thought I was.

We reached the bar at the far end of the club, and Bree hoisted herself up onto one of the iron stools. It was a weekday, so the place was pretty empty. A huge plus in my opinion. I wanted to dance, free and wild. Not get trapped in a sweaty mess of grinding college students.

Bree patted the stool next to her. "Come on, Norah. One drink won't kill you."

"No, but my mom might kill me if she found out." Still, I hopped up on the stool and dug my elbows into the slick iron surface of the bar top. Warehouse 27 was one of those trendy industrial places, set inside an old warehouse that had once been used for freight storage. Everything was iron or steel, and every wall was covered in intricately-designed graffiti.

Not only would my mom kill me if she found out I was drinking. She'd kill me if she even knew I was here.

"What'll you have?" The bartender strode up to the bar, giving both me and Bree a long stare before flipping two coasters in front of us. He didn't look much older than us, his dark shaggy hair falling into his eyes.

I glanced at Bree and raised an eyebrow. I certainly didn't know what to order.

"Two vodka and tonics," she said with a smile and a confidence that suggested she'd ordered drinks at bars a thousand times before. But that was all for show. She hadn't. We might live in the city that never sleeps, but we rarely stayed up past our bedtimes.

The bartender nodded and grabbed some glasses from under the bar before he gave me a nod, his eyes locked on something behind me. "Looks like you have an admirer."

An admirer? Was it that hooded guy from before? My heart lurched, and I slid my chin onto my shoulder to glance behind me. A tall figure in a deep green cloak now stood in the center of the dance floor, his eyes locked on my face. He wasn't dancing, a fact that made the chills sweep down my back again.

For a moment, I thought it was the same guy,

though his cloak was a different color. But there was something strange about this one. A sheen of light whispered across his skin, almost as if he were glowing from the inside out. I blinked and shook my head. That was impossible. The club lights were playing tricks on my eyes. But when I lifted my gaze to the dance floor again, he was gone.

"Norah," my best friend said as she leaned her face close to mine, her breath a cloud of vodka and cigarette smoke. "You okay?"

"Yeah. I just thought I saw something..." The world seemed to tilt sideways, and my vision went blurry. Ears ringing and mouth dry, I drew quick breaths in through my nose. Everything around me was suddenly loud, loud, loud, and the pulsing lights made my head spin. I pressed my hands against the bar top to hold myself steady, but that did nothing but launch a lump of nausea into my throat.

"Norah. What's wrong?" My best friend's voice sounded so far away, as if she were on the other end of a broken cell phone. A hand curled around my arm, pulling me away from the bar.

As soon as I'd made it three steps, my head began to clear, but the clammy sensation on my palms remained.

Bree's head ducked to mine. Her grip stayed tight around my arm, and I could see now that she was pulling me in the direction of the women's restroom. "What the hell's going on? Is it another one of those panic attacks?"

"Yes. No. I don't know." For the past couple of

weeks, I'd been experiencing increasingly overwhelming panic attacks, or so the doctors said. Heart palpitations, nausea, clammy hands, blurry vision, shortness of breath. It all fit. The problem—to me, at least—was that I never felt *panicked* when I had one of these so-called panic attacks.

They happened for no discernible reason, at least that I could tell.

One minute, I was fine. The next? I could barely see straight.

"Do you have your pills on you?" she asked as she pushed open the grimy black door that led into the women's restroom. I wrinkled my nose at the smell, my eyes darting from the yellow sinks to the mound of wet, crumpled paper towels that were spilling from an overflowing trash can.

"Yeah, I brought them just in case, but I can't manage to swallow them without some water." I pointed to the yellow sink. "And I'm not drinking from that."

She gave a nod without a moment's hesitation. "Okay, stay here and take some deep breaths. I'll get a glass of water from the bar."

She disappeared from the bathroom a moment later. Sighing, I leaned against the sink and stared at my reflection in the cloudy mirror. I looked about as good as I felt. There were dark circles under my eyes, and my complexion was so pale that my skin now matched my light blonde hair. Frankly, I looked like I'd seen a ghost that had been tormenting me for years.

These panic attacks were starting to seriously suck

ass, and the doctor had said I wouldn't improve until I figured out the trigger. She thought it might have something to do with my home life, but I wasn't home now. I hadn't even been thinking of my step-dad, much less feeling panicked about him. The only thing that could have set it off was the strange guy who had been watching me...

The door pushed open, and my shoulders relaxed. Whether or not these were actual panic attacks, the medicine *did* make me feel better. I could take the pill, splash some cold water on my face, and go back to swirling around the dance floor until the sun broke through the morning sky.

But a figure much taller and much more muscular than Bree stepped through the door. His dark hood no longer obscured his pale, gleaming face, though his black eyes were just as piercing, if not more so.

I sucked in a sharp breath and took a step back. My heart began to tremble in my chest. What the hell was he doing in the women's restroom? Had he followed me in here?

"Tonight's your eighteenth birthday," he said in a low rumble of a voice, one that was almost lyrical, like he had an Irish or Welsh accent. It sent shivers down my spine.

Swallowing hard, I stared at him. What was this? Some sort of strange pick-up line? I hadn't been out at clubs and bars enough to know the difference, but this seemed like a bizarre way to approach a girl who had caught your eye.

He let out an irritated sigh when I didn't respond.

"That is why you're here, yes? To celebrate your eighteenth birthday."

"Yes." A pause. "Why are you asking?"

He nodded. "Good. Can I see your ears?"

My mouth almost dropped open. "*Can you see my ears?*"

He took a step closer, a move I matched with a step away, forcing me closer to the wall behind me. I didn't dare move too far back. If I did, I would quite literally be backed up against a wall, and I was feeling more than a little freaked out—and, oddly, a little excited— by this strange guy who had cornered me in a women's restroom at a club.

Where the hell was Bree?

"Yes." Another impatient sigh. "I need to see your ears."

"Yeah, I don't think so, buddy." I crossed my arms over my chest and narrowed my eyes, hoping the stance made me look a lot more confident and in control than the trembling heart in my chest suggested. "I'm flattered, but I'm not interested. Now, if you don't mind, could you leave the women's restroom? I have some business I need to tend to in the toilet."

Inwardly, I groaned. *I have some business I need to tend to in the toilet? Why the hell did you have to say that?!*

His lips quirked, but the intensity of his gaze didn't falter. "Just let me see your ears, and I'll leave you to tend to your business. In the toilet."

For a moment, my resolve weakened, despite every logical bone in my body telling me to get the hell away from him. He was strange and unsettling. He'd followed me into the restroom, demanding to see my ears for reasons I didn't understand. And he wasn't being at all friendly. Instead, he seemed almost irritated, as if this entire exchange was some kind of chore, one that was very much beneath him.

But I still had this strange, inexplicable urge to give him whatever he asked. I felt almost drawn to him, as if my body recognized him even if my mind and my eyes did not. Had we met before? He wasn't someone from school, not unless he'd graduated several years before.

He stepped closer. This time, I did not take a step back. His cool hand brushed my cheek as he slid my long, blonde hair behind my ear. My heart hammered, so fast that I could barely breathe. Everything within me felt tight and tense, and a strange scent whispered into my nose. A combination of mint and frost and night.

"Ah, just as we thought," he murmured almost too low for me to make out the words. "It is you."

"Just as *who* thought?" My eyes were locked on his face, at the way his skin glistened underneath the yellow glow of the fluorescent lights.

He stepped back, and the strange magic of the moment vanished as he pulled the hood back over his head and the door swung open to reveal Bree. Her eyes bugged out of her head, and her grip on the water glass tightened, but the strange guy—whose name I still didn't know—completely ignored her presence.

"Don't take that pill." And with that, he strode

away, leaving me gaping after him. I slid my hand over my ear and gasped. It had a small bump near the top in the shape of a tiny pointed tooth. A bump that hadn't been there this morning. A bump that hadn't been there in all my eighteen years on this earth.

Was that what he had been looking for? And if so, why?

I needed to go after him and find out.

CHAPTER TWO

"Who the hell was that?" Bree stared at the door as if it had grown a pair of wings. "And why did he tell you not to take the medicine?"

"You know what? I wish I knew." I grabbed her arm and pulled her toward the door. "Come on. Let's follow him and ask."

But her feet didn't follow. Instead, she stayed rooted to the spot, her lips curled down into a frown. She held up the water glass and raised her eyebrows. "You need to take your anxiety medicine, Norah."

"I'll take it later," I said. "If we don't go after him now, we might lose him."

For a moment, I didn't think she would budge. Bree, as much as she was my best friend, had always had a protective streak when it came to me, more so than my parents. Hell, I hadn't even met my own dad. Sometimes, I appreciated that someone was looking out for me, particularly since my own family liked to make my life a living hell. Other times, like now, I just wanted her to be my partner in crime.

She must have seen it in the look on my face because she lowered the glass to the restroom counter and gave me a signature Bree grin. "Alright, I'm in. Let's find out what he's up to. But after that? You need to take your medicine."

I let out a sigh of relief, which made me realize just how much I'd been hoping she'd say yes. The strange guy was more than just a random creep. I could feel it in my gut. There was a reason he'd told me not to take my medicine. There was a reason he wanted to see my ears. He knew something about what I'd been going through, and I was determined to find out what it was.

For the past few weeks, I'd felt like I was going crazy. Maybe, just maybe, there was reason to think I wasn't.

Bree and I pushed through the restroom door to step back into the neon glow of the club. While I'd been inside, the space had begun to fill. The crowd had thickened, and the bar was surrounded by at least two dozen patrons in need of a drink. It made it almost impossible to pick out a single guy in dark clothes.

My eyes scanned the warehouse. There he was. By the door. He stood with three other guys, their heads bowed together as they spoke. Each of them wore those strange hooded cloaks, though all in different colors. Black, gold, red, and green.

As if they could sense my gaze, they all turned my way in unison, and my lungs tightened in response. Every single one of them was inexplicably gorgeous, just like the one who had cornered me in the restroom. Their eyes were bright and piercing, even at this distance. And their skin...they all had a strange sheen, though in differing shades of brightness. The one in red practically glowed like the sun.

"There they are," I hissed to Bree, pointing across the warehouse. "What the hell is up with their skin, especially the one on the far left?"

Bree frowned. "Yeah, I see him with some other guys, but I don't really know what you mean. Their skin looks normal to me. I mean, it's crazy clear, which I'm jealous of, but that's about it. I would kill to get rid of my damn acne."

"No, I don't mean that." Frowning, I shot a glance at my friend. "It looks like they're glowing."

Bree's eyes cut sideways, and her jaw flinched. "You sure you don't want to take your anxiety meds? I feel like maybe it's a bad idea not to follow the doctor's instructions."

"You think I'm making it up." I took a step away from her, shaking my head. "You think I'm going crazy, even if you like to pretend you think otherwise."

"I don't think you're crazy, Norah, but I think you aren't quite yourself." She gestured at the four guys who were still looking our way, watching our exchange with a strange detached curiosity on their faces. "You think they have glowing skin. Pretend for a minute that you weren't the one saying that. Don't you hear how strange that sounds?"

I blew out a hot breath and tried not to give in to the flicker of pain I felt deep in my gut at her words.

Yes, I knew it sounded crazy. And yes, I'd be skeptical if I didn't see it with my own eyes. And yes, maybe there was something very wrong with me. Normal people didn't go around thinking people had glowing skin. But I didn't *feel* crazy. This felt right. It felt real.

Though maybe no one ever really feels crazy, even if they are.

"Look, I have to talk to them, even if you think all of this is in my head." I shrugged and blinked back the tears that were beginning to well in my eyes. "Hell, maybe I am imagining everything. But if I talk to them, maybe I can at least find out the truth. Don't bother coming along."

I strode away from her, knowing full well that she was staring after me with a conflicted expression of hurt and worry flickering across her pixie features. I'd told her not to come along, so she wouldn't. Bree was like that. She always did whatever she could to keep the peace when it came to our friendship.

As I made my way across the warehouse, the four guys turned to each other before casting one last furtive glance my way. The one with the golden cloak opened the door, and they filed out of the bar quicker than I could reach them. With a frustrated sigh, I upped my pace, desperate to speak to them before I lost them to the nighttime city streets.

When I pushed open the door, a blast of hot summer air rushed into my face, bringing with it the cloying stench of rotting trash, exhaust fumes, and baking asphalt. The city could turn into a heat trap at the height of summer, even at night, when temperatures tiptoed into the mid-90's at times.

There were a few clusters of smokers camped outside the gray club, lazily discussing the most recent superhero film they'd seen in the theatre. They didn't even glance my way as I whirled in circles trying spot the four strange guys with the weird skin that apparently no one but me could see.

There they were, halfway down the one-way street, walking in the direction of Delancey Street. I rushed after them, picking up my pace to catch up with them. They walked side-by-side, their arms relaxed by their sides. One of their backs stiffened—the one who had followed me into the bathroom. He glanced over his shoulder and caught my eye. In an instant, he'd turned toward the others, and soon they were walking at a speed that was impossible to fathom. They didn't look as though they were running, but they were certainly moving faster than any normal person could.

They reached the corner within seconds and disappeared to the left. I kept following, though I knew it was no use. When I reached the corner myself, they were nowhere to be seen. They'd disappeared somewhere in the depths of the Manhattan streets, and I knew without a doubt that there was no way in hell I would find them. Not unless they wanted me to.

I shoved open my bedroom window with the tips of my fingers as I perched on the fire escape outside of our third-floor apartment. The chipped wooden frame shuddered at hurricane-level decibels.

I paused and sucked hot air into my nostrils. Closed my eyes and counted to ten. If the noise filtered out of my room, down the hall and into the ears of my sleeping parents, Mom would barrel right through the locked door, her intricately-painted nails clutching the fabric of her nightgown into a silky flower of panic. And then that panic would bubble into anger. And then pool into disappointment and distrust. Just like always.

Next time you sneak out, she'd told me last weekend, *you're grounded for a month.*

Even though I was eighteen-years-old, and even though I'd graduated from high school last month, Mom kept a tight grip on what I could and couldn't do. And if I got grounded for a month, I wouldn't be able to attend any auditions, my only chance of getting out of my rut of a life. And moving out of this hellhole of an apartment.

But despite the window's avalanche of noise, not a single whisper of movement stirred inside the apartment. I threw my legs over the window frame and hauled myself over the ledge behind it. After I closed the window, I padded over to my bedside table in boots that squished into the carpet, reaching for the neon blue lamp. And when I flipped the switch, several sights smacked me in the face all at once. Open drawers. Open laptop on my desk. Scribbled sheet of notebook paper on my pillow.

The paper held only three simple, non-threatening words. Well, non-threatening in most situations, anyway. But those three words on this particular night. On that particular sheet of paper. In that familiar loopy scrawl. Well, it was enough to make my stomach sink through the floorboards to join the rats that lived there despite the number of times the landlord had bombed them with poisonous fumes.

Living room. - Mom

Brilliant. For a split second, I considered ignoring the note and crawling under my whisper-thin sheets before Mom could realize I'd slithered back home, but deep down I knew it would be way worse if I did. She'd get my step-dad involved. And if she told him about it, my punishment would be far, far worse than a simple grounding.

I shivered at the thought of what he might do.

With a heavy sigh, I kicked off my boots and cracked open my bedroom door. It was silent and still in the apartment, like the calm before a storm. From down the hallway, I could hear the distant sound of snoring, a sound that set my frazzled nerves at ease. Mom might be awake and waiting for me in the living room, but Dan clearly wasn't.

I didn't have to be afraid.

My doctor had taught me a few coping mechanisms when it came to panic, though they really only helped when I wasn't already, you know, panicking.

Still, they slowed my rapid heartbeat at times like this, when I dreaded walking from my bedroom and into the rest of the apartment. I closed my eyes and took deep breaths in through my nose and out through barely parted lips, repeating it until the veins in my neck didn't feel as though they were throbbing against my skin.

I left the safety of my bedroom and tiptoed across the hallway to find Mom waiting for me on the sofa. She glanced up from her book, her long legs curled underneath a scratchy woollen blanket. Even in the dead heat of summer, she always had to have a blanket. Her black as night hair hung in natural waves around her bony shoulders, and her silver-rimmed glasses perched on the tip of her pencil-thin nose. Everything about her screamed librarian, maybe because she was one.

"Norah." She frowned and eyed me over the rim of her glasses before closing her book. She patted the empty spot on the brown leather couch. I bet she'd been waiting all night to make that exact move. "Come sit."

"I know what you're going to say." I held my ground and curled my toes against the hardwood floor. If she was going to take away the most important thing to me—my auditions, my dancing—then I needed to hear those harsh words standing up. Otherwise, they might knock me flat on my ass.

"I said, come sit."

My feet tried to grow roots, but it was no use. I made my way over to the couch while the AC buzzed like a thousand angry insects. Mom's dark brown eyes followed my every movement as I sunk into the soft leather and twisted my legs underneath me.

"By the stamp on your hand, I assume you went out to some club."

"I did."

"Did you have a nice time?" she asked.

I blinked at the words. They were a total 180 on her usual rapid-fire accusations and red-faced puffs. She must have found my empty room hours ago, and all the anger boiled off while she waited on this couch, like a whistling kettle left on the stove too long.

"Yes," I said slowly. "Bree took me out dancing to celebrate my birthday. Since, you know, you and Dan didn't care enough to want to do anything."

She winced and glanced away. "You know how your step-father is."

"Yes. I do." *And you should leave him. Tonight, if possible. Please, Mom. Get away from him.*

She let out a heavy sigh and shook her head, shoulders slumped forward in defeat. I hated that I'd been the one to cause her to look so weary, but I had to remember that it wasn't *actually* me. Not really. It was Dan, and the way he tried to run this household with an iron fist. And that was more literal than I wanted to admit.

"You know I need to ground you, Norah," she finally said, eyes still locked on the hardwood floor. "You snuck out. You didn't tell me where you were going. If Dan knew, he'd…"

She trailed off, not wanting to finish the sentence.

Truth was, she probably didn't know exactly how far he'd go, and I didn't either. I didn't usually disobey like this, and he flew off the handle if I was even five minutes late for dinner. There was no telling how he'd react if he knew I'd been out at a club all night long.

"Mom, you know I need to go to my auditions, and—"

She held up a hand and shook her head. "Two weeks. No auditions, but you can do your shifts at work."

"But Mom, I—"

"It's final," she said as she reached out to caress my cheek with her thumb. "Let's just keep what you did between us, though, okay? If your step-father found out…Norah, I worry it might be the thing that finally makes him snap."

"Then, leave him," I said, pleading with my eyes. "Don't stay with a man who would react that way."

But she wouldn't. If she hadn't left him yet, she never would.

CHAPTER THREE

Working at the theatre's ticket office had become a strange kind of exit from reality for me. There, my life was not the disappointing mess it normally was. My mom wasn't guarding my every movement, and my step-dad wasn't lurking menacingly nearby. None of the kids I'd gone to high school with ever came to see a show. It was an off-off-broadway place located on a small quiet side street with a name that no one ever heard of unless they were deep within the theatre community.

It was my haven.

"Four tickets to see *Belles and Brawls*," a deep lyrical voice rumbled from the other side of the glass. My eyes locked on the hand that slid four twenty-dollar bills across the counter. I sucked in a deep breath. The skin was luminescent, faintly shining beneath the fluorescent lighting in the ticket booth. With it came the otherworldly scent of frost and mint.

I looked up, heart hammering hard against my

ribcage. The four guys from the night before were standing quietly before me, and the one who had followed me into the bathroom was right in the front. They were each looking at me with an intensity that took my breath away, though their bodies reflected none of the tension. Their arms were slung into their cloaks; their stances were relaxed. It was as if they wanted the world to see one thing, and me another.

"You," I whispered, standing from the wooden stool where I usually perched the entirety of my four-hour shift. "Are you following me? Why did you ask me about my ears? Why did you tell me not to take my pills?"

A pause. "Four tickets please."

Out of the corner of my eye, I could see the owner of the theatre—and my boss—staring my way. She'd always been kind to me, and she'd given me this job even though I'd had zero experience in a theatre, or any job experience at all. Still, she was tough. She wanted attendees to be greeted with a smile and a chirpy hello, as I'd been told one too many times. Some days, I found it hard to be friendly. Some days, I just wanted to curl up and hide from the world.

She'd given me a lot of breaks, but I knew if I wasn't careful, she could easily lose her patience with me.

So, with a faux-smile pasted on my face, I tapped the ticket number into the computer and took the guy's money. I still didn't know his name, despite the fact he'd brushed his fingers against my skin. Despite the fact it felt as though I *knew* him, in some weird way.

When I slid the tickets across the counter, I held on for just a moment longer. Our gazes locked, and I dropped my voice to a hush. "Please just tell me something. I feel like I'm losing my mind, but I know there's more to it than that. And I can see it in your eyes. *You know*."

"Norah," came the sweet, smooth voice of my boss, Rachel. "Is everything okay here?"

I loosed a breath and released my death grip on the tickets, turning to Rachel with a smile. "Everything's fine. I just, ah…"

"We just had some questions about the show," the guy in front spoke up. "Thanks for your help, Norah."

They turned to go, taking with them any hope I had of getting answers anytime soon. The show was starting in ten minutes, and I'd most definitely lose my job if I interrupted it to demand some answers from four of the attendees.

Why were they here? There was no way in hell it could be a coincidence. And, if it wasn't, why pretend to watch the show? They wouldn't talk to me. They wouldn't give me anything but strange intense looks. What did they want? Were they just here to…to watch me?

I shuddered. It was the only thing that made sense. I had four stalkers. With glowing skin and piercing eyes, two important features that I might very well be imagining.

I would have to talk to them after the show. My

shift would be over, and I would no longer be obligated to smile and nod. It was going to be a long two hours.

When the show was over, I stood on the sidewalk outside of the theatre waiting for the strangers I should probably be more afraid of than curious about. The New York summer air was stifling, and the sun had only begun to dip behind the buildings in the west. I was still wearing my black pants and black t-shirt, along with my name tag for the ticket booth, which only amplified the heat. It made me dread going home.

Before my step-dad had moved in, Mom and I had a boxy air conditioning unit in every room, including the bathroom, which meant that we normally had five of them blasting all through the summer. But when my step-dad had moved in, he wouldn't hear of it, pointing out the astronomical utility bill. So, he'd downsized us to only two units. One for the living room and one for their bedroom.

I'd been stuck with just a fan.

Just another one of my step-dad's micro-aggressions toward me, his own special way of demonstrating just how much he wanted me out of that apartment and out of his hair.

Something crashed in the alley on the right side of

the theatre, and my mind was jerked away from my troubled thoughts of home. A heavy thump followed, and then a screech. I frowned and shifted sideways to peer down the side of the building, but it was drowning in shadows. The cast usually exited the theatre through the door at the end of the alley, and the crew would cluster together there for smoke breaks. But they would always flick on the light to chase away the darkness.

"Hello?" I called out.

Silence answered. With a sigh, I shook my head. Maybe I was imagining things. Again.

As I turned away from the alley, another crash exploded in the silence. Heart hammering, I glanced around. There was no one else around on this side street. No other businesses lined the skinny sidewalks. All the doors were shut tight, leading up into apartments that were buzzing from the echo of air conditioning units chugging along in the stifling heat.

A soft whisper drifted to me. "Help."

My heart squeezed tight, and I took a step closer to the alley. My boots brushed up against broken glass, likely from someone who had stumbled in here after a long night drinking in the city. The darkness that cloaked the alley seemed to pulse, and I swallowed hard. This seemed like a terrible idea. No one should go into dark alleys alone...But what if one of the cast members was hurt? What if someone had gone out to have a smoke, forgot to turn on the light, and had fallen after stumbling around in the dark?

"Hello?" I asked in a soft voice. "It's Norah. Are you okay?"

From within the depths of the alley, a hulking shadowy form rose from the ground. My heart pulsed, throbbing painfully in my chest. Eyes widening, I shook my head and stepped back. The...whatever it was, it had eyes the color of blood and teeth that were razor sharp. Thick saliva pooled on the concrete. It looked kind of like a wolf with long mangy hair curling off its bulky frame, but it was much, much larger than any normal wolf. It stood three times taller than me, and its muscular body was twice as wide.

It was a monster. One that had begun to let out a low rumble of a growl, a sound that made every hair on my arms stand on end.

Suddenly, the night was no longer stifling. It was no longer hot. Chills had consumed my skin, making my entire body shake.

"Norah, help," a strangled voice came from somewhere near the creature.

My heart shook in my chest, and I tore my gaze away from the wolf to stare at a small huddled shape on the ground by the wolf's massive feet. All the blood rushed from my face as I tried to make sense of what I saw. Lars, one of the sound technicians, with his bellowing laugh and hipster beard, stared at me from across the alley. His cheeks and arms had been gouged, and blood rushed from the gaping wounds. One of his hands was missing.

I couldn't breathe, and the stars that dotted my eyes made it next to impossible to see. Wildly, I glanced around the alley, desperate to find some kind of weapon that might work against this creature. A shovel. A two-by-four. A large concrete block that I could throw in its direction.

But there was nothing in the alley other than a few discarded cigarette butts and some styrofoam takeaway boxes from the Chinese place around the corner.

"Norah," Lars said in a gasp. "What is it? What attacked me?"

The creature's glittering red eyes looked down on Lars. It pulled back its lips, showing off the sharp points of its enormous fangs. Fangs that dripped with saliva, blood, and flesh.

My stomach turned, and I pressed my hand to my mouth. This couldn't be happening. It wasn't real. It was another one of my panic attacks, making me see things that weren't really there. As much as I'd wanted to believe I was okay, I clearly wasn't.

I was having a hallucination. The creature wasn't really there, and Lars wasn't hurt.

Stumbling back, I gasped when a soft hand landed on my shoulder.

"Norah, hon, why are you out here in the alley..." Rachel trailed off, and her face went stark white. The grip on my shoulder tightened, and the skin beneath her chin began to tremble. And then she was off, rushing down the dim alley to drop to Lars's side.

I tried to scream to stop her as she came within inches of the monster's sharp teeth.

"Oh my god, Lars. What the hell happened to you?" She pressed her hand to his cheek and choked out a cry. "Norah, call the police. Call 911. Tell them we need an ambulance." She glanced up, her eyes fierce yet full of tears. "Why are you just standing there? Do something! *Now!*"

Hands shaking, I nodded and pressed my cell phone to my ear. I couldn't take my eyes off of the creature that now loomed over Rachel, his saliva only seconds away from dripping onto her head. The creature was so close. So horribly, gruesomely close. If it shifted even an inch closer, its teeth could graze her cheek. Its sharp nails could slice through her back.

"It's not real," I whispered. "The monster isn't real."

"No, it's very much real." One of the strange guys whispered in front of me and charged down the alley, a dagger flashing in his hand. Bathroom Guy grabbed my arm and pulled me back, dragging me away from the mouth of the alley.

He shifted his body in front of mine and threw out his arms, holding them on either side of me. "Stay behind me, Norah. You interrupted its feeding, and it won't take that very well."

"His feeding." I blinked. "You can see it?"

"Of course I can see it," he said in an impatient tone of voice. "Just stay behind me. Liam, Rourke, and Finn should be able to dispatch it easily enough. As for your friend...even if he can survive the bites, the venom will be difficult to fight."

Fear churned through my gut as I watched the three strangers charge the alley. The creature crouched with claws and fangs bared. My heart trembled at the sight, but it did nothing to slow the men down. They quickly surrounded the creature, triple blades held high in the air.

The stranger from the club turned toward me, his eyes full of power and darkness. And then everything went black.

CHAPTER FOUR

Dishes clattered around me as silence rained down upon the dinner table. I couldn't get the images from the theatre out of my head. Blood splattering on the oil and grime stained pavement. Those empty eyes had that stared up at me, begging for my help, accusing me of being helpless to stop the creature. Or accusing me of causing the wounds myself.

I'd always felt like there was something wrong with me, like a strange shadow of darkness lurked behind me. And now I kept seeing things no one else could. My ears were turning into horns. Maybe it was my fault in some strange way. Maybe I was causing this.

"Adeline said you were grounded, but you got home late from your job. If you can really call that a job." My step-dad's deep voice cut through the kaleidoscope of gruesome memories, sending a sharp chill into my bones. So, my mom had told him she'd grounded me. That probably wasn't going to end well. Any time he thought I stepped even a toenail out of line? Well, he didn't react very well to it.

"The show doesn't end until eight. Rachel needed me to stay and help close up," I said after swallowing the lump in my throat. I hadn't told either of them what had happened. Because I couldn't. If I did, there was no telling how my step-dad would react. He would either try to pin the blame on me or force me to quit my job, citing safety as the reason. But the truth was, he'd take any excuse to exert more control over my life. He'd never had much respect for my job at the theatre. Probably because it paid shit wages, and he was dying for me to get out of his hair.

"Well maybe I'll just call Rachel to confirm that." He pointed at where my cell phone rested screen-down on the table and only showed the colorful music notes on the deep green case.

"Dan." My mom's voice was horribly weak and deferent, almost as if she were afraid to speak up against him. Which, of course she was. The man was horrible, terrifying. The worst kind of alpha male mixed in with what I swore were sociopathic tendencies.

I had no idea why she'd married him. No wait, that wasn't true. I understood it, in a way. When they'd first met, Dan had been different, though I'd always sensed an undercurrent of something *off*. He'd wined and dined my mom, made her feel like a million bucks when she'd been lonely and depressed before. And then, slowly, almost so slowly that it was hard to spot at first, he began to change. The small snide critiques of her figure. The random comments about other women flirting with him. The slow and methodical alienation from her other friends. He made her think she needed him and that she was lucky to have him, when really it was the other way around.

And now she was trapped.

I wasn't even sure she realized it, but I did. And that was why he hated me.

He dropped his fork on his plate and levelled his eyes across the table. Immediately, she flicked her gaze down to the flowery tablecloth, something she'd only bought since Dan came along. Before she'd met him, she wouldn't have been caught dead buying anything so feminine.

"Now, listen, Adeline. You said yourself that Norah needs to have some more discipline in her life if she's going to freeload off of us like this." He gripped the edges of the table, his eyebrows furrowing. Anger simmered off of him, like his body was full of a darkness so profound that it couldn't hold all of it inside of him.

"I'm not freeloading," I said. One thing I'd learned over the years: don't talk back to Dan. But sometimes, like now, I couldn't help myself, particularly when that rage was directed toward my mother. "I pay rent on my room."

He sneered, taking his attention away from my mom and placing it firmly on me. "You give us two hundred bucks a month. Do you know how much this apartment costs? Electricity? Cable? Internet? And let's not forget this damn food." He pointed at the cast iron skillet in the middle of the table, full to the brim with a delicious paella my mom had made from scratch. A dish that none of us were enjoying because of the dark tension in the room. "We live in Manhattan, for fuck's sake."

"Dan," came my mom's pleading voice. "Please. Let's not use that kind of language in front of Norah."

"She's eighteen years old, Adeline, and she's a high school graduate. You need to stop babying her. I'm fucking tired of her freeloading with no consequences. She either needs to get another job or get out." He shoved his finger at the paella. "Now serve me some of that food, or I'll start packing up her shit right now."

"*Dan.*" My mom's eyes had gone glassy, and her knuckles were snow white where she gripped the napkin in her lap. "I think that's enough. Norah is my daughter, and she's not going anywhere. Not until she decides it's time and she has the means to support herself."

I sucked in a sharp breath and sat up straight in the stiff dining chair. Well, this was certainly a first. Mom never stood up to Dan, not even when he transformed into the inner beast we both knew was beneath the handsome face.

His face darkened, and his voice dropped into a strange, eerie, quiet calm. "You pay less a month than she does, Adeline."

A quiet threat, one that made my mom blink in shock. I'd seen him do this before. Any time it might seem that Mom was grasping for some kind of control over a situation, Dan would turn the tables on her before she'd managed to find her feet. I didn't believe for a second he would ever kick her out, and maybe Mom didn't either, but there was enough fear there that it shut down her every objection. Because he was right. He supported her, fully and completely. She was broke without him.

"You know what?" I asked as I pushed back my chair and stood. "I'll serve you some paella. How's that?"

He pursed his lips, his gaze still locked on my mom, but then he nodded. "Maybe you aren't so useless after all."

Lovely.

Before Mom could object, I grabbed the skillet and moved to stand beside Dan so that I could spoon some paella onto his plate. But the moment my skin came into contact with the handles, the world became cloudy around me. Frowning, I blinked. Everything remained shifting blobs of dark and light.

I gripped the handles tighter, taking deep breaths in through my nose. I couldn't have another panic attack, not right now. Talk about the worst timing in the world. My step-dad would probably have me committed if he knew just how bad the attacks had become. But it was no use. Nausea churned through my stomach, my head felt light and full of swirling clouds, and my palms went slick with sweat.

And then I lost my grip on the skillet. It fell with a heavy thud onto the hardwood floor, and rice and seafood soared through the air. Some of it splashed into my face, but I didn't care. I needed some fresh air. I needed to sit down. I stumbled away from the dinner table, in the direction of my room.

But a strong hand shot out and wrapped around my arm. It lurched me back. His grip was so tight that it sent sparks of pain through my body. "Where the hell do you think you're going? You think you can just walk off and leave your mother to clean up your damn mess?"

"Dan, please." My mom's voice was soft, pleading.

Suddenly, the doorbell rang. Dan let out a grunt and threw his napkin onto the table, standing so abruptly that his chair almost toppled to the ground.

He pointed at me. "Stay here and start cleaning up. If that's one of your friends ringing our doorbell during dinnertime, you're going to be in even more trouble than you are already."

And then he stormed off, his fisted hands shaking by his sides.

As soon as he disappeared out of the room, I breathed a heavy sigh and slumped lower in my chair, thankful for the moment of sweet relief of not having my step-dad around, even if it would only last five seconds. Luckily, the person at the door wouldn't be any of my friends. Mostly because Bree was pretty much the only one I had, and she knew better than to stop by during dinnertime. Bree *knew* all about my step-dad.

"Norah, honey, you need to be more careful around him," my mom said quietly, hands pressed tight against the napkin in her lap. "You know how he gets sometimes."

"Mom. Maybe he's the problem and not me."

She hissed and flicked her eyes to the empty doorway. Deep voices drifted to us from the hallway, but thankfully, my step-dad hadn't returned just yet. "Don't say things like that. If you make him angry enough…"

Her words trailed away into nothing. The truth was, neither of us knew just how far he would go if he got angry enough. And while I certainly didn't want to find out, I was finding it increasingly difficult to keep my thoughts to myself. Things had to change and change soon. We couldn't keep living like this.

Footsteps thudded on the hardwood floor, and my step-dad darkened the doorway before stepping into the dining room. Behind him, two police officers stood with their hands resting lightly on the guns on their hips. My heartbeat roared in my ears, and a new kind of cloudiness began to creep into the corners of my eyes.

I wanted to ask why they were here, but I already knew.

It was about Lars's murder.

"Norah, these two police officers are here to ask you some questions about the death of one of the crew members at that theatre where you work." His eyes flashed, full of anger. I had blatantly not told him about what had happened, and he was going to punish me for it.

"Norah?" My mom rose from the table, her slender

hands pressing against the wood for support. "What's all this about? A death at the theatre? You didn't mention something had happened there. Why didn't you tell us?"

I winced.

"Yes, ma'am," one of the officers said. "Your daughter is a witness, according to another witness of ours. Norah, are you free to answer some questions, or will we need to take you into the station?"

I read between the lines. Either we could talk here, or they'd escort me into a police station where I'd be grilled in a little room with one-way windows.

"We can go into the living room," I said, pressing my sweaty palms against my jeans. "I'm happy to answer whatever questions you have."

Kind of. What could I say? A wolf monster killed Lars, but no one else could see it but me. Not even Lars had realized what had attacked him. And then four strange guys with golden skin fought the thing with swords and daggers before I'd passed out in the middle of the street, somehow ending up home even though I didn't remember getting here. The police wouldn't believe me. Hell, *I* wouldn't even believe myself unless I'd seen it happen with my own two eyes.

I didn't know how to explain what I'd seen without sounding crazy. Or guilty.

So, I lied. I weaved a story, one that sounded logical and realistic rather than something that sounded straight out of an episode of *Teen Wolf*. When I'd finished the explanation, both police officers jotted down notes, both uneasily silent about the whole thing.

"So," I said, clearing my throat. "It's like I said. I didn't actually see much. By the time I got into the alley, Lars's attacker was already gone."

One of the cops looked up, a woman who had called herself Deputy Franklin. "The owner, Rachel Harris, mentioned that you were shouting about a monster. Do you care to elaborate on that?"

From out of the corner of my eye, I could see the frown deepen on my step-dad's face. He'd insisted on sitting in on the conversation, as well as my mother. They were going to shit some actual bricks when the police officers left.

"I think she maybe misunderstood me," I said. "I just meant that whoever did this to Lars is a monster. There was a lot of blood." I swallowed hard and blinked back the tears that burned my eyes. "I think I was just in shock a little bit."

Deputy Franklin nodded, apparently accepting my scrabbled together answer.

"Just one more question," Officer Whitmore said, clicking shut his pen and resting it lightly on his knee. Something about that move struck me as odd, as if it wasn't entirely genuine, as if he wasn't actually relaxed about the question he was about to lob my way. And once he spoke, I knew why. "Rachel Harris also mentioned that your shift ended a full hour before she found Lars—and you—in the alley beside the theatre. I don't suppose there's a reason why you stuck around for so long after your shift?"

I swallowed hard. Shit.

Shit, shit, shit.

The first words I could think of popped right out of my mouth. "I was waiting to talk to someone I know who went in to watch the performance."

The officer clicked his pen. "And what's the name of this friend of yours? We'd like to speak with them just to confirm."

My heart shuddered in my chest. This was going far worse than I thought it would. Partially because I kept sticking my foot right in my mouth.

"Um...I don't actually know his name." I winced when the officer frowned. "See, the thing is..." I glanced over to my mom and her stark white face. Her eyes met mine, and they slightly widened, as if she knew exactly what I wanted—and needed—to say. She glanced at my step-dad and gave an imperceptible shake of her head. But I had no choice but to give a version of the truth. "It was a guy I met when I went out dancing last night for my birthday. I guess you could say I was...intrigued by him. So, when he showed up at the theatre with three of his friends, I wanted to talk to him since we hadn't exchanged numbers....or names."

"I see." The officer sounded skeptical, but I couldn't blame him. It sounded ridiculous, and she hadn't even mentioned the guys with the swords. It was almost as if...Rachel hadn't seen them either.

The police officers asked me a few more questions, and then finally stood to go.

"Thanks for your cooperation, but we'll likely need to speak to you again," Deputy Franklin said as the two of them hovered by the door. "It would be for the best if you didn't leave town until we've wrapped up the case."

I'd binge-watched enough police procedural shows that I knew exactly what that meant. I was a suspect. Maybe their main suspect. And if I tried to get the hell out of dodge, they'd probably arrest me.

When the door shut behind the cops, I had the sudden urge to fling it back open and beg them to take me into the station. Because I could just *feel* the piercing gaze of my step-dad on the back of my head.

Swallowing hard, I spun on my feet to face him. His eyes were so dark that my body shuddered in response. I took a step back, pressing up against the door, the metal knob digging into my skin.

"I don't even know where to start." He was using that strange eerie calm voice again, the one that caused tremors to engulf my entire body. "First, you outright lied to your mother and me about why you were so late getting home today. And then I find out you went to a club last night?" His jaw rippled from where he clenched his teeth so tight that I could hear a grinding sound coming from his mouth. "That's why your mother grounded you, isn't it? I should have known it wasn't for slacking off on your chores."

"It's not her fault," I said quickly. "I asked her to lie to you. I knew you'd be pissed if you found out."

"Damn right I'd be pissed. Here I am, paying your way and you're out partying all night. Probably drinking and doing drugs. Although that doesn't fucking compare to being a suspect for murder, now does it?"

A suspect for murder.

The words sounded alien to my ears even though I'd understood the truth of the officers' visit myself. Swallowing hard, I took a step back, only to find I had nowhere to go. The doorknob dug deeper into my skin, the cool steel of it pressing through my thin t-shirt.

"Well?" He stalked closer, so close that I could smell the hint of paprika on his breath. "What do you have to say for yourself?"

"Look, I'm sorry," I said, heart thundering. "I shouldn't have lied, I guess, but I was worried you'd overreact. Sometimes..." I took a deep breath and plowed forward. "Sometimes you can be a little intimidating when something goes wrong."

"Oh yeah?" He let out a chuckle. "Intimidating like this?"

He pulled back his fist, and I squeezed shut my eyes. This was it. The moment he lost it and finally broke a bone.

His fist slammed into the wall beside me, cracking through plaster and knocking right into the bricks underneath. The yell that erupted from his throat was so loud that my entire body began to shake. He'd punched the wall himself, but I knew what that yell meant. He was going to blame me for his own wound.

He stumbled back, and blood poured from his knuckles.

"Norah." My mother rushed into the entryway and

shoved her old suitcase into my shaking hands. "Go. Get out of here."

Tears sprung into my eyes, and I shook my head. "No. I'm not going to leave you here alone with him."

"I'll be fine." She jerked her head over her shoulder to stare at my step-dad, who was now wrapping his hand with one of my scarves from the coat rack. In an instant, my mother was close, and her breath was barely a whisper. She pressed a necklace into my hands, the one she'd worn almost every day of her life. "Take this and wear it always. Go to Bree's apartment. I'll let you know when it's safe to come back."

She yanked open the door and gave me a push. I stumbled out into the hallway, and my heart split in two. I wanted nothing more in the world than to get the hell out of here and never look back, but the look of hopelessness on my mom's face kept my feet rooted to the spot.

Until I heard my step-dad's voice through the thin door. "I won't let either of you disrespect me again, Adeline. You better hope she never comes back."

CHAPTER FIVE

Bree wasn't home. So, I snuck inside. She lived on the second-floor of a walk-up apartment building, and there was a fire escape ladder in the alley just behind it. For as long as I could remember, we kept a leaded rope hidden behind one of the dumpsters in case of emergency.

This was an emergency if there ever was one.

Once inside, I dropped the suitcase on the floor and plopped onto her tiny twin bed covered in *Frozen* sheets. Bree was a bit of a Disney fan, to say the least. I thought it was because she liked to imagine that she was a princess, though one of the ones who saved the day for themselves, not the kind who needed rescuing.

No, it seemed that *I* was the kind who needed rescuing. I wished it weren't so.

I must have fallen asleep like that because the next thing I knew, the overhead light was shining right in my eyes and Bree's face hovered in front of me. A hand reached out, gently, and shook me.

"Norah, what the hell is going on?" Her face blurred in before me as I blinked the sleep out of my eyes. "Don't get me wrong. I'm happy to see you, but you have to admit it's kind of strange that you're in my bed."

"Sorry." I pushed up onto my elbows and gave her a look, one that spoke far more than any words ever could. Realization immediately dawned on her face.

"It's the asshole," she said, matter-of-factly. "He finally snapped."

I blew out a heavy sigh. "It was like he'd transformed into a beast. He punched a hole in the wall and then threatened to do the same to my face."

She let out a low whistle. "So you left."

"So I left." I gave her a sad smile. "Though it was my mom's idea. I saw a flicker of something in her tonight. It gives me hope that maybe she's finally seeing him for who he really is, but that's scary in its own way. I don't want him to hurt her."

"Maybe we should call the police and tell them what's happened," Bree said. "They might be able to charge him with something."

I groaned, closed my eyes, and flopped back onto the bed. "Oh, god. The police. For two precious seconds there, I'd forgotten about the police."

"What are you talking about?"

With my eyes still shut tight, I said, "It's a long, long, long story that is going to sound absolutely insane. Like, even more insane than the time I told you that a stranger who cornered me in the bathroom held all the answers to my panic attacks."

"You mean that time that was last night."

"That's the one."

"Alright. Scooch over. Sounds like I'm going to need to be sitting down for this one."

With a laugh, I moved over and the two of us packed tight into her bed. It reminded me of when we'd been younger, and Bree would stay over at my apartment every Friday night without fail. We grabbed pizza from the corner shop and settled in for a movie marathon. There'd be talk of boys and crushes, but mostly we liked to talk about our dreams, about where we wanted our lives to take us. Bree had always wanted to leave Manhattan while I'd always wanted to stay. To her, this wasn't the concrete jungle made of dreams. She'd always thought there was more to the world than this tiny island. Sometimes, I thought she might be right.

So, I told her my story. I started out slow, unsure of myself at first. I was more than a little worried what her reaction might be. I was basically admitting to imagining a beastly monster killing people in alleys. The police thought of me as a suspect. My step-dad (and maybe my mom) thought of me as a suspect, too.

Would Bree think of me that way? I didn't know what I would do if the only person I had left in the world turned her back on me.

But when I was done telling my crazy tale, she wrapped her arms around me and pulled me close, the scent of lavender and roses swirling around us.

"Well, that is one shit-tastic day. I think this calls

for a pizza from Tony's and some Ben & Jerry's Rocky Road."

"Wait a minute." I pulled back to meet her eyes. "You believe me? You don't think I'm a killer?"

She snorted. "Norah, you're pretty much the opposite of a killer. Remember that I've seen you save spiders from your step-dad. Sneaking them out the window so he doesn't have the chance to squash them."

"Okay, but there's still the whole wolf monster in an alley thing."

"I'm not going to lie. I have no idea what to think about that." She plopped back onto the pillows and shrugged. "It doesn't make much sense. People don't go around seeing wolf monsters attacking people in alleys. So, honestly? I don't know what happened there. But what I do know is that you're not responsible. You saw something and that something killed Lars. Not you."

I loosed a breath, and my heart throbbed painfully in my chest. It felt so good to hear her say that, even though I knew I shouldn't have doubted her. We'd been best friends for so long that I couldn't remember a time when Bree wasn't in my life. Her family felt like my family. Sometimes, they felt even more like my family than my own flesh and blood did.

"Don't look so worried, Norah." She gave me a smile. "I'm on your side. Forever and always. You can stay here for as long as you need to. In fact, I insist upon it. I don't want you going back to that apartment as long as your step-dad is still in it. This is your new home, for as long as you need it to be."

And with that, I let out a heavy sigh and did my best to feel relieved. I had somewhere to stay. I had someone who loved me, no matter what kind of crazy things I said I saw. But beneath the tiny taste of relief, something darker lurked. My strange panic attack. The four eerie guys who were following me around, wielding swords. The wolf I'd seen in the alley. All that blood.

And that strange unsettling sensation that I was being watched. Even right now.

The next day, I showed up to work fifteen minutes early. I was feeling a bit jittery to say the least, and I wasn't entirely sure that the show would go on, so to speak. No one had called to tell me if the theatre was closed today, so I figured I'd better show up anyway. It was hard to imagine it being opened after what had happened, but I felt like I needed to be there. Just in case.

The lights were off, but I could see Rachel through the glass door. She was scrubbing at the walls so hard that paint flecks were raining down on the floor. I knocked, and she jumped almost ten feet in the air. When she saw it was me, I expected her shoulders to relax. Instead, they tensed up even more.

"What are you doing here?" she asked when she

opened the door. Now that the light was shining on her face, I couldn't help but notice the dark circles under her eyes and the frizzy hair that said she hadn't bothered to go through her regular hair care routine. Rachel used at least five different types of conditioning products in her hair every morning. So, that was saying something.

"I wasn't sure if we were closed today."

"Well, we are," she snapped. "And anyway, I won't be needing you back when we do reopen."

My heart dropped. "What?"

She rubbed her swollen eyes and sighed. "Look, I don't know what happened last night, but I do know that the police seem really interested in your part in it. Truthfully, I find it a little bit odd myself. Your shift was over. Why were you in the alley?"

I opened my mouth to try and explain, but she cut me off with a tutting noise I'd heard her use toward others but never toward me.

"I just think it's for the best if we end your employment here."

"You can't possibly think that I killed Lars," I said in a soft whisper as my eyes began to burn. I could understand the police thinking it. Hell, I could even understand my step-dad thinking it. But Rachel? She'd known me for years. Surely she didn't think I was capable of something like that.

"I don't know what to think, Norah. I walk outside, and there you are standing over his body. You were there when you should have been home. Something isn't right about that, and I hope to god it isn't what it seems like. But until the cops prove otherwise, I would feel a lot better if you weren't here."

I blinked and stepped back. Her words were a slap in the face. She was scared. Of me.

"Okay, if that's what you want," I finally said.

She gave a nod, and then she slammed the door right in my face.

I was starting to understand Bree's opinion on Manhattan. The city that dropped dreams from the top of the Empire State Building where they smashed onto the grimy concrete sidewalks. As I wandered through the gray-laden downtown streets, the buildings rising high on either side of me felt as though they were pressing in close, and the scent of hot steel swirling into my nose made my head spin.

Everything was gray and hot and smelly. Even the cracks in the sidewalks didn't have hints of green. Nothing about the city felt alive.

I turned the corner and stopped short when I was confronted with an unfamiliar street. It didn't look much different than any of the others I usually passed on my way around downtown. Two Chinese takeaway restaurants with their neon lights buzzing in the windows. A pawn shop, a bagel shop, and a hair salon that looked like it had seen better days.

Problem was, I didn't recognize any of them. Somehow, I'd gotten turned around. I'd been wandering aimlessly for at least an hour, and while I knew the city well, I'd ended up in a chunk of blocks I'd never explored.

Footsteps echoed on the pavement behind me, and a strange eerie sensation settled over me. The feeling of being watched. With a slight hitch in my breath, I continued to move down the street and cast a furtive glance over my shoulder. A dark form hovered at the end of the block. The clouds overhead cast the streets into grey shadows, and he—or it—hovered beside the edges of a building, making it impossible to make out more than that.

My heartbeat picked up speed. Was it that creature from last night? Or was it one of the strange guys who had clearly been following me around? Or maybe it was a cop, keeping an eye on their number one suspect.

Whoever it was, I didn't want to stick around to find out.

My footsteps were heavy on the concrete, echoing in time with the thud of those that followed. A part of me felt the strong urge to take a look behind me again, but another part was too afraid to see. I just had to keep moving.

When I rounded the next corner, I set off into a sprint and then turned onto the next street before the stalker could catch up. It was the only way I knew how to lose him. Breath heaving, I slowed and ducked beside a black wrought-iron railing that led up to the front landing of an apartment building. There were some trash cans just in front of me, blocking me from view of anyone passing by.

Surely I had lost him. Surely he wouldn't know I'd turned down this street.

With my heart still racing, I grasped onto the railing and peered down the street in the direction I'd come. As soon as my fingers came in contact with the railing, my entire body was slammed by an overwhelming tidal wave of nausea. I jerked away, my head ringing, my chest heaving, my eyes blurring.

This was worse than before. *Way* worse.

And this time, I wasn't getting any better. I grasped onto the railing to keep myself from falling over, and another wave of nausea pummelled me right in the gut. Darkness stormed into my eyes, and I couldn't hear anything in the world but a sharp, high-pitched ring.

Maybe I really did need help. Maybe I was going crazy. Because nothing about this was normal.

I struggled to stand, and my knees buckled underneath me. It sent me tumbling onto the grimy pavement, my elbows and knees slamming into the concrete. A cry of pain ripped from my throat, and a blinding pain shot through my arm. Breath heaving, all I could do was lie there, trying to squeeze the darkness out of my eyes. But it wouldn't be gone. It consumed every part of me, and my grasp on the world began to fade. My eyes slid closed, and I couldn't even move the tip of my finger.

As the ringing began to subside, I heard the heavy

thud of footsteps. They stopped right by my ear, and I screamed inside at myself. *Move, Norah. Run.*

But I couldn't move at all. I couldn't even open my eyes.

"Well, this isn't ideal." A male voice, one that wasn't familiar at all, though the lyrical tone of it alarmed me. "You really need to stop touching iron. Otherwise, you're going to end up in the hospital, and they won't be able to fix you."

I tried to open my mouth to respond. My muddled thoughts were trying to form questions. *Iron? Hospital? Who are you?*

I had no idea if I spoke the questions aloud.

"Right, well. I can't very well leave you in the middle of the street like this, can I? Especially not when you keep attracting the attention of Redcaps."

Red caps? What the hell was that? Little men who wore red caps?

The rustle of clothing sounded by my ear, and then two strong arms slid underneath my body. The pavement fell away, and a sweet, sweet smell filled my nose, one of fresh grass, honeysuckle and lilac, and the forest air after heavy rain. This strange man who had found me was now...carrying me. To somewhere. I started to struggle, desperately trying to crack open my eyes, but it was no use.

He chuckled. "You know, the guys and I have been making a bet about who you belong to. I'm betting on Spring, of course, with those brilliant green eyes of yours. That blonde hair. But you do have a little fire in you, so Liam is convinced you're his. And of course Kael thinks you're his, what with the way the Redcaps are so drawn to you, though he doesn't seem particularly happy about it. And Rourke? He couldn't care less, but that's an Autumn fae for you."

He was speaking gibberish. Pure nonsensical gibberish. English yes, but none of it made any sense. It was as if he'd jumbled up normal words and put them together in a way that made them sound as if they were a completely different language. Or maybe that was my scrambled brain.

Regardless, I didn't hear any more of it. There was something soothing in the soft sweet scent of him and his strong arms that gently held my body. It dulled the panic and fear that had been raging through my gut.

Consciousness left me, and the next thing I knew, I was back in Bree's bed. Alone. The only thing that made me feel as if I hadn't imagined the whole thing was the single lilac flower stem left behind on the bedside table.

CHAPTER SIX

"I've found the answer to all your problems." Bree was practically bouncing up and down, even though it was stupid o'clock in the morning. The sun streamed in through the thin gauzy curtains. Apparently, today was the longest day of the year, which meant sunrise had happened at an ungodly hour.

"Since when were you a morning person?" I asked as I shielded my eyes from the glare of the sun. "And also, I think we need to get you some thicker curtains."

"Time to get up," she said, eyes sparkling. "You have a world to conquer. Or a theatre, at least."

She shoved a bright purple flyer into my hands, the kind you found on cork boards in university buildings. Sighing, I took the page and began to read, and then immediately sat straight up, the covers falling off my shoulders.

"You see?" Bree asked in a gleeful tone of voice that

matched the new hectic beat of my heart. Because I did see. Very, very much so.

"A choreographer, for an Off Broadway theatre," I breathed. "No previous experience required. It sounds too good to be true, Bree."

"It's right there on the flyer. In bold Helvetica." She grinned. "I called them and got you a slot for tonight."

I dropped the paper, as well as my chin. "*What?*"

"They're doing things in an audition style, I guess. All you have to do is go and show them what you've got. It should be a piece of cake for you. I've seen your dance routines. You're the best damn dancer I know."

"Yeah, but Bree," I said, shaking my head. "They're going to get a lot of 'auditions' for this. It says no experience required, but there are going to be people going for this who have actually choreographed shows before. I can't compete with that."

"You can, and you will," she said. "It doesn't hurt to try, does it? Show that asshole step-dad that he's wrong about you."

With a deep breath, I gave Bree a nod. Lately, it felt as if my entire life was spiralling out of control. It was time to do something about it, and getting a full-time choreographing job would be a great start.

We were at the entrance of the theatre at eight in the evening. Apparently, they'd been doing 'auditions' all day, and were planning to go until ten. A lot of competition. Way more than made me comfortable. I felt jittery and unsettled, and my palms were slick with sweat. I was in the exact opposite frame of mind that I needed to be in, and I couldn't help but remember that I often felt like this before one of my weird panic attacks, hallucinations, or whatever you wanted to call them.

The guy who had carried me home yesterday had felt so *real*, but Bree was convinced that I was conjuring things in my imagination because of the stress. But that didn't totally explain what had happened and how I'd been able to smell such a vivid scent. The honeysuckle, the post-rain freshness of the air. He'd felt solid, steady. And if he hadn't carried me back to Bree's? Then I had no idea how I'd gotten there by myself.

Still, I needed to push those thoughts aside until this interview-slash-audition was over. My best dancing was always done with a clear, fresh head. When I was emotional, my dancing reflected that. It was more chaotic, more strange. Technique didn't matter as much as dancing out all the pain.

Inside, the lobby was hushed, and voices echoed from a door held ajar by a box full of props. My heartbeat flickered, and I pressed my palms against my black jeans. My dreams were inside that theatre, ones

I'd had for as long as I could remember. If I screwed this up...

"I need to go to the bathroom before I go in there," I finally said, turning to Bree. "Meet you in a bit?"

She gave my arm a squeeze. "You'll be fine, Norah. You're good at this. Go splash some cold water on your face, and then go in there like you own the place. I'll see you after. Break a leg."

I cracked a smile, grateful for Bree's words. Quickly, I found the bathroom and took in several deep breaths to steady my nerves. She was right. I was good at dancing. I might not be good at anything else, but I knew I was good at that. All I had to do was go up onto a stage and perform the steps I'd done a hundred times before.

It was time to stop hiding behind my fears.

After splashing some water onto my face, I stepped back into the empty hallway. All of the overhead fluorescent lights had been cast off, and the hall formed a dark, empty tunnel to the metal doors leading to the rest of the building. Pinpricks of light shone through the cracks. Other than that, there was no sign of life.

Something didn't feel right. It was the absence of noise. It was the absence of any movement at all. Not even a breath of sound in a place that was normally full of activity. I shivered and paused in my steps to feel the pointy tips of my ears. They were still there.

A long, painful wail bounced off the walls. An animalistic sound. Goosebumps stampeded my arms. Every hair on my neck stood on end. With frozen lungs, I turned to stare down the hallway behind me. A dark shadow hovered at the far end.

And then the shadow charged.

I twisted on my heels and stormed toward the door. A loud hiss filled my ears, and the tangy scent of blood swirled into my nose. The air pressed in tight around me. Whatever chased me would dig its claws into my feet and take me then.

But it didn't. And once I was out of the hallway and into the rest of the theatre with the glaring lamps shining light onto my head and the murmur of ordinary voices, I wasn't sure anything had even been there at all.

A heavy thud echoed from behind me. Shivers slid down my spine, and I rushed through the theatre doors. Two expectant faces turned my way from the front seats. The directors I needed to impress, but I wouldn't be doing any impressing tonight.

Bree had taken a seat near the back, and I grabbed her arm. Frowning, she yanked out of my grasp, her eyes wide.

"Norah, what are you doing?" Her voice was low, soft. She didn't want the directors up front to overhear our discussion, even though they could clearly see I was trying to drag my friend out of this place.

"We have to go," I said, grabbing her arm again. "Don't fight with me on this."

"Norah—"

No time to argue. I pulled her along the red carpet and back out into the lobby, kicking open the front doors of the theatre with my heavy boots. Once we were out in the fresh night air—if you could call the trash-infested air fresh—she wriggled out of my grip and shot me a dark frown.

"Honestly, Norah. What the hell was that all about? If you changed your mind or something, you could have at least said something to them instead of dragging me out of there like that."

"One of those monsters was in the building."

Her eyes widened, and a heavy sigh escaped through her parted lips. And then she shook her head, crossing her arms over her chest. "Not this again."

"I know you think I'm imagining things, but I *saw* it, Bree. It chased me down the hall."

"I love you, Norah. You know that right?" She dropped her hands onto my shoulders and squeezed. "But think about when this happened. Right before doing something that was making you so nervous that your entire face went white. I should have known not to push you into a stressful situation, not when you're going through...whatever this is. I thought you'd be able to handle it. And I'm sorry I didn't realize how tough it would be for you."

Frowning, I stepped back. "You don't believe me."

"No, I believe that you're seeing it," she said in a sad voice.

"But you don't believe it's real."

She winced and glanced to the side as if the fire hydrant was suddenly the most interesting thing she'd ever seen. Her gaze was locked on it, and her jaw rippled as she clenched her teeth. Tears sprung into my eyes.

"Bree," I said. "Please. You have to believe me."

She shook her head. "No. I'm sorry, Norah. I don't believe it's real. I know it's not what you want to hear, but you need to hear it. I love you, and I want to support you, but I don't know how to do that when you're making up monsters in your head."

I flinched and stepped back. "If you told me this was happening to you, I would believe you."

She flicked her gaze back to my face. "Would you? Or would you think that maybe it was time I booked another appointment with my psychiatrist."

That hurt. More than I expected it to. With tears filling my eyes, I sucked in a sharp breath and said, "You know what? Maybe it's better if I don't stay with you after all. I'll go pack up my stuff and stay in an Air BnB until I can find a sublet I can afford."

I couldn't afford a sublet, especially not after I'd run out of that theatre. But I also couldn't stay with Bree. She didn't believe me. She thought I was crazy. How could I stay with her when she thought I was losing my mind?

She jerked back, almost like I'd slapped her, and then her voice turned to ice. "If that's what you want, Norah, then I won't try to stop you."

"Fine," I said. "I'll go back now and pack my things. I'll be gone within an hour."

"Right." She sniffed. "Well, I'm hungry, and there's a pizza place on the corner. I'll go grab something to eat. That way, I'll be out of your hair while you get your things."

This was awful. I hated fighting with Bree, especially when it felt like we were splitting up for good.

My heart hurt worse than any physical wound I'd ever had. But it felt as though we'd climbed onto a runaway train, and neither one of us could get off. I wanted to stop this. I wanted to wrap my arms around her and hear her say that this was all some kind of horrible joke. But that would be a lie.

Bree turned and strode away, her feet aimed away from me. With a sigh, I followed suit, letting my body take me in the opposite direction. It was hard to see the sidewalk through my tears.

And then a scream ripped through the night, freezing my feet in place. My blood roared in my ears, and I knew what I would see even before I turned. Down the street, Bree stood in the shadow of a towering wolf-like creature. Her eyes were wild with fear, and her fists shook by her sides. The creature loomed over her, fangs flashing against the bright street-lamps that illuminated the empty street.

"Bree!" I choked out the word and began to stumble toward her.

She flicked her eyes my way, her face as white as a sheet. The sorrow and fear I saw in them would haunt me to my grave.

The creature raised its sharp claws in the air, and my feet moved faster.

"NO!" I shouted, but it was too late. There was nothing I could do to save Bree. There was nothing I could do but watch the creature's claws slice right through her neck. Blood soared through the air, and I stumbled onto my knees. Bree crumpled onto the ground, her eyes distant, her face slack.

The creature jerked its head to the right, and then launched down the street, disappearing into the night.

They found me on my knees with blood all over my hands. I couldn't remember anything after the moment that I'd seen Bree's broken body fall onto the pavement. My entire body was numb and cold, and the world felt like a distant memory. Nothing felt real. Not even the blood on my hands.

"Miss, we're going to have to ask you to come away from the body." A woman in blue knelt before me, shining a flashlight into my eyes.

I blinked and glanced away. "I can't leave her. I'm trying to stop the blood."

Her voice went soft. "I know, honey, but we can't help her if you don't move away."

"Can you stop her bleeding?" I asked.

A pause. "We'll do our best. Now, come on."

Body still numb, I stood. A sharp crack echoed in the night, and I peeled my eyes away from Bree to find myself face-to-face with a police officer. His gun was pointed right at me.

"What's going on?" Deep within my muddled mind, I knew I should be alarmed and afraid. Someone was pointing a gun at me. But I felt nothing. Nothing but the need to make sure Bree was okay.

"Norah Oliver, yes? You need to turn around and

put your hands in the air." The officer glanced at the woman who had found me next to Bree. "Martha, I'm going to need you to search her for a weapon."

A weapon? I frowned, confusion rippling through me until my mind began to piece the clues together. My blood-stained hands. Me kneeling over the body. The number one suspect in another similar brutal murder.

Murder.

Revulsion shook through me, and I grasped at my shirt because I didn't know what else to do with my hands. This couldn't be happening. Bree couldn't be dead. And I wasn't about to be arrested for her death.

A loud shot rang through the neon-lit streets, and the gun clattered out of the cop's hands. His eyes widened as he stared down at his gun, and then he moved his eyes to me. My heart hammered. What the hell was going on? Was someone shooting at us? At me?

And then I heard a soft quiet voice whisper into my ear, from somewhere far, far away. Somehow, it sounded so near. "Run."

I didn't know why I listened to the voice, but I did.

Before the cop could grab his gun, I ran.

CHAPTER SEVEN

I ran. I didn't know where I was going, but I ran. At first, I flew down the streets with a sense of determination and purpose. *Get away from the cops.* But as the minutes ticked by and the pulsing red lights faded into the background, my feet began to falter as a horrifying realization washed over me.

I'd just run from the cops. They'd found me at a murder scene, and I'd done the worst thing in the world I could do.

With my heart constricting inside my chest, I swerved into the nearest alley and ducked behind a dumpster. Sobs heaved from my body, my mind engulfed by grief and fear. Bree was gone. She'd been killed right before my eyes, and I hadn't been able to do a thing. And our final conversation had been so fraught with barely contained anger.

"We're sorry about what happened to your friend," came a foreign voice.

"We didn't realize another Redcap was tracking you, or we would have taken care of it." But that voice... that was the one from my dreams.

I looked up, peering through my tears to find the four strange guys standing before me. The ones from the club. The ones from the theatre. The ones who had battled the monster. But their fighting hadn't helped. Because another monster had come along and killed my friend.

"Who are you?" I asked in a harsh whisper. "Why are you following me? And what the hell was that thing?"

"That's a lot of questions to answer in one conversation," the golden one said. "It would be easiest if you just came with us. I'm Rourke, and this is Liam, Kael, and Finn."

"Came with you?" I fisted my hands. "Are you insane? After what just happened, do you really think I'm going to go with four random strangers who cornered me in a dark alley?"

Rourke frowned, and my gaze caught on his eyes. They were a deep golden color that matched his hair. There was something strange about him, more so than the others. He reminded me of dry cracking trees and the smell of fresh dirt. He was mesmerizing, a fact that I found more than a little annoying. Right now, I needed to get answers.

"I suppose that means you don't remember your little tumble yesterday," Finn said in that quiet, curious voice of his. He was the opposite of Rourke. His eyes were a sapling green, and everything about him seemed vibrant, as if death and despair were foreign things to him. But, just like Rourke, he was tall with broad shoulders and a strong, square jaw.

The other two hadn't spoken, but I couldn't help but stare at them, too. The one from the club's eyes were still that strange endless black, his dark hair curling around pointed ears. I sucked in a sharp breath when I finally registered what I'd seen. Yes, his ears were very much pointed. Like...what mine were becoming.

I looked to the next, the fourth, the last. He was alight, his eyes a bonfire red with hair that matched. I'd never seen anything like him before. Everything about his presence was full and commanding, the very opposite of soft and weak. He looked like someone who you didn't want to get in the way of...of course, none of them seemed particularly meek. Every single one towered over me.

"I need to know what's happening," I finally said. "What killed Bree? Please tell me what's going on."

My voice cracked as tears refilled my eyes. The shock of her death was beginning to wear off, and with that came emotions I didn't know how I could handle. My entire body ached, as if a part of it had been ripped from my guts and thrown all over the pavement. I couldn't imagine life without her. I couldn't imagine that smile as brilliant as the sun never brightening up the world. She had been a star amongst a world full of darkness, and now she would no longer shine.

"Shit," Liam muttered. "She's crying again. I don't know what to do with crying girls."

"Here's a thought, Liam. Be a little more sensitive. Understand that she just saw her best friend get killed by a Redcap."

Sniffling, I glanced up. "You said that before. A Redcap. What is that?"

The guys exchanged gazes before Rourke stepped forward. Suddenly, my nose filled with the scent of forest mushrooms, rotting leaves, and dirt. So much dirt. Why would someone smell like that? I glanced at his ears again, my eyes locked on the sharp points. A strange thought was beginning to sprout in my brain, but I didn't dare let myself believe it.

I'd heard stories growing up. Anyone who had been born in the city had. Legends of the fae folk. Mysterious sightings in Central Park at dusk and dawn. Men and women who were not men but something more. Something other. Of course, they had only ever been stories with no more realism than *Little Red Riding Hood*. But I couldn't help but make connections between those stories and these four boys.

No, not boys, but not men either. They were fresh-faced and young, probably around twenty, but they held a strange kind of strength and power that made them appear older than that.

As if they were ancient, as if they weren't really men at all.

Finn was finally the one to speak up. "What attacked your friend was a Redcap. What attacked the man at the theatre where you work was a Redcap. Though, I don't believe they were the same one. It seems they are drawn to you, and they're coming out of the woodwork."

My heart thumped hard. "But what are they? Some kind of wolf? And why would they be attracted to me?"

The guys exchanged glances again. Clearly, there were things about these Redcaps that they didn't want to tell me. They were hiding something, and I was determined to find out what. One of those things just killed my oldest friend in the world, and I was barely able to concentrate on the conversation with the grief consuming my mind. I needed to know what the hell was going on.

"We should probably give her some more details or she's not going to come with us willingly," Finn said.

Rourke pursed his lips and frowned. "That's not typically how we do things, and we still need to collect the other two."

Kael spoke, ignoring the others. "Long story short, Norah. You're a changeling, a fae who was swapped at birth with a human child. Now that it's the Summer Solstice of your eighteenth year, it's time for you to return to the faerie realm, Otherworld, and train at the academy to learn how to use your various...gifts. You'll belong to one of four courts, but we won't know which until we test your abilities. That said, Redcaps are typically drawn to Winter fae, like me."

I gaped at him, his words tumbling over each other in my head. A changeling swapped at birth. A fae. A realm where they expected me to go. None of this was logical. None of it could be real. But words from the stories also tumbled through my brain, melting together with what he had said. The legends had talked of this, too. Of children stolen from their cribs to be replaced with baby fae.

But how could this be true? How could magic be real? And how the hell could *I*, of all people, be one of them?

"You do realize this sounds crazy," was the only thing I could say.

Kael lifted his shoulder in a slight shrug. "Perhaps. But tell me, deep down inside, do you not sense this as the truth? Are you anything like your mother? Have you always felt as though you were an outsider? You've seen things, felt things, that no one else could. The Redcaps, your ears. It's really not difficult to see the truth if you just open your eyes to it."

"There must be some other explanation."

"Usually it's much easier to introduce a changeling to our world, but your situation has turned out to be... unfortunate." Kael sighed. "Normally we just take you straight to the Faerie Ring, so you can see it for yourself."

Finn nodded. "Why don't you come with us, and we can show you some proof."

I shook my head, crossed my arms over my chest, and took a step back. "I'm not going anywhere with you. My best friend was just..." My breath hitched. I couldn't say the words out loud. "And then you four strange stalkers, who just happened to be there, I have to add, expect me to just go along with you? When you're spouting nonsense about faeries?"

Rourke scowled, and Kael merely let out a sigh. It was the one with the flaming red hair who stepped forward, his eyes sparking with a dangerous kind of fire. One, I had to admit, made my breath get caught in my throat. His eyes made me feel as though he could see right into my soul.

"Look, I know what you're feeling. You're devastated. You're confused. And you're angry. You're so angry about what happened to your friend that you wish you could punch that asshole Redcap right in the throat. Am I right?" He crossed his arms over his muscular chest and raised an eyebrow.

My heart thumped. He was right. A hot anger burned through me, nothing like I'd ever felt before. The only times I'd ever come close was when my stepdad turned his rage toward my mother. It boiled through my veins, threatening to burn me from the inside out.

I nodded, swallowing around a thick, painful lump in my throat.

"Good," he said. "Use that anger to do what you need to do. If you come with us and train at Otherworld Academy, you can learn to fight these Redcaps. We'll give you all the skills you need. Hell, there's even a team of Hunters you can join once your Court has been assigned to you. You can fight these things. You could even find the creature who killed your friend."

"There are Hunters?" I whispered.

He nodded. "Hunters who track down these things and kill them."

Pain ricocheted through my gut like a stray bullet as Bree's face filled my mind. Her sparkling blue eyes, her infectious grin. I'd been able to nothing to save her. I'd been helpless, forced to watch her slashed down by a beast I could never hope to fight.

I'd been helpless all my life.

My heart had been racing before, but it was going at light speed now.

I didn't want to be helpless anymore.

"My mom..."

"Your mother is fine," Liam said. "We've been keeping an eye on things. And don't forget that you'll learn how to stand up to that asshole step-dad of yours, too, if you're ever inclined to return after your training."

My hands fisted.

"I do find it necessary to add that you're now wanted for murder," Kael said in an icy voice, dousing some of the flames in my gut. "You have no job or home. If you stay here in the human realm, your life will turn to ash."

"Okay, we don't need to pile it on top of her, guys," Finn said. "She's had a rough few days. Have a little heart."

"She needs to understand the gravity of her situation," Kael replied. "We've been protecting her for the past few days, but we can't stay in Manhattan after tonight. She'll be on her own."

On her own.

I shivered, despite myself. I'd had a sneaking suspicion that they'd been following me, watching me, but I hadn't known what that had truly meant. And as insane as it sounded, I knew deep down in my bones that it was the truth. They'd tried to keep me out of danger, but the danger had only kept following me around. And I couldn't fight those monsters, those Redcaps, on my own. And I'd certainly never be able to make Bree's death right unless I learned to fight back.

I could learn to fight back.

I didn't have to be weak anymore.

"Okay," I said after taking in a long, deep breath. "I'm not sure I completely believe you. This still all sounds totally insane. But I'll come with you to see your proof, if you have it. You have to keep your distance though. The second one of you comes too close, I'm gone."

Finn pursed his lips in amusement. "She thinks she can outrun us."

I opened my mouth to let out a retort, but Rourke held up his hand and shot Finn a sharp look. "Agreed. We'll keep a reasonable distance."

For a moment, I hesitated. I was so torn. On the one hand, it seemed impossibly stupid and dangerous to go with these four guys. On the other hand, I had no idea what other choice I had. Because they were right. I'd run from the cops. Monsters were stalking my every move, my step-dad never wanted me to step foot in my apartment again, and I had no job. No money. No nothing.

All I had was myself, someone who might end up being the impossible: a changeling fae.

I had to go to Otherworld. I just had to hope this all wasn't some sort of trick. I had to hope it was real.

I would learn to fight. I would become a Hunter. And I would never again watch someone I love get destroyed.

CHAPTER EIGHT

The fae—if that was what they truly were—kept their promise. They led me through the city streets and into Central Park, never coming more than ten feet near me. They all stood tall and alert, their eyes darting across every shadow and passerby, as if they were on guard against unseen attackers. Maybe they were.

Within Central Park, they led me off the paved pathways that wound through the lush greenery. And my nerves began to falter. One thing I'd always learned growing up. Don't go anywhere with strangers, and especially don't go into the park after dark. And here I was doing both of them at once.

"Here we are," Finn said in a cheery voice as we reached a clearing in a cluster of trees. It was pretty much a perfect circle, blooming red flowers lining the entire perimeter. The grass was perfect, lush, and a bright vivid green that almost glowed against the cloying darkness that surrounded us.

I hovered on the outskirts of the circle of flowers, unsure of what was supposed to happen next. "This is pretty and all, but I don't understand how it's supposed to prove that this whole faerie thing is real."

"Step inside the ring," Kael said in a soft, quiet voice that sent shivers down my spine.

"You mean, inside the circle of flowers?"

"That's right," he said with an eerie smile. "It's called a Faerie Ring. When you step inside of it, you'll see the proof that what we've told you is real."

"You do realize that this sounds creepy as hell." My feet were frozen to the ground. Logically, I knew stepping forward onto a patch of grass was not dangerous in the least. It was just grass. Those were just normal flowers. But my heart was pounding so hard against my chest that I could barely breathe.

Bree's death still lingered in my mind, and a dull ache had filled my bones. I didn't know how I could go on. I didn't know how to move forward. The only thought keeping me moving was the idea of becoming the kind of girl who could hunt one of those monstrous creatures down. Because there was a truth that I'd tried to ignore, one that would make the ache explode into excruciating pain.

The Redcaps were drawn to me, if these four guys were to be believed.

If Bree hadn't been with me, she wouldn't have died.

And I had been unable to do anything to stop it.

So, I stepped forward onto the grass. For a moment, nothing happened. In the distance, I could still hear the familiar honk of yellow cabs, and I could see the lights of the buildings casting an orange glow on the cloud-studded sky.

But then everything began to change. The world rippled, the ground shook. And suddenly, everything went strangely, eerily silent. Night turned into day, and the dark sky morphed into light. I whirled in a circle, heart stuck in my throat. I was still in the Faerie Ring, in the clearing between the trees, but it was quiet now, so quiet. And everything had gone strangely bright.

It was as if the city had vanished and had been replaced by an endless sea of trees.

The four guys blurred in before me, and I jumped back with a sharp cry. One moment, they hadn't been there. The next, they were mere inches away.

"Welcome to Otherworld," Finn said with a wink. "So, now you see we weren't lying."

"I don't understand. Where did everything go?"

"It didn't go anywhere," Kael said, voice gruff. Almost as if my very existence irritated him. "Manhattan is still where it's always been. *We're* just not there anymore. The Faerie Ring transported us into Otherworld."

"Which is the...fae realm." It sounded so insane that it felt like it wasn't my own voice that said the words. We'd been transported to a fae realm through a ring of flowers? Maybe I really was going insane. Maybe this entire thing was a hallucination, a result of seeing my only friend in the world killed by a vicious wolf.

I felt a little lightheaded now, a dizziness sweeping

through my body. Stumbling forward, I pressed my hand to my mouth and tried to breathe around the panic in my throat.

A strong pair of arms encircled me, saving me from face-planting onto the dewy grass. "Whoa there. Can't have you passing out on your first night at the Academy."

I twisted to look up into a pair of sapling green eyes. They were kind but mischievous, and a strange thrill went through me. He'd caught me once before. I was sure of it now. He'd been the one who found me passed out in the alley. And he'd caught me again now. I felt a strange tug toward him, a need to have his arms hold tight just a little bit longer.

My face flushed, and I yanked my gaze away. That was ridiculous. I didn't want him to hold me up. This guy was a weird stranger who was calling himself a fae, and calling me a....changeling.

"Right." I pulled myself out of his arms and brushed off invisible specks of dirt, hoping he couldn't see the red in my cheeks. "So, you've convinced me that maybe the fae realm is real, though I don't know how I'm supposed to know that this is really it. Still. Even if all that is true, it doesn't necessarily mean I'm a changeling."

Finn laughed and shook his head. "Norah, only fae can travel through Faerie Rings. If we want to bring a human here, we have to carry them through ourselves. In our arms. Kind of like how I was just holding you."

He winked. He actually winked. The redness in my cheeks deepened another shade.

"So, because I was able to travel through by myself..." I trailed off, understanding immediately the implication of his words.

He nodded. "It was your final test. You're fae. And you've got the ears to match, though they're still growing."

"But why now?" I couldn't help but ask. "If I'm really one of you, wouldn't I have noticed a long time ago?"

"Fae don't begin to reveal their abilities until their eighteenth birthday. It's a right of passage and cause for celebration here in Otherworld. For changelings, it's a bit more complicated. You were lucky that your birthday was a mere few days before the Solstice, which is the day all changelings return to their realm. Otherwise, you would have had to deal with all of this on your own for months, like some others."

I frowned. "Okay. But why? And why was I swapped at birth? What happened to the human baby? Does my mother know about this? Oh my god."

My heart stopped as a new realization slammed into me.

"Does that mean...?" I whispered.

Kael gave a curt nod. "Your mother is not of your blood. As for the rest of your questions, all will be answered at Orientation this evening. If you go with Finn, he'll take you to your room where you can settle in while we collect the other two changelings who are still in Manhattan."

"The other two? There's more?"

"Four from Manhattan. Sixteen in total each year,"

Finn said, gently taking my elbow in his hand. "The four of us were tasked with collecting the Manhattan recruits this year. One is already at the Academy. She's sharing your quarters with you. We collected her first, though that might have been a mistake…"

He trailed off, leaving the rest of his sentence unsaid, though I knew the meaning of his silence. If they'd come for me first, Bree wouldn't be dead. It took everything within me to move my feet forward, out of that circle, and to leave my old life behind. Not that it was much of a life anymore.

A trail led through the thick forest. As we walked along the soft dirt, I began to notice just how different this place was to home. Specks of silver hung in the air, blowing this way and that along a soft breeze that smelled like sunflowers and the thick hazy musk of summer. Strangely, it was warm but not the same kind of heat that made the New York pavements feel so claustrophobic. This was a much different kind of warmth. One that felt soothing and soft rather than cloying. There was humidity, but not too much. It was neither dry nor wet. It was, strangely, perfect.

My heart squeezed tight. Bree would have loved it here.

Insects buzzed around our heads, but not any kind of insect that I'd seen before. They were like tiny golden birds with giant translucent wings. One let out a whistle as it darted in front of my face, a sound that was repeated by hundreds of others. It was like a song. A familiar song. One I felt as if I'd heard before.

"What are those?" I finally asked.

Finn had kept quiet, almost as if he could sense my need for silence. Right now, there was still so much I had to process. And while I had so many questions, I didn't even know where to start.

"Slyphs," he said. "In the summer, they fill the forest, singing songs that can sometimes even be heard inside the Academy."

Another slyph whispered by my ear and whistled a series of high and low notes that made my heart lift in my chest.

"They seem to like you," he said with a smile. "Maybe you're not a Winter fae after all. They don't much like the cold."

"And you...you're a Summer fae?"

He let out a low chuckle. "Thank the forest, no. Summers are...hotheaded, to say the least. Fiery, passionate, easily angered. They're far too dramatic for my tastes. No, I'm a Spring fae. Liam back there is a Summer. The one with the red hair."

I nodded. "I see what you mean. He got a little worked up about the Redcaps."

"To say the least," he said, casting me a sideways glance. "And his speech seems to have convinced you to come to Otherworld. You want to learn how to fight so you can avenge your friend. Like I said, maybe we were wrong about your Court."

My heart dipped. *Bree.*

"But the Redcaps are attracted to Winter fae, right?" I whispered.

"Indeed." He pursed his lips. "Truthfully, it's far too early to tell where you'll belong. It usually takes the first full year to identify a changeling's Court. Your abilities have not fully come to you yet, so you may demonstrate qualities of several Courts for awhile. Many do."

"So, this training thing, it takes a year?"

"Oh, no." He flashed me a smile. "Once we've identified your Court, you move on to more specialized training to hone your skills. The Academy is a three-year school. So, you should know that it will be your home for a long while to come."

"Three years?" I stopped in my tracks. "No one said anything about three years when I agreed to come along. That's not an option. My mom is stuck there with my step-dad. Bree's killer is just out there in the streets. I can't be gone for three years. I'm going back."

"Ah..." Finn trailed off, giving me a bland smile. "Unfortunately, that's not an option."

I took three steps back, fisting my hands. "The hell it isn't. What are you going to do? Pick me up and carry me to the Academy, kicking and screaming?"

He lifted his shoulders in a slight shrug, and then flashed me a pair of perfect white teeth. "If that's what it takes."

"You wouldn't," I said, taking two more steps back down the path. Finn followed, mimicking my moves with a strange kind of fluid ease. Two more steps back.

And then he followed once again, as if we were caught in some sort of magical dance routine.

"You're really testing me, aren't you, Norah?" He gave me a wink. "Fine. We'll do things your way. If you take one more step toward the Faerie Ring, I'll have no choice but to throw you over my shoulder. Be careful not to doubt me, Norah. I never lie."

I narrowed my eyes. Surely he wasn't serious. He couldn't very well force me to stay here against my will. Then again, he was a fae. They all were, and there was no telling just how good or evil they might be. I mean, they swapped human babies with changelings. That in and of itself was wrong in more ways than I could count. And yet, I'd come with them willingly.

There's nothing for you back in the human realm, Norah, a soft voice whispered in my ear. His voice. But he hadn't opened his mouth to speak.

Frowning, I glared at him. Was he throwing thoughts into my mind? Whatever it was, I didn't like it.

I took a step back.

With a laugh, he rushed toward me at an impossible speed, wrapped his arms around me, and threw me over his shoulder before I could even utter a yelp of surprise. I kicked my legs and pushed at his chest, but it was no use. His grip was iron-tight, and all my flailing did was make him squeeze tighter.

"Fighting this won't do you any good, but continue to wriggle against me all you want if it makes you feel better." He let out a light chuckle.

Irritation flickered through me. "It's not funny. Put me down. Now."

"Oh, it's impossibly funny. And enjoyable, I might add."

"Let me guess," I snapped. "While Summer fae are hotheaded and passionate, Spring fae are annoying and irritating and frankly rude."

He laughed again. "Curious. Mischievous. We are prone to see the lighter side of things than the dark."

"So, you're a big jokester," I grumbled. "Makes sense. Though I really think you should add annoying to the list."

"Some find us annoying, particularly those who don't belong in the Spring Court," he said. "It's a shame. It would have been fun to have you by my side."

Have you by my side. His words sent a sharp thrill down my spine. Which was weird. And annoying. Nothing about this fae thrilled me, especially not the thought of him being by my side. Nope. I wanted nothing to do with him. Nothing to do with his beautiful green eyes, his gorgeous glistening skin, that mouth that looked as though it knew how to...

What the hell, Norah?

"So, what about the others? What are they like?" I asked, desperate to change the subject, though there was a part of me that was also desperate to know what he meant.

"Rourke, the Autumn fae, is...strange, as I'm sure you've gathered. Strong, devious, fixated on darkness." He cleared his throat as we bounced along the path.

"People assume that's how the Winter Court fae would be, but Autumn is the season when the leaves pack up and die."

"Well, then what are Winter fae like?" I asked. "I mean, he seemed a little unnerving, I guess, but you all do."

He laughed again. "Trust me. We know how we come across to those who have spent their entire lives in the human realm. Kael is...sensible, I guess you could say. He focuses more on logic than on emotions, so he comes across as cold and unfeeling. He doesn't have much patience for frivolous things."

I shivered, remembering how annoyed he'd come across when he'd asked to see my ears. "Yeah, that sounds about right."

"The opposite of Summer."

We fell silent after that. The buzz of the thick forest rose up around us, sounds of insects and birds and rustling leaves. It was a nice sound, one I felt could lull me to sleep if I wasn't careful. Maybe I really was part of the Summer Court. At the thought, I almost laughed out loud. How quickly the strangeness of this world and these people had begun to fade. Already I was beginning to feel as if I'd stepped out of a dream and into the true reality of my world.

And it gave me a sudden burst of bravery.

"So about that whole 'stand by my side' thing," I started to say just as Finn came to an abrupt stop and deftly lowered me to my feet. The second my toes touched dirt, I stumbled away from him, glaring at his stupid sparkling eyes.

"Ah, here we are." He dusted off his hands and grinned. "It's probably best if the other students aren't introduced to you by me carting you inside the Academy on my shoulder. Start off with a good impression, if you know what I mean."

My heart began to thunder in my chest. The whole training to fight monsters thing had drawn me here, but I hadn't really considered that I'd be training with *other people*. High school had never really been a pleasant experience for me. I'd been the weird girl, the one no one really liked. Sometimes, I'd made friends, but they'd only stuck around until they realized that I just wasn't like other people.

The thought of going straight back into a school atmosphere? Well, it wasn't making me excited, to say the least. I'd never planned on going to college. I thought school was in my past. Not in my future.

"I know what you're thinking. Want to know how?" He grinned. "Because every single changeling who has come here has thought the same thing. You didn't enjoy school. You didn't have many friends. You got bullied, made fun of. Don't worry. Everyone here has been through the same as you. You'll fit right in."

"If I try not to go inside, you'll just sling me over your shoulder again," I said. "Won't you?"

He cracked a grin. "See, you're catching on already."

CHAPTER NINE

The actual Academy itself was something out of a gothic horror movie, minus the dark and rolling clouds lurking in the background. The ancient stone castle was the color of the steel Manhattan buildings, but a tapestry of thick green moss covered the bottom half. Spires rose up from every corner, and a large archway commanded the entrance. Through one of the thin rounded windows on the third floor, I spotted a hazy figure staring down at us. I shivered but kept my chin high as I strode through the archway behind Finn, who I could have sworn was chuckling under his breath.

Inside, we climbed a curving staircase that was carpeted in a deep red that reminded me of the color of Liam's hair. Framed painted portraits lined the wall. Fae, I was guessing. They sat on thrones with various crowns decorating their heads. Twisting branches of bright and vivid flowers sat on one while another crown was nothing more than the deep gold of autumn leaves.

"Our Royals," Finn said with a flick of his wrist at the paintings. "There's the Spring King and Queen, and there's Autumn." We passed two more. This one had a crown of roses, and the thorns had remained intact, something that seemed a bit like a hazard to me. "And that's Summer."

"Right," I said with a nod. "Makes sense. I guess. Actually, none of this makes sense. You have royalty?"

Finn grinned and pointed to the next painting. "And this here's our Winter Royals." Their crowns had no leaves, no flowers. Only knotted brambles twisted tightly together.

The expressions on their faces were cold and uncompromising. Was I really like them? I'd never thought of myself as unfeeling, as calculating, or as cruel, but maybe I didn't know myself that well. After all, it turned out I was a fae, something I'd never known about myself until now. Maybe there was more about me I didn't know. Maybe I really wasn't the kind of person I thought I was.

Maybe I wasn't as weak and as helpless as I'd always thought.

"Who's that?" I asked when we passed the last portrait on the wall.

For the first time since we'd met, Finn's face crumpled, and the lighthearted expression fell away. He clenched his jaw and kept moving up the stairs, his eyes turned away from the portrait.

I jogged to keep up. "Wait, who is that, Finn?"

His voice was hard when he spoke. "Marin. She was our Queen for three hundred years, but her rule was overthrown by members of the Autumn Court. At that time, there was only one Queen, and the Autumn fae wanted change. Four Courts. Four rulers. So, they killed her."

I gasped.

"Out of respect, we keep her portrait on the wall, but some would consider it treason to display any amount of loyalty to our dead Queen. We may one day need to remove it."

"That's...terrible," I finally said.

He stopped short, spun on his feet, and placed a finger to my parted lips. I almost stumbled down the stairs from the sudden contact, and my heart froze in my chest. Our gazes locked, and a strange emotion flickered in his eyes, one I was sure was reflected in the flutter in my stomach.

Something about this Spring fae felt strangely alluring. It was as if some unseen force had drawn me to him. And suddenly, a mere finger to my lips didn't seem like enough at all. I wanted more.

Where the hell were *those* thoughts coming from? Him? Or me? It was insanity. I'd only just met him. He was a fae. He'd stolen me away to another realm. And my heart still felt cracked in two. How could I possibly be thinking about anything but how much I wanted to scream and cry and run?

I shook my head, and that strange tugging sensation snapped away.

"Don't say things like that, especially not in front of

anyone who isn't me. Don't even say it in front of Liam or Kael, and especially don't say it in front of Rourke," he said, voice suddenly dark and empty. "We must fully commit to our current Royals. It's the only way we can survive."

My heart thumped. "You're kind of freaking me out here."

"Good." He gave a nod before that familiar lopsided smile of his reappeared on his face. "I couldn't let you get too comfortable, now could I? Got to keep you on your toes on your first day."

Something told me I would *never* be comfortable around Finn, no matter how long I was here.

"Norah, meet your new roommate, Sophia." Finn's green eyes sparkled as my new roommate came bundling out of the door. She wrapped me in a tight hug, and my breath whooshed out of my lungs. When she pulled back, she smiled, and I couldn't help but smile back. Everything about her was bright and cheerful. She had long, glistening hair that reached her waist, and her eyes were a bright sparkling green. And she seemed a lot happier about our strange new world than I would have expected.

"Good," Finn said as he began to walk away. "I'll leave you two to catch up. Orientation will be downstairs in about an hour. See you later, Norah."

He winked as he disappeared, and the bright spots in my cheeks rushed back in full force.

"Seems like he likes the look of you," Sophia said with a grin as she pulled me into our quarters and shut the door. "You have the green eyes and the fair hair. Maybe you're Spring."

I was pretty certain I wasn't Spring, but the idea of it sent a rush of warmth through my gut.

Her eyes tripped down to my empty hands, and she cocked her head. "Where's all your stuff? Didn't you pack a bag?"

"Erm…" I said, suddenly nervous. What would she think if she knew that the Redcaps had been chasing me around Manhattan? I got the feeling that the Autumn and Winter fae weren't as well liked as the sunnier seasons. And she definitely seemed like a sunny, happy one. The kind of fae who everyone would like.

"I didn't have time. There was this whole fight with my step-dad, and I couldn't go home to get my clothes."

"It doesn't matter," she said with a kind smile. "I'm sure the fae will be able to get some clothes for you. I mean, they *are* ancient, magical beings after all. Surely they can conjure up some kind of wardrobe."

"*We*," I said. "We're fae, too. As strange as that sounds."

"I know," she said, eyes lighting up. "Can you believe it? I mean, at first, I thought maybe they were crazy. It wouldn't be the first time I'd met some weirdos. But then they made a good point. I've always been weird and different, and the past six months have been really bizarre."

I lifted my eyebrows and perched on the edge of the antique red sofa. It looked as though our quarters were a lot different than the dorms on college campuses. We had a living area full of antique furniture with a patchwork rug spread across the stone floor. Two doors hung open, both leading into lofty rooms with four-poster beds.

"Have you been seeing strange things, too?" I asked.

"Seeing things?" She shook her head and sat next to me. "My ears got all pointy, and I kept passing out all the time when I touched iron. Went to the doctor and everything, and they couldn't find anything wrong with me. In fact, they said I was healthier than the average eighteen-year-old. Why? What have you seen?"

"Ehm..." Should I try to explain it? And *how* could I? I wasn't even entirely sure I knew how to describe the Redcap. Plus, introducing myself as someone wanted for two homicides probably wasn't the greatest idea in the world, especially when I'd be spending who knew how much time with my new roommate.

Homicides. A fresh wave of pain smacked me in the face. My eyes burned with unshed tears, and the painful lump in my throat returned. Bree was dead.

My oldest friend in the world was dead.

And it was all my fault.

"It's okay," she said, giving my arm a squeeze. "I understand how you feel. It just started happening to you, didn't it? I was scared to tell people about it, too. I thought they'd think I was crazy. And well...some did." She let out a heavy sigh and gave my arm a squeeze. "I won't think you're crazy, Norah. When you're ready to talk about it, I'll be here to listen."

I gave her a weak smile.

And that was when I decided that sharing quarters with another changeling wouldn't be so bad after all.

An hour later, we entered the Great Hall for Orientation. The vaulted room was located on the ground floor of the academy, sandwiched between four wings that spread out like the long points of a compass. Golden light streamed in the arched windows along one wall while banners of gold, red, black, and green hung along the other. Our footsteps echoed as we drifted inside, and my eyes widened at the motes of glistening dust that drifted through the sweet-scented air.

At the far end of the room sat a wooden table, parallel with the small stage where a cluster of powerful fae stood watching. I spotted the four guys who had saved me in Manhattan. My stomach flipped as my gaze caught with Finn's. He winked at me from where he stood next to the other three guys, along with about a dozen more fae. Some men, some women.

Five more tables stretched across the center of the Great Hall. Four held what I assumed to be other students. At each table, many had similar features, and they wore cloaks of similar colors. A cluster of deep red hair on one. Several students with gleaming black eyes on another.

The final, fifth table was full of nervous-looking students, cloak-less and confused. That would be where we would sit.

Sophia and I eased onto the wooden bench and waited while one powerful female fae stood and stepped to the edge of the stage, her lilac gown rustling around a lithe yet toned frame. Magic shimmered across her skin, and her deep golden hair gleamed beneath the sunlight that streamed in from the large windows. She looked no more than five or ten years older than the rest of us, but there was something ancient and wise in her dark eyes.

"Welcome to Otherworld Academy. I'm Alwyn Aldair, your Head Instructor," she said with a wide smile that felt more eerie than welcoming. "As always, we have sixteen new changelings with us this evening, from four different origins in the human realm. So far, you may have realized that four is a common theme here. And that's because we have four courts. From each human origin, there will be a Spring, a Summer, a Winter, and an Autumn amongst you, giving each Court four new changeling fae a year."

We all nodded and murmured. The fae who had saved—or captured, depending on how you looked at it—me had explained most of this to me, though they hadn't gone into much detail. I guessed it made sense, though I still didn't understand the how or the why of it. It was also one more point in the Not-Spring column, since I was pretty certain my new roommate was the embodiment of all things Spring.

"For some of you, it will be quicker to determine your Court. Fae in each season tend to have certain traits and certain dispositions. That said, it's not always the case. Many times, a changeling recruit will start her first year believing she's of one Court and find she's of entirely another. It's a process, one we'll determine through training and challenges."

A hand shot up near the end of the table. With a frown, Alwyn nodded at the student. "Yes?"

"Why don't you know what we are?" the guy asked. "I mean, you guys keep saying we're changelings, and that we were swapped at birth. So, we were born here, right? Are we not in the same Court as our, uh…" He trailed off, swallowing hard.

Our parents. My skin and neck began to tingle, and a heavy rock tumbled down into my gut. I still hadn't come to terms with the fact that my mother wasn't my birth mom. And I had a feeling that most of the new recruits here felt the same.

"Excellent question." Alwyn steepled her hands underneath her chin and smiled. "Yes, your Court is hereditary. Only in rare—and I do mean rare—cases does the son or daughter not fit within their natural born Court. And yes, we do keep meticulous records on each of our changelings. Unfortunately, Magnus Farrow, our previous record-keeper, died in a fire seventeen years ago. With him went all of his records and knowledge about the changelings. We don't know who each of you are. That knowledge was lost. So, that's why we must perform these tests. The changelings who come to the Academy two years from now will no longer need to undergo the introductory first year since our current record keeper is alive and well, and the files are routinely copied down. We won't make the same mistake again."

Well, that was certainly interesting. And, in response, half a dozen more hands shot up.

The Head Instructor held up her hand with an irritated sigh. "Let me guess. Your next question is why we've been swapping out human babies with fae. Well, here is the very long answer made short. There are more realms than just the human and the fae. There is a realm of darkness, of demons. Each year, we must pay a Tithe to that realm. Sixteen fae babies must go into the human realm, and sixteen human babies must come here. If we do not keep up our Tithe, the darkness will not only descend upon us but it will descend upon the humans as well." A tense, uneasy silence followed, and she smiled. "So, you see. We must do this. Or else we would cause the Apocalypse to arrive in both our realms."

Every single one of the new recruits stared at Alwyn with a mixture of confusion, horror, and fear. Including me.

"Luckily," she continued as her face slightly brightened, "we can make the swap back during the Summer Solstice. You will each be trained in the ways of the fae, and you will each be trained to fight. Once your training is complete, you will join your Court along with your male or female mate, those of which are on this stage and will be working with you throughout your time at the Academy."

Hold up. My eyes widened. Had she just said *mate*? The words from Finn began to tumble over me. *By my side*. I swallowed hard, and my heart began to race. Murmurs began to echo all around me, the rest of the changelings as thrown by this new information as I was. In fact, it almost felt more shocking than the reveal about the demons and the Tithe to hell.

Almost.

A girl stood from the table, her long fiery hair swishing around her shoulders. "You can't just assign us mates. Don't we get some choice in the matter?"

"It will be your choice, eventually," Alwyn said coolly. "You're from Manhattan, yes? Then, one of these four males here will be your mate. Finn, Rourke, Liam, or Kael. And trust me when I say that you'll be happy for it, as strange as it may seem to you now. The magic of Otherworld has brought you here together at the same time. You may not understand it yet, but you will in time."

"But wait," another girl said, standing from the table, her voice a heavy Irish accent. "First, you're telling us that we were taken from our homes at birth. Then, you're telling us that we have no choice in what we do from now on, including what Court we join, and the person we end up mating with? You can't honestly expect us to have sex with someone just because you say so."

Alwyn let out a low chuckle. "We're not forcing you

to do a thing. At the end of the year, you'll be so bonded to your male, naturally, that you will be glad he is your mate. And if you're not, then you are welcome to go your own way."

The girl narrowed her eyes. "I'm gay."

"Oh." Alwyn's lips twisted up as she glanced over her shoulder at one of the female fae behind her. "Well, then your Court will certainly be easy to determine."

When another round of questions rose up, the Head Instructor clapped her hands and frowned at us all. I'd quickly determined that she was either Autumn or Winter. She didn't have the temperament to be one of the sunnier types of fae. "There will be plenty of time for more questions, and plenty of time to learn what you need to know. But first, what better way to introduce you to life at the Academy than through your first challenge? You'll divide into your origin groups and go outside where your instructors will lead you through a test with the bow and arrow, to determine whether or not you're a natural shot. That will give us some indication about the strength of your powers. Now, go."

We stood in the expansive lush gardens behind the Academy's main building. Rolling hills tumbled in the distance, meeting the orange and red streaked sky. For a moment, I stared at the dying glimmer of sunlight, wondering at who and what I had suddenly become.

Bree would love it here, I decided. She'd dive head-first into training, and she would without a doubt have her eye on one of the fae, hoping he was hers. She'd be a Spring or a Summer, most likely. Nothing about Bree was dark or cold.

"All right," Liam said, clapping his hands as he stood before our little rag-tag group. "Time to get started. Who wants to go first?"

On the way over, I'd introduced myself to the two other Manhattan recruits. All girls, all wide-eyed, and a little shell-shocked. So, kind of like me. The girl with the fiery hair was named Lila, and a quieter girl with golden eyes was named Sam. She watched the entire group, sizing things up with a quiet kind of intelligence that suggested she wasn't the kind of person to miss much, even if she never really spoke up.

"I'll go first!" Sophia said, her hand shooting high in the air. Finn chuckled from where he watched from the side, and he shook his head. His laugh was such an annoying sound, mostly because I couldn't get it out of my head once I'd heard it. It was so lyrical, so poetic, almost, like a song that kept repeating over and over again in the most perfect way imaginable.

But that was stupid.

It was a laugh, an annoying one at that.

And *he* was annoying.

But a part of me felt like I could dance to the tune of his laugh.

"Alright, looks like we have our first volunteer." Liam waved Sophia forward and slid the bow into her hands. It wasn't the kind of bow that you'd see in any kind of modern hunting shop. Instead, it looked old and weathered, as if made from ancient trees. Hell, it probably had been.

"There's the target," Liam said, pointing at a bulging sack at least a hundred yards away. "You've got three shots. Good luck."

Sophia wrinkled her nose. "Aren't you going to show me how to use this thing? I've never shot an arrow in my life."

"Nope." He crossed his arms over his broad chest and stepped back. "The challenge is to see how well you can shoot without any training. That means no demonstrations from me. Yet."

She shrugged and slid an arrow into the bow. At first, she fumbled a bit. The arrow slid this way and that, but after a few minutes of wobbly trembling, she finally managed to get it to stick. With a deep breath, she raised the arrow and loosed it in the air.

And then it sunk into the sack with a heavy thump.

My mouth dropped open, and Sophia pounded her fist in the air.

"That was awesome!" She whirled toward me with sparkling eyes, and I couldn't help but grin back. "Maybe this whole fae thing isn't so bad after all."

Her next two arrows hit the mark, but that wasn't much of a surprise after the first. Lila went next. She managed to get her first two shots within a couple of feet of the sack, and the third finally hit the edge of the mark. With every second that passed, the more my palms began to sweat. I'd never been particularly good at anything but dancing, and this seemed about as far away from dancing as something could get.

Up next was Sam. She was a little better than Lila but didn't reach the same heights as my new roommate, and she huffed and muttered beneath her breath. Clearly, she wasn't used to not being at the top of the class.

Finally, it was my turn. Liam stepped forward and slid the bow into my hands. As he gave me an arrow, our fingers brushed. A jolt went through my body from the connection of our skin, like a static shock times ten. I sucked in a sharp breath as his eyes locked onto mine. Those eyes that were as bright and as brilliant as the red-and-golden summer sunset. Despite myself, my gaze dropped south. To his chest. His very broad and muscular chest. I could see the ridges of his abs through his tight, black tunic, and it was impossible not to notice his perfectly formed pecs.

Heat poured through my stomach like molten lava. Swallowing hard, I dragged my gaze back up to his face where he watched me with an intensity that made my knees weak.

His lips curled up into a devilish smile. "Something wrong?"

I blinked and stepped back, dropping my hand

away from his. "No. Of course not. I've just never handled a bow and arrow before."

My voice sounded rough. I hoped he didn't notice.

He lifted a brow. "None of the other Manhattan recruits have either."

"Right." My cheeks burned with embarrassment. He'd clearly caught me sucked in by his impossibly orange-red eyes, and the tremble my body had instinctively made when his hand had brushed mine. And Liam, I was quickly understanding, was the kind of person whose ego relished in even the slightest of compliments.

Not that I was complimenting him. I was just *noticing* him, the same way any other girl with blood in her veins would.

Sucking in a deep breath, I forced my gaze away from the Summer fae and fumbled to fit the arrow into the slot thingy. I mean, who was I kidding? I didn't know any of the terms for a bow and arrow. So, a slot thingy it was.

"By the way," Liam suddenly spoke up, his lips only inches from my ear. In the few seconds I'd had my attention turned away from him, he'd snuck up on me, and the cloying scent of summer rain and sunflowers swarmed into my nostrils. "Whoever loses this first test gets Watch Duty tonight. Which means you'll get very little sleep, and you'll become intimately acquainted with what goes bump in the night." He gave me a wink. "And there are many things that go bump in the night, including me. Good luck."

CHAPTER TEN

Trembling, I lifted the bow and stared down the aim at the bulging sack. Liam's words echoed in my ears, no matter how hard I tried to block them out. His stupid smug smile. His bonfire eyes.

Gritting my teeth, I thought of Bree. I remembered her terrible scream as the beast bore down on her. I focused on how I'd done nothing but stand there, fear tumbling through me.

I focused on my step-dad's face, remembered the sound his fist had made when it had punched the wall by my head. I heard my mother's warbling voice, her fear.

The bulging sack became everything I hated and feared. This was my chance to become better than what I was. To be strong.

I loosed the arrow.

It went flying off into another section of the garden, landing nowhere near the sack.

My mouth dropped open. "What?"

Liam chuckled, a sound that irritated my very bones. "Nice one. Try again, darling."

"Stop calling me darling," I snapped as I grabbed another arrow.

"You have two more tries. Make them count. Darling."

I let out a low growl of irritation and turned back to the target. The next two arrows didn't fare much better. They stayed in our lane, but they were about as far from the sack as I could get. It was as if my arms and hands were playing a different game than everyone else: get the arrow as far from the target as possible.

Liam was still lurking over my shoulder when I was done. He'd been standing like that the entire time I'd been attempting the shots. I felt his breath whispering across my neck, and I heard the laugh I swore that no one could hear but me.

When I lowered the bow, I whirled on him, my own eyes as fiery as his. "You did that on purpose. You wanted to see me fail, so you made me lose."

His grin widened, and I wished I could punch his face. This wasn't fair. He'd been nothing but nice to the other changelings. It was only me whose life he wanted to make miserable. Anger boiled inside of me, but at least it was better than pain.

"I did nothing of the sort. And, don't forget, I'm one of your instructors. You need to show me the proper respect. Otherwise..." His eyes sparkled. "I might have to add some more punishment on top of your Watch Duty."

My mouth dropped open, and anger curled in my stomach. "Oh, so is that how things work around here? Women mates get punished if they don't obey their men? What kind of archaic bullshit is this?"

"Oh, you're not my mate yet, darling." His voice was deep and dark as he curled a finger underneath my chin. "But I see that fire in you. Maybe you will end up mine."

"Sorry about what happened out there," Sophia said as we strolled back into our shared quarters. I only had an hour to "unpack" and settle in before I had to meet up with the other losers who had been assigned Watch Duty for the night. All the changelings who had come in last in their groups were suckered into a long night of watching the dark forest for any sign of dangerous creatures. Since we sucked so bad at the whole bow and arrow thing, we weren't there to fight. Instead, we would waste away our sleeping hours by keeping watch.

I shrugged and slumped down onto the bed in Sophia's room, watching her unzip the first of three massive suitcases. A twinge went through my gut. I wished I'd had a chance to pack my things. Instead, I was here with nothing from my past, except Mom's necklace which dangled from my neck. Nothing else to remind me of who I really was.

Except the pain and anger still burning in my veins.

"It wasn't your fault, Sophia. It's not like you cursed me to be terrible at being a fae." I sighed and looked around me. Compared to hers, my room would be brutally empty. No clothes. No signs of life. "And I could really use a shower and a fresh change of clothes."

"Maybe if I'd been worse, it'd be me keeping watch tonight instead of you." She pulled a black t-shirt from the depths of her bag. "Want to wear this? It's sufficiently guard-like, and we're about the same size."

I lifted my eyes from the stone floor. "Really? You wouldn't mind?"

"Nope, not at all." She tossed me the shirt with a smile. "Until the fae manage to round up some clothes for you, feel free to wear anything of mine. We've got to stick together, right?"

I let out a relived sigh and nodded. "We've got to stick together."

When I returned to the Great Hall an hour later, I expected Liam to be waiting to greet me with that egotistic smile of his. He'd been the one who had assigned me Watch

Duty, after all. Instead, it was Rourke, the Autumn fae. The weird one who, I had to admit, made me feel a little nervous. There was something so unnerving about him. He was quiet and cool, his lips pressed together in a firm line. Next to Finn's boisterous nature and Liam's fiery flirting, Rourke just seemed...

Chilling.

"This may be your first evening at Otherworld Academy, but we don't ease changelings in slowly here." Rourke strode to the wall and took four binoculars off a wooden shelf before passing them out to each of us. "Each night, students assist with Watch Duty, an essential task for ensuring the safety of this Academy. And while you may feel this is a punishment for losing your challenge, it's an integral part of your training. You should consider it a privilege to guard this place."

A guy with fair reddish hair scoffed and crossed his arms across the kind of chest that could only be built from hours spent in a gym. "Right. A privilege. Then, why didn't you give it to the so-called 'winners' of today's challenge?"

Rourke turned to the guy and stared, his eyes glittering with a ferocity that almost made me gasp. I was certainly glad he wasn't looking at me like that.

"Griff, is it? From Wales?" Rourke said quietly. "Their time will come. You need to focus on your own training. Be appreciative of this opportunity."

"Well, we should at least get some kind of weapon," said Griff. "What good are we going to do just wandering around with some binoculars?"

"No weapons yet," Rourke said firmly. "This is your

first night here. You aren't ready. If you see anything out of the ordinary, you'll sound the alarm, and the instructors or guards will take care of the issue."

Griff snorted, and I frowned. I knew I should keep my mouth shut. Rourke was more than a little intimidating, but I also had questions that he needed to answer.

"So, all we're doing is standing around keeping watch with these?" I lifted the binoculars. They were black and heavy and clearly from the human realm. It seemed the fae stole more than just babies.

His glittering eyes turned my way. "Yes, Norah. That's why it's called Watch Duty."

My cheeks flamed. I was glad I wasn't an Autumn Court fae. I couldn't imagine spending the rest of my life with this guy by my side, his eerie unnerving way of speaking, those golden eyes that I swore felt as though could see past my skin and into my soul.

Not that I could imagine spending the rest of my life with any of them. I mean, we'd just met. Yeah, they were all insanely gorgeous in their otherworldly way they had, and I had a feeling they looked amazing with their shirts off, too. But it was just too bizarre, imagining that one of them would end up my lifelong mate.

And that I would somehow end up *thrilled* about it.

Of course, it was hard to believe that *any* of this was real.

"So, what are we watching out for anyway?" another one of the changelings asked, a girl with dark wavy hair that curled around her pixie face. "Are there actually things out there we need to be worried about?"

Rourke's lips curled into a devious smile. "Oh yes. Why do you think it's a requirement for all changelings to be trained once they return to Otherworld? You're in the land of the fae now, and not all creatures of this realm are like us."

He waved at himself, and his words sent a chill down my spine. I couldn't help but think of the wolf monsters who had killed Bree. Was he talking about those? Or were there more things out there? Things that were even worse?

I swallowed hard.

As if reading my mind, he flicked his eyes my way and nodded. "There are many types of dangerous creatures in Otherworld, Norah. You'll begin to learn more about them tomorrow when classes begin. For now, all you need to do is keep an eye out for anything with fangs and fur. If you spot one, sound the alarm."

At first, my palms were almost too sweaty for me to keep my grip on the binoculars, but after two uneventful hours where there was nothing but buzzing crickets and endless dark, glittering skies, I began to relax.

Rourke had given each of us a small squat watch tower in the corners of the Academy grounds, so I didn't even have anyone to keep me company for the six hours that darkness would permeate the skies. Once Watch Duty was over, we'd have just enough time to go back inside for an hour's nap and a shower before classes began for the day.

A privilege, my ass.

A soft cool breeze whispered across the back of my neck, and my body stiffened instinctively. Not because of anything I saw or heard but because I felt something nearby me. Something dark and dangerous and cold.

"Norah," came a shiver of ice from behind me. "All quiet on the northwestern side?"

It was just Rourke, though that knowledge did little to calm my nerves. My pulse began to throb in my veins, bouncing dangerously quick in my neck.

I lowered my binoculars to the stone ledge before me, but I didn't turn to face him.

"Yep, no sign of murderous wolves," I said after swallowing hard. "That's what I'm looking for, right? More of those wolves that killed Bree?"

A part of me desperately hoped he'd say no. I wasn't sure I was ready to see another wolf beast so soon. But another part of me wanted nothing more. I *needed* to see one. And I needed to take it down. Not that I'd succeed, at least not with a bow and arrow.

"Yes and no." He stepped up beside me and peered out across the thick forest. "Redcaps are sometimes attracted to this place due to the presence of the Winter fae who reside here, but there are more creatures than Redcaps to worry about. Many of them are much, much more dangerous."

My heart tripped in my chest, and I glanced up at

his strong and steady profile, horrified by his words. "*More* dangerous than Redcaps? But they...they..."

"You're right to be afraid." He nodded. "And that's why you're here. You need to learn how to fight."

"I want nothing more than to learn how to fight. I want to learn how to kill them," I found myself saying aloud. I clamped my mouth shut, shocked I'd been so blunt and open with this stranger, with this *fae*.

"Because of Bree?" he asked quietly.

"Yes," I said, voice catching. "To know that there are creatures like that out there killing innocents..."

I closed my eyes.

"There are far worse things in the world than Redcaps, Norah," he said, voice eerily calm and quiet.

My heart squeezed tight. "Obviously, I never thought the faerie realm was real, but I never would have imagined it to be like this."

He raised his eyebrows and cast me a strange smile. "And how would you imagine it, Norah? All puffy clouds and rainbows? Dancing and merriment? Everyone holding hands and singing songs?"

"Well...yeah, actually," I said, heat creeping into my cheeks. He made it sound so stupid when he put it like that, but it *was* what I'd imagined when I'd thought of faeries. "I never would have thought it was a place full of dangerous creatures who went around murdering people."

His eyes flashed, and something in his expression darkened. But just as quickly as it had come, it was gone again. What was that all about? A part of me yearned to know. This fae was...odd, unsettling, strange. And it made me want to figure him out.

"There is much to love about Otherworld, but there is also much to hate. At one time, our world was better than this. There was the merriment, the dancing, the songs. We do still have that now, though not nearly as often as we used to. Otherworld is changing. Ever since we split our Courts, a darkness has begun to creep in. With it comes more violent attacks and much more danger."

Frowning, I glanced up at him. His eyes were locked on something in the distance, and his strong, square jaw clenched tight. Every part of his body was stiff and straight, radiating with pure tension. I thought back to my conversation with Finn on the way into the Academy. Four Courts. Four rulers. When there had once been only a Queen.

"You don't seem particularly happy about the division of the Courts," I finally said. "I thought it was the Autumn fae who led the revolution."

He leaned forward, his fingers tightening on the stone ledge of the watch tower. "It wasn't a revolution, Norah. It was..." He stopped short and sucked in a sharp breath through his flared nostrils. "It matters not. But you see those storm clouds on the horizon?"

Rourke shifted behind me, took my hand in his, and pointed my finger toward a dark shape beyond the furthest edge of the forest. His touch was cold and electric, and it was my body's turn to go tense. Why was he touching me? Why could I feel the caress of his breath on my skin? A whirlwind of scents enveloped me: crackling leaves, rotting wood, and deep damp earth. In my chest, my heart began to shake.

He smelled like the very earth itself, and it was almost overwhelming. I wanted to rip my hand out of his grip, but I couldn't. Every cell in my body stilled, waiting desperately for…I didn't know what.

"See it just there?" he asked in a low whisper with his lips only inches from my ear. He was so close. Why was he so close? And why didn't I *move*?

Swallowing hard, I ripped my gaze from where his fingers were curled around my hand and followed the line. "Yep, I see it. There it is."

He let go, but I still stood frozen in place with my hand outstretched before me. I was losing it. Something about these fae guys had a strange effect on me, one that couldn't be normal. Every single one of them was either irritating, annoying, or kind of weird, but they were all really getting under my skin. I mean, I was practically a trembling mess when Rourke had barely touched me. Not to mention the way that Finn had made me want to punch and kiss him at the same time. And Liam, with his deliciously fiery eyes.

No, I wasn't having these thoughts. Not about these fae. It was just some kind of magical allure they carried around with them. That was the only logical explanation. They had magic, and they were using it on me. And I hated every single second of it.

Rourke had begun speaking again while I'd been distracted by my ridiculous reaction to his touch, and I only tuned back into his words in time to add another terror to the increasingly-growing list of things to worry about in Otherworld.

"Those storm clouds were never there before, particularly not during the Summer," he said with a deep frown. "But they've been increasing these years past. Sometimes, the storms are quite violent. We don't know what's causing them, but I believe it has something to do with what we did all those years ago. We killed the Queen and tore the Courts apart. Otherworld was stable, and now it no longer is."

My eyes caught on his sharp profile, outlined by the light of the moon. "Finn told me it was traitorous to question the new ruling situation."

"Yes, he would say that." Rourke sighed. "And truth be told, it *is* best you don't question it, Norah. If Viola got wind of a new changeling being rebellious, she could make life incredibly difficult for you."

Great. Another thing to worry about.

I raised my eyebrows. "Who's that?"

But his answer was cut short when a boom shook through the night. We both turned toward the sound, only to get blinded by lightning that split the sky. As I frowned at the rolling clouds, something dark blurred in the corner of my vision. Something from within the forest. I lifted my binoculars to my eyes. There, just between the trees, a small creature charged across the forest floor, its clawed hands kicking up bright green leaves. Its slick emerald skin rippled beneath the light of the pale moon, and its veiny, pointed ears flopped against its wrinkled face.

"I see something in the forest," I said, though the

little creature didn't look all that dangerous. Just...kind of weird. "It's probably nothing though. You said to look out for furry things, and that's not furry."

Rourke held out a hand, palm up. "Let me see."

After he held the binoculars to his eyes, he let out a low whistle. "That's not nothing, Norah. It's a pooka, and it's been a long time since one has come anywhere near the Academy."

Shivers coursed down my spine. "That doesn't sound good." I paused. "So, what the hell is a pooka?"

"Pookas thrive on mischief and trickery. Sometimes, they'll transform into horses and carry riders to the nearest stream where they'll drown and then devour them."

I blinked and tried to still the frantic beat of my heart. "Right. So, definitely a danger."

He gave a nod and set the binoculars on the stone ledge. "Interested in some one-on-one training? I can give you a demonstration on how to take care of a pooka."

My mouth suddenly went very, very dry. "I thought we were supposed to sound the alarm when we spotted something dangerous out there."

"You are. But I'm here, and I'm perfectly capable of taking out a pooka. It would be a good experience for you." A beat passed as his lips curled into a devious smile. "Or are you too afraid to face the beast?"

"I'm not too afraid." The words popped out of my mouth before I could stop them. Truthfully, I *was* a little afraid, but I wasn't about to say no and stay here in my safe little tower out of harm's way. I wanted to learn how to fight, and here was my chance. It had just come far sooner than I'd expected.

I was all too aware of what had happened when I'd tried to shoot an arrow at a fake target. I didn't want to know what would happen when I tried to take on a real creature, one that sounded pretty freaking terrifying. At least Rourke would be there. Not that I really trusted him.

"Then, shall I show you how it's done? It might give you an edge in training, one you're going to need."

My heart thumped. I could read between the lines on that one. I'd screwed up with the bow and arrow, and this was my chance to get some important one-on-one training before classes started. I might have failed the challenge, but maybe this would keep me from failing the next. And maybe, just maybe, I wouldn't suck this time.

"Okay," I said in a small voice.

His laugh only added to my terror. "Good. Then follow me."

CHAPTER ELEVEN

The forest looked different at night than it did in the day. The brilliant, verdant trees had transformed into dark and twisting vines that choked out the sky above, and a heavy fog drifted through the undercurrent of leaves. Gone were the sparkling lights and the singsong of the birds. In its place, darkness had come.

Twigs snapped beneath my lace-up, leather boots as I followed Rourke deeper into the woods. He'd been quiet since we'd left the watch tower, and I couldn't stop staring at the muscles in his back, and at the way he held his sword as if it were merely an extension of his arm.

Yep, he had a sword. For some reason, that unnerved me even more. He hadn't given me one though.

"Shouldn't I have a sword?" I whispered, trying my best to keep my voice as low as possible. I didn't want that pooka creature to hear us coming. I distinctly remembered Rourke saying it liked to *devour* its prey. Much like the Redcaps I'd encountered.

"Not happening."

"Why not?"

"I saw what happened with the arrows."

A flush went through my cheeks. "Honestly, it's not like I'd be *throwing* the sword."

"Maybe not on purpose."

I growled, fisting my hands.

"Shh," he said sharply. "Just follow me. Don't say or do anything."

Right. Because I was really only here to watch and learn. As far as Rourke was concerned, I was a useless girl who had failed her first challenge. One who needed to be dragged into a forest so she could stand by helpless while he took care of the pooka.

My hands twitched. I really wished I had my own sword.

Suddenly, he stopped short and held up his hand. He jerked his chin over his shoulder, and his glittering eyes met mine. My breath caught at the look in his eye. He pointed at a spot just to my right. When I turned, there it was, lurking between two thick tree trunks, the color of its skin melting into the forest surroundings.

And it was staring straight at me with a pair of bright red eyes that were the color of blood. I swallowed hard, my heart trembling beneath my ribcage.

"What do we have here?" it asked in a hiss. "A girl who dreams of vengeance. A girl who doesn't belong here. Well, then this is your lucky day, my dear. Take a ride with me, and I can return you to your native lands where I will give you the strength to smite your enemies."

Swallowing hard, I glanced at Rourke, but he'd disappeared from my side. Heart shaking in my chest, I swung my head left and right, desperation and fear rising up from deep within my bones. Where had he gone? Had he left me here to face the creature by myself? *Without a damn sword?* Surely he wouldn't. He was one of my instructors. He was tasked with keeping me safe.

My heart thumped hard.

Or was he?

He'd seemed chilly to me from day one. Maybe he didn't want me around. Maybe this was his way of disposing of me quickly and easily, without any witnesses. I didn't know these fae. How could I be certain they were trustworthy? I'd gone along with this whole thing without question. And maybe, just maybe, I'd only been walking straight into a trap.

The pooka's sharp grin widened, and it scuttled forward. I yelped and jumped back.

"What do you say then, Norah of Manhattan?" it hissed. "Will you come with me?"

As it took another step closer to me, I bent my knees and fisted my hands. It had sharp teeth and claws, but it was small. It had no weapon but itself. Maybe if I gave it a good kick in the face it would leave me alone.

It scuttled forward. I shouted and swung my foot into the air. My boot made contact with nothing but air. Another dark form lunged from the depths of the forest. It all happened so quickly, and the shadows around me blurred at an impossible speed. One moment, the creature was before me, extending its hand toward mine. The next, a sword protruded from its neck, and a waxy blood dripped down onto the forest floor.

Rourke yanked his sword from the pooka and wiped the blade across a cloth he pulled from the depths of his golden-hued cloak. "And that's how it's done."

My heart hammered as I stared up at him open-mouthed. "You just left me out here with the pooka. It attacked me while you were lurking around in the bushes."

"No, he was trying to lure you away from here. Away from me," he said with a quick shake of his head. "He wouldn't have attacked you until he led you back to his den. But, well done." He glanced up, his eyes glittering. The look in them made my heart tumble. "You were brave. I didn't expect that. Most first-year changelings would have run."

I narrowed my eyes. "So, what were you doing then? Testing me?"

"No." A pause. His gaze flicked down. "It's next to impossible to kill a pooka head on. They need to be distracted long enough for someone to sneak up on them from behind. It's the easiest way to get in a killing blow without things getting messy."

Realization dawned, and I had the sudden urge to show the fae what a messy fight could really look like. "You used me as bait. This wasn't about giving me a demonstration on how to kill a pooka. It was about making your life easier on you." I shook my head and took a step back away from him. "I can't believe it. I actually believed you were trying to give me some training. I'm an idiot."

His smile was pure ice with a hint of that fae mischief I was beginning to really despise. "Two birds with one stone. I needed someone the pooka would be interested in, and you needed to learn how to approach one."

"You know what?" I fisted my hands and took another step away from him, whirling on my feet toward the Academy. Anger sliced through my gut. "Next time you want to help me, don't bother."

His quiet, eerie chuckle followed me all the way back to the watch tower, and I could have sworn he kept stopping by my corner for the rest of the night, though he stayed hidden. The cloying scent of crackling leaves and rich, dark earth stayed with me until I stumbled onto my bed for my precious hour's sleep.

The next week passed with more of the same. We spent our days holed up in classes, learning about all the various types of fae and faerie creatures that called this realm their home. Our physical training also began. Fight moves and strategies were discussed, though they didn't introduce weapons just yet. It was clear we were all very much beginners, and the only one of us who seemed particularly good at anything (and everything) was my roommate.

If she wasn't also my best friend in the whole of the Academy, I might be kind of jealous.

Okay, so maybe I was jealous, but I didn't hate her for it.

For the third night since I'd arrived, I found myself prepping for a long, quiet stretch in the northwestern watch tower. Lila and I kept coming last in the tasks for the Manhattan recruits, so it was always either her or me who ended up having a sleepless night. Rourke hadn't visited me again after that first night, though I'd always partially held my breath, wondering if he was somewhere nearby.

I was still angry that he'd used me as bait, but the dance with danger had also been thrilling in a way I couldn't define. I'd tried to kick an asshole pooka in the face. I'd failed miserably, but at least I'd tried.

It was more than I'd ever done before. It felt like a very small step toward...something. Something more than what I'd always been and who I'd thought I was.

A knock sounded on the door just as I slid my feet into the dark leather boots I always wore during my Watch Duty shifts. Just in case I got another chance to take on a creature. I glanced up, heart in my throat, half-expecting to see Rourke's golden eyes boring down on me. But it was only Griff, the changeling fae from Wales who seemed to *enjoy* coming last in tasks so he could spend his nights on Watch Duty.

I kind of couldn't blame him. It was the closest us changelings came to real hands-on training.

"Yep, I'm coming," I said as I finished lacing up my boot. "I don't even want to imagine how Rourke would react if we were late."

"Came here to tell you that Watch Duty has been postponed for tonight," Griff said with a frown. "Really sucks."

"Wait, what?" My heart dropped.

"You heard me. No Watch Duty tonight for us. We've got to entertain some royals or something instead."

"Royals?" My ears pricked up at the words. While we'd spent many hours learning about Otherworld—the creatures, the ancient history, the types of weapons we would one day learn to use—my instructors had been strangely silent about the political side of the faerie world. It was almost as if they weren't yet ready for us to know. That coupled with the strange dark clouds in the sky that Rourke had pointed out...well, my curiosity had been piqued. Like, seriously piqued. I was dying to know more about the four Courts.

"Some members of the Winter Court have come to meet the new changelings or something," he said with a shrug. "We're supposed to go to the Great Hall and be on our best behavior or something. Sounds dumb. I don't care about royalty or politics. I just want to learn how to fight and keep everyone safe."

"Same, Griff," I said, giving him a soft pat on the back. "But trust me. I'm sure you and I will be right back on Watch Duty tomorrow night."

Griff and I were the last two changelings to enter the dining hall, and I could see that we were somehow late even though I'd just learned about the visit from the royals five minutes ago. The fourteen other first-year changelings were sitting quietly and tensely at the table where we usually gathered for breakfast, lunch, and dinner while a cluster of extravagantly-dressed strangers turned their gazes toward me and Griff.

"Ah, here we are," Kael said as he flashed me a tense, irritated smile that made my toes curl with annoyance. It wasn't my fault I was late. "These are our last two changelings, Norah and Griff. They were assigned Watch Duty for this evening, hence their late arrival to meet you."

A tall thin male strode forward and sniffed. His coal black hair hung in loose curls around his angular face, and his eyes were a deep black that seemed almost endless. A crown perched on his head made from glistening knotted brambles. I sat hard on the bench next to the other first-year changelings, struck by the aura of power that radiated off his golden skin.

"This is the King of the Winter Court, Brannon Glass," Kael said as he gave the ruler a half-bow. He then turned to gesture at the woman who stood just behind the King's shoulder. Her hair was nothing like his. It was a bright, brilliant blonde that lit up the entire room. "This is his Queen, Orla Glass."

The changelings and I merely sat silently, staring at the two royals. They were dressed in varying shades of gray and black, with the male in an elaborate, billowing cloak and the woman in a sparkling gown that touched her toes. I glanced down at my black tee, my black jeans, and my muddy boots. Clearly underdressed, as always.

Kael cleared his throat and gave us all a strained smile. His eyes drifted to me. For a moment, the world seemed to stop around us. Something strange sparked within my chest. An almost...recognition. And then it was gone again as Kael pulled his eyes away.

I shook my head. What the hell was *that*?

"The Winter Court was interested in seeing the new changelings for the year. As you know, four of you will be joining them after you graduate from the Academy, so your development and training is of interest to them. They wish to see a bit of a demonstration from you."

Blood drained from my face, and I shifted uncomfortably on the hard bench. A demonstration? Surely he didn't mean that we had to show the Winter Court what we could do. Because...we couldn't do much. Not yet, at least. And certainly not me.

And this could be my court. As the days passed, it seemed more and more likely that Winter was where I belonged, and I didn't want to look like a fool in front of them. My roommate was very obviously a Spring fae while Lila and her fiery temper could only fit into the

Summer Court. That left me with either Winter or Autumn, and seeing how those Redcaps were drawn to me...

Fingers crossed this demonstration had nothing to do with a bow and arrow.

"King Brannon," Kael said, turning back toward the tall, commanding male fae, and his crown of twisted brambles. "What would you like to see from our recruits?"

"Skill with the bow and arrow is essential, particularly for our Court." His words solidified the dread around my heart. "Our fighters specialize in long-range attacks."

Kael bowed his head. "Bow and arrow it is."

Outside, the moon was obscured by thick, rolling clouds, and thunder echoed in the distance. There was no moonlight to help us this evening, only a few torches the instructors had rounded up from the Academy grounds. I stood shivering, sandwiched between Griff and Sophia, though I wasn't cold. My nerves were rocketing around in my gut like a bullet ricocheting from one metal object to the next.

"Norah." Kael flicked his fingers at me, of all people, motioning me forward. "Let's start with you."

Why? I wanted to ask, but I kept my mouth shut. I could feel the eyes of the Royals watching my every move. If they'd come here to see the new changelings, then there was no doubt in my mind that they had an idea of who and what I might be. Kael had probably filled them in on everything, including the Redcaps' strange attraction to me. They would be sizing me up, seeing if I had the chops to join their Hunters after my graduation.

I did not have the chops. Not yet. But I wanted to prove myself to them regardless.

I stepped forward and took the bow. Kael pressed the arrow into my hands and locked eyes with me. No words came from those strained lips of his, but it felt as though he spoke to me. Through his eyes, through his mind, through the intense connection I suddenly felt with him.

Stop pushing it away. Accept what you are and fight back.

Frowning, I slid the arrow into the bow and lifted the aim to my eye. If only it were that simple. If only my mind and my acceptance could make my body perform. I *wanted* this. More than anything. With a deep breath, I pulled back the bow string and loosed the arrow across the field.

And then it just sank into the ground two feet from where I stood.

Disappointment burned in the back of my throat. I didn't dare look at the Royals. I knew what their faces would say. *She is not one of us. She's not good enough.*

She's helpless.

Kael let out a heavy sigh and ran his fingers through his coal black hair. The two Royals muttered something to each other, too low for me to hear. But I didn't need to hear their words to know what they meant. I sucked ass. They probably didn't want me in their court. I blinked away the burning tears that threatened to fall from my eyes.

Kael's hand landed on my arm, and he gripped tight. "Come with me."

Suddenly, the world blurred around me and a deep cold settled over my bones. Everything went pitch black. The summer night became nothing but a darkness so pure that it felt as though we'd entered a black hole.

And then the world was right again, the buzzing insects roaring up around me. Blinking hard, I stumbled back. "What the hell was that?"

Kael's eyes were pools of night. He gazed at me with such an intensity that I could not help but flush in response. "I know you can do more than what you're letting us see, and if you don't improve, things are not going to go well for you."

"What are you talking about?" I glanced around me, but the Royals and the changelings were no longer there. And neither was the Academy. Instead, we stood high on a cliff that plunged low on every side but one. One that led to a cave set deep into the side of a mountain. No lush greenery. No swaying trees. It was all rocks and mist. Panic bubbled up in my chest. "Where have you taken me? How did you do that? What the hell is going on?"

Kael edged in close. So close that only an inch of air wafted between us. I sucked in a breath and tipped back my head, staring up into his endlessly dark eyes. My heart pounded in my chest. Why was he so close? He didn't need to be this close. Did he? My eyes snagged on his lips. They were full and curving up, revealing two rows of teeth that almost looked...sharp. I shuddered, dragging my gaze up the length of his strong, square jaw and up to where his silky strands of raven hair curled over his pointed ears.

He was...not terrible to look at. But he had also somehow transported me through air to steal me away to a cliff so that he tell me just how much I sucked. He no doubt thought I was a Winter fae. Everyone did. And now I was embarrassing him in front of his King and Queen.

With a shuddering breath, I took a step back. But then he just took another step closer.

"There's something we haven't told you all yet because we didn't want to frighten you," he said in a low growl, and his breath whispered across my cheek.

My heart thumped at his words. "Okay, well, that's not really making me feel any better."

"It's possible to fail at the Academy. Those who do not pass are banished from the Courts. You must join the Wilde Fae, and it's a fate I do not wish on anyone, Norah."

"The Wilde Fae," I repeated. "So, they're...not part of any Court?"

I mean, that didn't sound *that* terrible. Just so long as I could still learn how to fight.

"They're savages," he said, eyes flashing. "Vicious and cruel and violent. You wouldn't survive."

"Okay. Not ideal," I said, wiping my palms against my jeans. "But also...thanks a lot for having absolutely no faith in my ability to survive. I'm stronger than I look, Kael."

He leaned closer then, his eyes sparking with something I didn't quite understand. "I know you're stronger than you look. Rourke told me about your bravery when faced with the pooka."

I snorted. "And now you're bringing Rourke into this? He used me as *bait*."

"And you didn't run. You tried to fight it, and you might have succeeded if it wasn't impossible to take on a pooka head on. Which makes me think you're holding back." He slid a quiver of arrows from his back and dropped them to the ground in front of me. He took a step back. "You're better than you think you are. Good luck."

Before I could ask him what he meant by *good luck*, Kael disappeared from the cliff. As in, he *actually* disappeared. One moment, he was there, and the next, he was gone. A shimmer of darkness surrounded him, and then there was nothing left but the quiver of arrows he'd dropped onto the ground. A low growl sounded from behind me, a sound that skittered up the back of my spine. It was coming from the depths of the cave.

There was definitely something inside of that cave. And it definitely wasn't human or fae.

In an instant, I understood far too well what he'd done. He'd left me here with some arrows, thinking I'd be able to shoot the creature if I had no other choice.

One had used me as bait. And now one had abandoned me to fight a monster on my own. I was really starting to hate these fae.

Mouth dry, I grabbed the quiver and slowly spun on my feet to face whatever lurked behind me. A beast stalked out of the cave, its massive claws punching the ground. Deep black eyes glimmered from beneath a mess of mangy fur. The beast stalked closer, hot breath curling from its fangs. My body began to tremble, and my heart shook so hard it felt as though it might burst through my chest.

It was one of the creatures. It was a Redcap.

The monsters who had killed my best friend.

And now one would kill me, too.

Hands trembling, I grabbed an arrow and tried to aim the bow, but my body was shaking so hard that the arrow bounced all over the place. The creature growled and edged forward, dark saliva dripping off its sharp fangs.

"Shit," I whispered, stumbling back. One swipe of those paws. One bite from those monstrous fangs. That was all it would take to end me. "Kael?"

No answer. There was no sound at all. Nothing but the scrape of the Redcap's claws against the rocky cliff. The beast leaned closer, opened wide its massive jaws, and roared. Shivers coursed across every inch of my skin, and I lifted my bow once again, desperate to find a steady aim.

I could do this. My heart thumped once. My eyes zeroed in on the Redcap's monstrous face. I didn't have to run. I could fight. For Bree. For my mother. For the helpless girl I used to be.

I loosed an arrow. It soared through the night air and sunk heavily into the Redcap's left paw. Mouth opened wide, it roared and lunged toward me. I was too slow this time. Its mouth closed around my leg, its teeth slicing through my skin. Pain exploded behind my eyes, and I dropped to the ground. I couldn't breathe. I couldn't think. The pain was unbearable.

I closed my eyes and sucked deep breaths in through my nose.

With a strangled yell, I grabbed another arrow and punched it into the Redcap's claw once more, like a sword. It sunk through flesh. Blood poured onto the matted fur.

The beast roared, a sound that shook the very ground.

Wind whooshed around me. Darkness filled my vision. I ground my teeth together and squeezed my eyes tight as the air seemed to *shift*.

I heard a clap. And then another. And then a light chuckle that came with the scent of burning leaves and damp dirt.

When I opened my eyes, I was no longer on the cliff with the creature bearing down on me. I was back in the Academy courtyard with the changelings staring at me wide-eyed and open-mouthed. The Royals stood just to my right, softly clapping and nodding while Kael, the horrible fae who had abandoned me to face a monstrous creature alone, was nowhere to be seen.

Rourke was suddenly there, holding out a hand as he leaned over me, his stupid golden hair falling into his equally stupid golden eyes. "Well done. You're the first new recruit to shift. That means you're likely mine."

I smacked his hand aside and stood, my entire body trembling, my leg burning from the pain. Lifting my chin, I gave him a shuddering growl. "I am no one's."

I winced and braced myself for his reaction. I'd hit his hand and stood up to him, in front of Royals no less. My instructors had made it clear that they wanted to be shown respect. But I was all out of niceties. Not after what had happened. Not when I'd almost just died.

Both he and Kael had thrown me to the wolves. Literally. If they thought I would go along with this whole mating thing willingly after all they'd done, they had another think coming.

But instead of scolding me, his eyes glimmered. He stood a little taller, if that were even possible. He already towered over everyone else.

"Indeed," he murmured. And then his gaze flicked down, darkened. "You're hurt."

He scooped me up into his arms. I tried to wriggle away, but it was no use. The pain was blinding. In fact, everything seemed a bit fuzzy now. I would tell him exactly how I felt all about this...but later. I couldn't find the energy to do anything other than drop my head against his chest. He smelled so strange. Like the very earth itself. My nostrils flared as I breathed him in, and a strange sense of calm flooded my painful limbs. And as he strode away from the Royals, darkness filled my mind completely.

CHAPTER TWELVE

"So, let me get this straight. Only Autumn and Winter fae can shift?" I sat in the infirmary bed, flipping through a book my roommate had brought for me. Sophia had found it in the library, the sole copy of a book we'd be covering in one of our classes next semester: The Magic of the Four Courts.

I was desperate to know everything I could. Partially because...I didn't want to end up in either of those two Courts. Not after Rourke had used me for bait. And especially not after what Kael had pulled.

Not that Liam or Finn were much better, but at least they hadn't put my life in danger. Yet.

"That's what it says," she said with a nod, pointing at the book. "All fae have access to certain powers and strengths, like the whole bow and arrow thing, apparently. Every fae is supposed to be pretty good with weapons..." She cleared her throat, knowing it was still very much a sore subject for me. "But then there are specialized gifts, like shifting."

I wrinkled my nose and crossed my arms over the thin infirmary sheet. "Why do they call it shifting? I would have thought that term meant changing into something else. You know, like werewolves or something."

She let out a light laugh. "Wouldn't that be something? Well, apparently it just means you're shifting through space. From one location to the next. And only Winter or Autumn fae can do it."

"And that's what I did," I said softly. "So, that means I'm definitely not Spring."

A strange feeling passed through me, a mixture of both dread and disappointment. Knowing that I was a member of one of the two darker courts meant I'd end up with Kael or Rourke, a prospect that did not fill me with glee. But it also meant that the strange connection I'd felt with Finn was really nothing at all. Those moments where he passed me in the hallway and winked, there was no reason I should blush in response. He belonged to someone else. Most likely my roommate.

I'd known that deep down inside, but having it confirmed made me feel more disappointed than I would have expected.

I frowned. "I can't believe I'm probably going to end up mated to the fae who was willing to leave me for dead just to prove a point."

She pursed her lips and leaned back into the old wooden chair. "I don't think he left you for dead, Norah. He didn't shift back into the courtyard before you got back."

"Are you sure? He disappeared right in front of me. And he left me those arrows so that I had to fend for myself, *knowing* there was a Redcap in that cave."

Anger burned through me. Kael could not be my mate. He just couldn't.

"Yeah, he did." She shrugged. "But I don't think he actually left you. He probably shifted, like, five feet away. Didn't you say there was a cave? I bet he was hiding in there, watching. He would have stepped in if you weren't able to handle yourself."

"Well, if that's the case, then why didn't he come back when the Redcap bit me? I got injured, and he did nothing," I said, frown deepening. "Face it, Sophia. I'm probably stuck with Kael, a fae who couldn't care less about what happens to me."

"I don't think Winter fae are as unfeeling and emotionless as you think they are. Maybe he'll end up surprising you as much as you surprised everyone when you appeared in the middle of the courtyard like that." She grinned. "Remember what Alwyn said? We're going to end up thrilled with our mates."

I scowled. "Unlikely."

"How's the wound?" The sweet scent of sunflowers whispered in from the open doorway of the infirmary. I glanced up from my reading. I had gotten pretty engrossed in the book about the four different powers and gifts, to the point where I hadn't realized that several hours had passed until I spotted the full moon outside the window.

"It really fucking hurts," I said with a half-wince, half-smile. "How long do you think it's going to take to heal?"

He eased into the room and shut the door behind him with a click. There was something about his movement that made my breath catch. Liam was like a graceful lion, stalking his prey, which meant...what was his prey? Me? I swallowed hard, trying not to notice exactly how well his dark tunic fit his perfectly-sculpted chest and arms.

"Unassisted? It could take weeks." He shot me a mischievous smile.

My stomach tumbled. "You mean, without medicine?"

His eyes flashed as he strode across the room and pushed the chair around so that the back was facing me. Then, he perched in it, legs spread wide on either side of the wood. "Looks like you've been doing some interesting reading. Have you gotten to the chapters about the Summer fae gifts?"

"No," I admitted. "I've been kind of engrossed in

the parts about the Winter and the Autumn fae. I guess because..."

"Because you think you're one of them," he finished for me. "And you'd be right. You're an Autumn or a Winter. Rourke is going around telling everyone you're Autumn, though I'd place bets on you being Winter."

"Because of the whole Redcap thing."

I couldn't help but notice how easily he spoke about my Court, as if it didn't matter to him at all where I belonged. But why would he care? And why should I care that he didn't care? I stared at him, at his bonfire eyes and hair. That sizzle I always felt around him was there again, tugging me toward him. That magic. His hidden allure.

He nodded, shooting me a wink. "It's a shame, really. There's a spark in you I like, Norah. You're brave and feisty. I could have seen us doing well together. In fact, I could have sworn I felt a..." He shook his head and squeezed his fingers tight around the chair. "Nevermind that. Clearly, I was wrong. The Winter Court will be lucky to have you."

I swallowed hard at the look in his eye. What had he been about to say? He'd felt...something. What? Was it the same thing I felt when I looked at him? But that was impossible. He was just using his magic on me. I was certain of it.

"So, do you think I should be reading up on the strengths of the Summer fae?"

His smile was so bright, it was almost blinding. "You've had a hard past few days. I'll make it easy on you." He leaned forward and whispered into my ear, sending a swarm of goosebumps storming down my neck. "Summer fae are known for their healing powers."

I pushed myself up higher on the pillows, wincing when a new blast of pain went through my leg. "Well, that would sure come in handy right about now." A pause. "The nurse is a Summer fae, right? Why didn't she heal me, then?"

"Technically," he began as he shifted closer to the bed, his movements as graceful and purposeful as a lion's once again, "we're not to use our healing gifts unless absolutely necessary. It can drain us, you see."

"Drain you how?" I asked, trying to focus on the conversation rather than how close his body was to mine.

He lifted a shoulder in a shrug. "It can make us tired and weak, particularly if the injury is serious. We then need time to recover, which isn't ideal when we have foes to fight or academies to run."

"Right." I sighed and leaned back onto the pillows. "That makes sense."

He grinned and slid a hand onto the bed, resting it a mere inch from where my thighs were covered by the thin white sheet. "That said, I'm feeling inclined to help you, Norah. You've had a tough first week, and it'd be a shame for you to miss any of your classes. Why don't you and I make a deal? I'll heal your leg, and you can give me something in exchange."

Both his words and the tone of his voice sounded full of danger. A flashing red light blazed in my head, blinking furiously in an attempt to stop me from making a very stupid move. Liam didn't unnerve me as much as Rourke and Kael did, and he certainly hadn't used me as bait or abandoned me on a cliff to face a Redcap on my own.

Yet.

He was his own kind of dangerous. One that I should probably run far, far away from.

But this damn leg…

I winced at the pain.

Also, I was…curious. I couldn't help myself. His hand was so close to my thigh. Did that mean he had to touch me to heal me? My skin buzzed with excitement.

I clearly needed to get a grip.

But then I gave Liam a nod with my breath held tight in my throat. "All right. Are you going to touch me?"

Oh god, that sounded far more suggestive than I'd meant. Partially because my voice was practically a strangled whisper.

His smile widened.

Before I knew what was happening, Liam slid his hand underneath the sheet. His fingers whispered across my bare thigh, tracing lazy circles around the bandages that had been wrapped around my wound. I couldn't move. I couldn't breathe. I couldn't even blink. Blood roared in my ears as every single part of me focused on where his skin met mine.

I felt on fire. Delicious, exquisite fire.

It took every ounce of self-control not to squirm.

"So, would you like me to heal you then?" he said in a teasing voice. "Or shall I remove my hand?"

My breath shuddered from my lungs. "Healing, please."

It was all I could say, and even those words sounded strained and whispered, like the sound of the wind rattling through the trees.

"Very well," he murmured. He dragged his fingers from my skin and onto my bandage where he continued to caress my leg. I tensed at the expectation of pain, but none came. Instead, a soothing warmth flooded through me. It felt as though the sun had risen from behind the clouds, beating down on my skin as I soaked up the summer rays. My whole body felt alive and electric. Warm and soothed and free of pain.

That warmth slipped up my leg and built between my thighs. Sparks dotted my visions as I stared up at the ceiling, not daring to look at Liam's face for fear he would know exactly how he was making me feel. His fingers continued to caress my thigh. Gently, softly. An aching need built inside of me. A need for his touch. A need for...him.

Oh god.

What the hell am I doing?

Was this really how fae healed? Because it felt like a hell of a lot more than that.

"Look at me," he said in a soft growl.

I pulled my gaze from the ceiling to meet his eyes. His eyes sparked; his thumb swept across my skin. I bit my lip, swallowing down the moan that threatened to escape from my throat. How did this feel so agonizingly good? How did I feel as if I were two seconds away from shattering beneath his touch?

It was the magic, I thought, heart racing in my chest. It had to be the magic and nothing more.

When he finally slid his hands out from under the covers, my chest was heaving. I could feel the imprint of his hand still on my skin. The ache between my thighs burned.

"How are you feeling now, Norah?" he asked with a lazy grin.

"Yep." I swallowed hard, cheeks flaming. "Pretty sure that fixed it."

"Good." He winked, leaned forward, and dropped his voice to a hush. "Now, if anyone asks, I wasn't the one who healed you. You're going to make sure I don't get in trouble for helping you."

I nodded my head vigorously and tried to find my voice. "I guess I owe you a favor or something, right? What do you want?"

He chuckled. "I have an errand to run that requires a trip to the Autumn Court. I'd like you to accompany me, but you'll need to pretend as though you're my *companion*."

"Your companion?" My face drained of all feeling, except for the heat that still dotted my cheeks. I wasn't over the whole healing thing yet. "You mean you want me to pretend I'm your mate? But won't they know I'm a new changeling at the Academy?"

"The fae I'm visiting do not know about my role here at the Academy, so no. There's no reason for them to suspect you're a changeling, nor one who is clearly not of the Summer Court."

Not of the Summer Court. I needed to remember that. Which was hard after…the whole healing thing. I was still buzzing from his touch, as little as it had been. I wanted more. But he wasn't my mate, and he never would be. Someone else would. The high I'd gained from his healing magic suddenly dipped. Kael or Rourke would be my mate instead.

"All right, I guess I can do that," I said with a frown. "But don't I need to be here for my lessons? I mean, I may have shifted or whatever, but I clearly need as much training as I can get."

"Tomorrow's Saturday." He pushed his auburn hair back from his face. "So, you have the day off from lessons. I'll have you back long before Monday's training begins."

"All right, I guess that's okay, then," I said, still frowning. "What is this errand anyway?"

"It's important," he said. "Trust me."

Trust him. Ha! That was rich. Not a single one of them had done anything to convince me to trust them. And yet…I wanted to go. It was another chance for some hands-on training. Another chance to learn more about this world.

I would never be able to fight the Redcaps unless I took every chance to learn that came my way.

With a brilliant smile, Liam pushed up from his chair and strode to the door before pausing to hold his finger to his lips.

"Now, remember. I wasn't the one who healed

you." And then he disappeared out the door with a wink.

The next morning, I snuck out of the Academy just before daylight. Liam was waiting for me in the courtyard. And he was...sitting on a horse, one with sleek green-gray skin that rippled as it stomped its hoof on the dewy grass.

I slowed to a stop in front of them and frowned up at Liam's bonfire eyes. "You didn't tell me there was going to be horse-riding involved." A pause as I scanned the horse, noting the green-gray color. Dread pooled in my stomach. "Is this one of those pookas?"

He tipped back his head and laughed before giving his horse's neck a soft pat. "Sapling here is about as far from a pooka as she can get. Trust me. When you've seen one up close, you'll be able to spot the difference."

I decided not to tell him I *had* seen one up close, though in its weird goblin-like form. These fae sure were fond of keeping secrets from each other, of sneaking around, and of breaking the rules. Doing things unknown, things they knew the others wouldn't approve of. Rourke had told Kael, but he clearly hadn't filled the others in on how he'd used me as bait, probably because it had been a pretty asshole thing to do.

Though come to think of it...every single one of them would probably do it, too. A thought that didn't leave me feeling much better about our secret trip to visit the Autumn Court.

I crossed my arms over my chest. "So, then where's my horse? You don't expect me to walk the whole way while you get to take it easy."

He flashed me a grin. "You're on this one with me, darling. Mates would never take a ride on their own."

I wasn't usually the type to have a dirty mind, but there was something so suggestive in the way he said his words. My cheeks boiled under his heated gaze, and I cleared my throat, desperately casting my eyes around for anything at all to look at that wasn't him.

With a chuckle, he held out his hand. "You're so easily flustered. Keep it up. The Autumn Court won't have any trouble believing in our coupling if you keep blushing like that."

I narrowed my eyes. "I'm not blushing."

"Then, why are your cheeks so gloriously red? They practically match my hair."

He yanked me up onto the horse as if I didn't weigh a pound. My legs slid in behind his, a perfect fit. Timidly, I wrapped my arms around his waist, tensing when I could feel the hard planes of his stomach through his thin shirt. He felt even more muscular than he looked, and that was...that was saying something.

"It's just warm out here," I finally said, realizing I hadn't replied. "It's summer. You know, the hottest season of the year? Maybe I even have a sunburn."

I didn't have a sunburn.

"And you like the warmth?" he asked as the horse took off across the courtyard lawn in a prancing trot.

"Of course," I said, tightening my grip around his waist as the horse took off. "Who doesn't? Long, warm nights. Lazy days. Swims that make your muscles ache." My heart panged at my words. So much of that reminded me of Bree and our trips to the beach. We had gone every year. "Though I guess summer isn't like that here."

"Oh, summer is very much like that here," he said, casting his words over his shoulder. "There's a small river down the hill behind the Academy. You can go there for a swim anytime you'd like. We train you hard, but we like you to have time off, too."

"Really?" I peered over his shoulder to see him turning the horse onto a dirt-packed road that led away from the eastern side of the Academy. "What about all the dangerous creatures that we're supposed to be watching out for?"

"Well, those are easy enough to avoid. Don't go swimming at night." His body stiffened. "And get your swimming in while you can. It will be perpetual Winter when you head to your assigned Court in a few years. Not much sunshine there. Just lots of snow."

"Perpetual Winter," I repeated, not quite knowing how I felt about that. "You mean, there will be no other seasons there? But…does that mean the Academy is located in the Summer Court?"

"The Academy is located on free territory, which means it doesn't belong to any one Court. That means it gets to experience all of the fae seasons," he said. "It's the best kind of situation for training changelings. Even though you'll only belong to one Court, it's good for you to experience what each of them are like... though there are some who would disagree with that."

"Like who?" I couldn't help but ask. So far, the whole Court system had felt like a bit of a mystery, but Liam seemed pretty talkative today. Might as well use that to try and wrangle as much information out of him as I could.

"The Autumn Court, for one," he muttered, his body tensing underneath my arms once again. "They're all about full separation. They don't like the Winter Court, and they truly hate the Summer and Spring fae."

"Then, why do you want to visit them?"

A beat passed. "I suppose I should explain our mission, but you need to promise me that you won't say a word about this to anyone else."

My heart charged a little faster. "Why does that sound like Finn, Rourke, and Kael don't know about this?"

"Because they don't," he said, jerking his chin over his shoulder. His gaze locked on mine, so intense that it made me shiver. "Look, I know you're destined to end up as Kael's mate, but you aren't his yet. Can you do this one thing for me and not tell a soul about it? If one day, years down the line, you feel as though you do need to tell Kael, fine. But just not now. Not yet. Okay?"

My heart pounded in my chest, and I swallowed hard. This sounded serious. Yesterday, this quest had all felt like some kind of joke. Like he'd been playing around, almost. Like our mission wasn't really a big deal.

Now, I wasn't so sure.

It sounded a hell of a lot like a big deal now.

"All right, I'll keep it to myself," I said after taking a deep breath. "But just so you know, you're kind of freaking me out here."

"Maybe you should be freaked out." His voice rumbled beneath my hands. "Before I became an instructor at the Academy, I was a fighter in the army for the Queen. And no, before you ask, it wasn't for the Summer Queen. It was for Marin, the Queen of all Fae, the one who was assassinated by Viola, the new Queen of Autumn. They kept me prisoner for several years until they decided that I was no longer a threat, only releasing me if I agreed to become an instructor at the Academy."

My eyes widened. "So you were loyal to Marin?"

He gave a nod. "I was. And because of my connections, I've heard word that the Autumn Court has something else planned, though they're keeping things very hush hush. Only Viola knows what I look like, so I should be able to get in and out without being recognized. Today's trip will be an attempt to find out what they have planned, and I'll stand out much less if I have a mate by my side."

"Something planned..." I trailed off, skin buzzing. "You don't mean they're going to try to do something like they did before? Kill another Queen?"

"Well, that's the question, isn't it, darling?" Liam said. "If the Autumn fae are planning another assassination, the other Royals need to be warned."

CHAPTER THIRTEEN

It was easy to tell when we moved from the free territory and into the lands of the Autumn Court. The sapling green forest morphed into a reddish brown, the sweet brilliant life of the trees fading into a tapestry of reds and golds and browns. It was beautiful in its own way, though I could tell by Liam's grumbling that he wasn't much of a fan.

Several hours after we'd left the Academy, we entered a small village set amongst the autumn trees. There were about thirty buildings in total, all made from the same dark branches that rose high into the sky. Fae bustled about, some carrying baskets of leaves or moss, others chattering in groups. When we approached, a plainly-dressed female glanced up from where she was gathering fallen berries, her long golden strands glistening beneath the dappled sunlight.

Her eyes were quick and intelligent, glancing first at Liam and then to me. "Her I can't be sure of, but you're a Summer if there ever was one. State your business."

"I'm a half-breed," Liam said. "Mother was Autumn and father was Summer."

"Was?" The female arched an eyebrow, dusting her hands on her linen skirt.

I tightened my grip around Liam's waist, questions piling on top of my tongue. He wasn't a full Summer fae? He was part Autumn? And where were his parents? What had happened to them? But I pressed my lips together, swallowing the questions down. I knew I couldn't ask them now, not in front of these fae.

"Both killed when the Courts split," he replied. "This is my mate."

She sniffed and gave a nod. "Nasty business that war, but it gave us a better way of life."

"Aye." Liam shifted on the horse. His back was toward me, but I had the strange sensation of knowing exactly how he looked in that moment. Smiling, slightly flirtatiously. He was turning up the charm as best he could, and by the softening look on the female's face, it was working. "Anyway, my mate and I are just passing through on our way to Esari where we're hoping to find a life and a home for ourselves."

The female's golden eyes flicked my way. "Newly-weds then, I see. Well, I guess the city is the easiest place to start a family, but it's definitely not what it used to be."

"Oh?" Liam asked, all casually, though I could tell his interest was more than piqued by her offhand comment. "How so?"

"Haven't you heard? Storms. Sometimes I swear the sky will split in two." With a sigh, she shook her head and motioned for us to pass. "Go on then. Just make sure you aren't out and about when the lightning comes, or else it might just strike you dead."

We reached the fae city of Esari after another couple of hours spent trekking through the autumn woods. I was beginning to think it might be a bit of a reach to assume we'd be back to the Academy by Monday morning's lessons. It had taken us almost all day to arrive at our destination, and we still needed to round up the information that Liam was desperate to find.

Esari was unlike any city I'd ever seen. It rose up high on a hill, spread out behind the sprawling autumn forest. There was so much gold, from the streets to the rooftops to the large castle that loomed at the highest peak, its twin towers reaching high into an orange-streaked sky. Every building had been crafted from the wood of the forests, a dark brown that only highlighted the glistening gold of everything else. There were at least three thousand homes, if not more. Plus, bakers and butchers and pubs. All around us, life pulsed from the hundreds of fae who roamed the cobblestone streets.

"Welcome to Esari," Liam said quietly as I awkwardly dropped from the horse and fell right onto my knees. It was the first time I'd ever ridden one of these things, which meant I didn't know what the hell I was doing or how to get off of it without falling flat on my face. With a chuckle, Liam wrapped his strong arms around my waist and hauled me to my feet. I flushed, hating that it took so little for him to fluster me. "Looks like I'm going to have to keep a closer eye on you than I thought."

"I'm fine," I said in as peppy of a voice as I could manage. Truth was, I was blown away. The Academy was one thing, but this...this was something entirely different. The city was huge, and there were so many fae. And this, I realized, was only a small part of them. There were dozens of other smaller villages within the Autumn Court alone, plus all the fae who lived in the other seasons.

How had humanity gone so long without knowing all this was here?

Liam pulled a golden cloth from the satchel he'd strapped onto the horse. "Here. Wear this. It'll keep you from standing out too much."

It was a golden cloak, much like the one that Rourke always wore.

"What about you?" I asked as I slid the cloak over my shoulders. It was a soft material, like silk. "Your hair kind of gives you away, you know."

He flashed me a grin. "I'm not trying to fit in. The easiest way to get information out of someone? Provoke them. Piss them off."

My mouth went dry. "I feel like there should be a better option than that."

"Trust me, Norah. I've done this before."

And I didn't doubt it.

Overhead, the sky was beginning to darken. As Liam led me through the bustling streets, he explained the different seasons of the fae. They were much like those in the human realm. Autumn was colder with crisp air and rattling leaves, the days short and the nights long. Winter, he said, was even worse, but I expected him to feel that way. He was Summer, after all. Anything but warm hazy days and short nights would seem torturous to him.

We came to a pub called the Rotting Horse, a name that did little to instil a sense of ease in me. Inside, dozens of fae were sitting at long oak tables, but it wasn't the kind of raucous merriment that I expected from an establishment like this. They were calmly and quietly sipping their pints, exchanging murmured conversations.

"Members of Viola's Court often come here." Liam leaned forward and whispered the words into my ear, and shivers coursed along my skin. He noticed my trembling, and he must have taken it to mean that I was cold. Because somehow, his arms were suddenly around me. He pulled me close to his hard chest. His body was so warm, like a radiator that had been left on for hours. Trembling, I had the strange urge to curl up against him and breathe in the scent of fire and rain. Here we were, in strange and potentially dangerous territory, and yet I'd never felt safer than I had in this moment. As if nothing in the world could go wrong, not when Liam's arms were wrapped around me. Swallowing hard, I glanced up to his eyes, half-terrified to see what I would find in them. His gaze burned.

"All better now, darling?" There was an undercurrent of amusement in his voice, and it snapped me out of my strange reverie.

I pulled myself out of his arms, stumbled back, and hurriedly began to straighten my cloak. There was nothing wrong with it, of course, but I was suddenly in desperate need of something to do with my hands. Anything to distract me from Liam's smirk. From his hands. From his eyes.

"The cloak will do, thanks. You don't need to paw at me to keep me warm."

His lips quirked. "I wasn't *pawing* at you. Don't believe me? I'm happy to give you a true demonstration of what pawing means."

My entire face flamed, which succeeded in doing two things. First, I wasn't cold anymore, so that was great. Second, Liam could see just how much his words had gotten to me. That wasn't so great.

"Like I said." Liam winked. "Keep on blushing, my beautiful bride."

"I'm not blushing," I said through gritted teeth. "And I told you, stop calling me darling!"

Liam ignored me. Instead of responding, he opened the door and ushered me inside the tavern. Rows of lights were strung up across the ceiling, and candlelight flickered on every table. A soft music whispered out from invisible speakers. It was an eerie type of folk music mixed in with a clanging piano that sounded out of tune. I tried my best not to wrinkle my nose. I definitely wasn't a fan.

"Care to sit?" Liam pulled out a wooden chair for me at the nearest table, pretending as if he were some sort of gentleman, but I knew the truth. He was anything but.

Still, I followed his lead and settled onto the chair. It was hard and somewhat spiky.

"Now, what would you like to drink, *darling*?" he asked with a wink, speaking loud enough for his words to drift toward the tables around us.

I leaned forward and dropped my voice to a whisper. "Vodka tonic?"

I mean, it was the only drink name I knew.

He let out a low chuckle. "I'm afraid that's not an option. Don't worry. I'll find you something you like. Now, why don't you drop back your hood and make yourself comfortable while I grab us a couple of drinks?"

I frowned, but I kept up my end of the bargain and did what he asked, pushing the hood away from my face.

"Good girl," he murmured. "Don't want to hide that pretty face of yours, now do we?"

In spite of every desire otherwise, my stupid face flushed again.

As soon as he was gone, I began to look around the room. I didn't get very far though because another fae male took Liam's seat within seconds. With a sharp gasp, I scooted back in my chair. This fae was...well, he reminded me a lot of Rourke, only...somehow, this one was even more unsettling.

In fact, I'd take it past unsettling and go for flat-out creepy.

His lips were a strange orangey-red, split into an eerie grin that showed off two rows of very pointed teeth. Was he a different kind of fae? None of the Autumn fae I'd met at the Academy so far looked anything like this. His eyes were even a reddish hue, the color of old, dried blood.

I shivered when he leaned forward and traced a long, sharp nail across the surface of the table. "Why would a pretty little thing like you be here with a Summer fae?"

"He's a half-breed," I blurted out, though I wasn't entirely sure that was the truth. It was what Liam had told several fae along the way here, but I had no idea if it was a lie meant only for us to gain access.

"Even worse," he sneered. "Surely you would be better off with a pure Autumn fae such as myself."

"I ah..." Desperately, I cast my eyes around for any sign of Liam. He was at the bar, lifting two glasses of orangey liquid into his hands.

"I'm happy where I am." I turned back to the fae. "So, you can be moving along now."

"You might think you're happy, but you're not." The male wrapped his long fingers around my wrist and squeezed tight. With a growl, I yanked away and slapped him right on the face. The sound echoed through the quiet tavern. My palm stung, and a big blotchy red spread across the fae's pale cheek.

I sucked in a sharp breath.

Whoops. I hadn't meant to do that.

Liam suddenly appeared and slammed the drinks down onto the table. Wood splintered. The murmured conversations fell into a quiet hush, and every head in the tavern turned our way.

I swallowed hard. This wasn't going well. And I had a feeling it was about to get a lot worse.

"Are you coming on to my mate?" Liam bellowed, his voice a boom against the wooden walls. "Are you trying to steal her away from me?"

The Autumn fae folded his long, thin hands into his lap and looked up at Liam with a chilly smile. "Your mate informed me you're a half-breed. I was merely suggesting that she might be in a better position if she turned her romantic interests elsewhere."

"So, you *were* trying to steal her." Liam leaned down and snarled into the fae's face, his body trembling from barely-contained anger. "You. Were. Trying. To. Steal. My. Mate!"

Oh my. Well...this was certainly an interesting reaction, one that should have made me cower in fear. Liam was kind of scary. But...instead of flinching away from him, I leaned forward, enthralled by the fire dancing in his bonfire eyes. I had never seen anything like him before. He was pure fury. Pure *power*. If he'd told me in that moment that he could rip the very sky to shreds, I would have believed him.

The Autumn fae didn't even flinch. He merely tsked and rolled his eyes. "Honestly, the Summer temper tantrums are so tiresome."

Liam leaned forward, bracing his fists on the table, which shook beneath the force of him. "You think this is a Summer temper tantrum? Trust me, it gets a hell of a lot worse than this. Now, get away from my mate or you'll see what the true force of my anger can do."

"Liam," I said in a harsh whisper, the heat on my cheeks deepening. Even though his reaction had intrigued me, it probably wasn't a great idea for him to continue on like this. We'd never find out what he needed to know if things escalated.

Besides, I didn't know why Liam was reacting like this. I wasn't *actually* his mate. And both of us knew I never would be. So, why was he getting so pissed off that another fae was talking to me? Was he...*actually* jealous?

The Autumn fae pushed back his chair and stood, crossing his arms over his golden-cloaked chest. All around us, the entire bar did the same. Dozens of Autumn fae stood from their tables, the room a hush that was louder than the murmur of voices from before.

Uh oh.

"I think it's time you leave. Your mate is welcome here, but you are not." The Autumn fae rested his hand on the ornate, golden hilt of a sword that he'd somehow kept hidden until this moment.

Double uh oh.

I swallowed hard, my heartbeat flickering a frantic beat. Eyes wide, I glanced from the Autumn fae to Liam's fiery eyes. Both men looked on the verge of a violent fight, though they were so different in how they held themselves. Liam was visibly angry, his fists trembling with his passionate emotions, as if he were two seconds away from pummelling the fae with all the strength of his body. The Autumn fae, on the other hand, was still, quiet, calm, like a dangerous predator ready to pounce on its prey. Like a snake prepared to strike.

"In Otherworld," Liam began in a low, dangerous voice, "we do not attempt to steal another male's mate. It's devious and cruel. But I guess I shouldn't be so surprised, should I? Not here, in the Autumn Court. You're soulless assassins. Failing ones, at that. When was the last time you managed to get a worthwhile kill?"

My eyes slightly widened at his words, though I kept the rest of my face blank. I understood what he was doing now. Provoking them. Inwardly, I rolled my eyes at myself. I couldn't believe I'd thought he was actually angry that another fae male was talking to me. Of course he wouldn't be jealous. What an idiotic thing for me to think.

He didn't *like* me. There was no real connection between us. Just meaningless flirty banter that would go away just as soon as he figured out who was his mate. And that wasn't me.

Come on, Norah. Get a grip.

The stillness of the room deepened, and the Autumn fae's eyes flickered with a strange, eerie darkness that hadn't been present before. "Perhaps the reason you believe we're unsuccessful in our assassinations is because you never hear of them, being a Summer half-breed and all."

Liam leaned forward just the slightest of breaths and dropped his voice even lower. "Oh, I hear about them alright. And I know what you've got planned against the other Courts. But you'll fail. You lot always do."

The Autumn fae let out a low chuckle, a sound that sent a storm of goosebumps over my entire body. "Doubt us, if you like, but you won't be mocking us when your entire stifling season has been replaced by the cool breeze of Autumn."

I jerked back in my chair, shocked by his words. Which had the unfortunate side effect of drawing the fae male's attention—as well as the rest of the fae in the tavern—away from Liam and right to me.

"You look as though you don't approve," he sneered, his fangs flashing against the dim overhead lights. After a moment, he waved dismissively. "Your time with this Summer half-breed has made you weak, and I have no time for soft little things." He shifted his attention back to Liam. "Now, take your mate and get out of here, or we will put our swords to your necks, starting with hers."

CHAPTER FOURTEEN

Outside of the tavern, Liam was silent as we bustled our way through the city streets and back toward where we'd dropped off his horse. His shoulders were tight, and the skin around his jaw rippled with tension. He didn't have to say a word for me to understand what he was feeling.

On the one hand, we'd gotten the information we'd come to get, but it had turned out to be far worse than Liam must have been expecting. The Autumn Court was planning something, alright, and it sounded as though they wanted to take down the entirety of the Summer Court.

I half-expected the fae from the tavern to follow close behind us, waiting until the right moment to slide their swords into our backs. But, somehow, we managed to reach the stables safely. We were back on our horse before the darkness had fully deepened, though the heavy storm-clouds overhead crackled with fierce and dangerous lightning. Any moment now, the clouds would open up, and rain would pour down on our heads.

When we reached the forest's tree line, Liam pulled on the reins to slow the horse's trot. He cast a glance over his shoulder at the fading city behind us, his entire face a grim knot of worry and anger.

"Here's a good training exercise for you, Norah," he said in a quiet, dangerous voice. "What did you make of that?"

"It sounded like the attack they have planned will target the Summer Court Royals," I said without letting a beat pass. "Like maybe they want to merge your Court with theirs?"

"Close," he said after a moment. "But I don't think *merging* is what they have planned. Notice what they said about the seasons."

"About the stifling heat turning into a cool breeze?" I asked with a frown. "I thought he was just being dramatic."

"If only that were the case, Norah." Liam stiffened and shook his head. "Autumn fae are not dramatic. If one says that the seasons will change, then that is likely precisely what he meant."

"Can they do that?"

A crack split the sky, and torrents of rain slashed sideways onto the dirt-packed ground. Liam flicked the reins, and the horse began to trot again, but the increased pace did little to outrun the rain. It splattered my face and my hands, soaking into the golden cloak I still wore, the material clinging to my shivering body.

After what felt like hours, Liam stopped the horse in one of the small villages we'd passed through on the way. Every single inch of me was drenched and frozen, so much so that I could no longer feel my toes in my leather boots. The rain had even soaked through them, sneaking in to turn my socks into a soggy mess.

"There's an inn here where we can stay," Liam said after he led the horse into the village's stable. He slid to the ground and held a hand out for me, which I promptly ignored. When I jumped off, my landing was even worse than before, mostly due to the fact I couldn't feel my feet. I stumbled forward with a yelp of panic, but Liam kept me from toppling into the mounds of hay. His strong hands held me upright, and that sparkle in his eyes returned for the first time since we'd left Esari.

My heart dipped.

"We really need to work on your dismounting technique," he said with a light chuckle. "Otherwise, we won't be able to trust you to go for a ride without breaking a bone."

"I'll admit, I'm not the most horse-savvy person around. I didn't even know it was called dismounting." Liam's hands were so very warm. Even though we'd been riding through the rain for the past hour, none of his heat had disappeared. It was as if it was deep within his core, and it emanated from his skin in a delicious, soothing way. Hell, no need to go in an inn. We could stay here in the stables as long as he kept his arms wrapped around me.

"What in the name of the forest did you think it was called then?" He arched an eyebrow, still chuckling.

I grinned. "Tumbling off?"

His laugh deepened, but it trailed off just as quickly as it had come. "You really are an enigma, Norah, and you're so different than any Winter fae I've ever met. They'd rather be caught dead than laugh about their own weakness. Don't ever change, regardless of how they say you should be."

A thrill went through my gut and I pressed in closer to him, snuggling against the warmth of his body. Against me, his body tensed, but he didn't push me away.

"You're so warm," I said, voice tight, breath hitched. "The rain was freezing, but I don't feel cold anymore."

His arms tightened around me, and the musky summer scent of him filled my nose. "Be careful, darling. You're playing with fire. The others might care about the rules, but I'm nothing like them."

My heart pattered in my chest. I pulled back and looked up into his orange-red eyes. "What rules?"

His grin widened as he traced a finger across my cheek. Despite the warmth from his body, I shivered in his arms. "It's against the rules for the instructors to be intimate with any of the students, not until after graduation. It's to ensure that things don't get complicated if and when a changeling ends up being in a different Court than originally thought."

Intimate. The word echoed in my frazzled mind. He'd said intimate.

I suddenly felt very, very shy, like I needed to launch to the other side of the stables where piles of hay had been stacked along the wooden walls. The thud of the rain on the roof over our heads was drowned out by the heavy beating of my heart, and the flickering torches on the walls highlighted the dangerous glint in Liam's eyes.

He didn't really mean it, I thought. Surely this fae didn't want someone like me. I fell all over myself trying to do pretty standard things, and he'd seen firsthand how terrible I was with the bow. Not to mention the fact that I'd shown no signs of being a Summer fae.

He knew I wasn't his mate.

With a light chuckle, he shook his head. "Come on, let's get you inside the inn and out of those wet clothes."

It turned out the inn only had four rooms, and three were taken. So, Liam and I were forced to share. Luckily, the bed had a double mattress instead of a twin, so we didn't have to battle it out for space, though a part of me kind of wished we could. That said, we would still have to share a bed, and the room itself wasn't particularly large. It was a tiny little space in the corner of the top floor with a single window overlooking the village square.

I was feeling a little...out of sorts, to say the least. Liam's words from the stables had gotten under my skin, and I couldn't help but wonder if he truly did want to break the rules. Rules that, I had to admit, made a lot of sense. There was clearly some sort of magic tied in to the whole idea of mates, yet it didn't seem to fully kick in until changelings had spent some time in Otherworld. What if you were drawn to the wrong fae, only to find out you had a bond with another? It seemed like a lot of unnecessary drama.

"This was all they could find for us," Liam said when he opened the door to the room. I'd stayed inside, perched on a knotted wooden chair, shivering while he went in search of some clean, dry clothes. He held up a white linen pillowcase and grinned.

I arched a brow. "You don't really expect me to wear a pillowcase."

"It's not a pillowcase," he said, chuckling, and then he closed the door behind him. "It's a nightdress. It belonged to the owner's ex-wife, but it's the only thing she left behind. Unfortunately, it's either this, your wet clothes, or your birthday suit."

Cheeks flaming, I frowned down at the drenched clothes that were clawing at my skin. As much as I hated to admit it, I really did need to change. If I stayed like this, not only would I spend the whole night shivering, I'd have to wear damp, dirty clothes all the way back to the Academy in the morning. If I didn't hang them up, they'd never get dry.

And I *definitely* wasn't going to wear nothing at all.

As tempting as it was.

"Okay." I held out a hand toward the pillowcase gown. "I'll change, but not because you said so."

He smirked and tossed me the gown. "No, I know why you're changing. It's because you don't think you'd be able to control yourself if you were naked in the bed with me."

I rolled my eyes and shoved the wet cloak off my shoulders. "Has anyone ever told you how full of yourself you are? It's like your ego is ten times the size of your head."

"My ego is *exactly* the right size, as is everything else about me." He leaned forward and slid his finger along the hemline of my trousers. I froze, lungs squeezing. "Do you need help with those or are you just going to stand there gawking at me?"

Irritation flickered inside me, an emotion that was mixed with a hint of excitement. Somehow, Liam was able to simultaneously annoy the shit out of me and draw me in at the same time. That fact alone made me want to throttle him. And then make up for it by snuggling in close to his chest.

No, my inner voice roared at myself. *Stop getting so distracted by the gorgeous fae.*

I hadn't come to Otherworld to flirt with every fae male who gave me attention. I'd come here to learn out to fight, to find out how to battle the monsters who had killed my best friend. At the thought of Bree, all the excitement and annoyance I felt toward Liam disappeared into a cloud of bitter sadness.

I stepped back and gave him a pointed look. "Turn around, please. I'm not going to change when you're standing there watching me."

His eyebrows furrowed. "What's wrong, Norah?"

"Honestly, is it that hard to believe a girl doesn't want to change in front of you? There has to be something wrong?"

With a sigh, he shook his head and turned his back my way. "Of course not. It's just that two seconds ago, you had a look in your eye, one that made it seem like you wanted to climb on top of me. And then out of nowhere, you looked...well, sad."

I shimmied in the trousers and pushed the soaking material to the floor before shrugging my damp t-shirt over my head. I took off my bra for good measure, but I kept my underwear on. After slipping the linen gown over my head, I tapped Liam on the shoulder. He hadn't even tried to sneak a peek while I'd been changing, a fact I was strangely grateful for. I hadn't expected him to show much respect for my wishes.

He turned and silently watched me drape my clothes over the a wooden railing by the window. He didn't even make a crack about my lacy black bra. Instead, he strode toward me and tucked a finger beneath my chin, his fiery eyes searching mine for the truth.

"What's wrong, Norah?" he asked. "And no, this isn't about my ego. It's not difficult to tell that something is wrong when your entire demeanor changes within the blink of an eye."

With a sigh, I gritted my teeth and glanced away.

"It's Bree. I can't stop thinking about the creature that killed her. I can't stop thinking that maybe I could have done something to prevent it. And I can't stop thinking that I need to focus on training instead of getting distracted by other things. It's not fair to her."

"I see," he said quietly. "It sounds as though you haven't had a chance to mourn her."

"How would I have?" I asked, throwing up my hands. "Within an hour of her death, I was on my way to Otherworld, and I've barely had a moment to think since I arrived. Watch Duty, challenges, lessons. And now, trips to Courts. It's been good to keep busy, but when the thought of her enters my mind, I feel like I've been punched in the gut. I didn't even get to go to her funeral."

I started crying. Liam winced and awkwardly rubbed my shoulders, clearly unused to comforting crying girls. After a moment, he pulled me close to his chest and rubbed the back of my neck, silently holding me while the grief poured out of my eyes.

The warmth of him cocooned me, the strength and steadiness of his body holding me together when I'd been so close to shattering apart. Bree's death was still a sharp pain, a ripping in my gut. But Liam's presence was almost like a salve spread across the very worst of it.

"I'm so sorry, Norah," he said softly. "I know how much it hurts to lose someone you love to such a terrible gruesome death. You want to do something to avenge her. You want to fight back."

I tipped back my head to gaze up at him. "You sound like you're speaking from experience."

His jaw rippled, and he nodded.

"Your parents," I said softly, hoping that I wasn't treading on ground that might break beneath the weight of my words. "Was what you told the Autumn fae true?"

"Every word of it," he said bitterly. "Both fought in the war. For Queen Marin. Both died at the hands of the Autumn fae. I saw it happen with my own eyes. They were…ripped to shreds. By beasts the Autumn fae controlled. It was then I vowed I would do whatever it took to destroy the Autumn fae."

My heart pounded in my chest. It sounded so painfully familiar.

"But I was reckless," he said, shaking his head. "I got caught, along with dozens of my friends. They let me go after many, many years, but the others were not so lucky."

"I'm so sorry, Liam." Tears had filled my eyes as he spoke. I could feel the pain, as if it were my own, as if it had taken up residence within my own heart. Liam had lost so much. And yet here he was. So powerful. So strong. It had not broken him.

Suddenly, I became very aware of how close our bodies were. My chest was pressed against his. Our thighs were brushing. And my hands were splayed across his biceps, the strong curves of them tensing beneath my fingers. I swallowed hard, trying to control the rapid beating of my heart, but it was no use.

It was impossible not to notice Liam. Everything

about him *demanded* attention, from his flaming hair to the way he moved. No, the way he *prowled*.

"You're looking at me that way again," he murmured. The hands around my waist tensed, fingers tightening just enough to make my breath hitch. "Does talk of death excite you, Norah?"

"No," I said, lungs shuddering. "I just couldn't help but notice how you survived and came out stronger on the other side of it."

A low growl rumbled from his throat. "I could say the same about you, darling."

"Me?" I snorted. "The girl who can't shoot an arrow straight?"

He smiled. "The girl who decided to fight instead of run when she was told what she was. You didn't let your grief consume you. If that isn't strong, then I don't know what is, Norah."

"I want to be strong," I whispered. "I don't want to be weak. I don't want to be helpless ever again."

His thumb brushed my cheek, and pleasure curled down my spine. "You are such an enigma. There is so much passion in your eyes."

He was one to talk. His eyes practically blazed, scorching my skin from where he dragged his gaze across my face. I wet my lips, despite myself. Flaring my nostrils, I leaned closer and sniffed. The smell of summer filled my nose, and my mind reeled as if I'd downed half a dozen vodka tonics.

"Did you forget what I said about playing with fire?" he murmured, and then his mouth found mine. I gasped, curling my hands around his tunic. His lips were surprisingly soft and gentle. They moved softly against me, exploring. His hands tightened around my waist as I leaned into him, letting go all the pent-up fear and anger and uncertainty that had plagued me the past weeks.

All that existed was Liam. His strong chest was ridged with muscles. My hands drifted across it, and then settled on his broad shoulders. His kiss deepened, sending a flare of pleasure through my gut.

Suddenly, he lifted me from the floor. My thighs spread and curled around his hips instinctively. Between us, I felt the unmistakable bulge that said he was enjoying this just as much as I was. Heat pooled between my legs, and a heady ache settled in my core.

His mouth moved to my neck. The feel of his lips on my skin made me entire body tremble with a kind of need I'd never felt before. I think I must have moaned out loud, because he let out a light chuckle. "I think someone is enjoying herself."

"You really do have an impressively big ego," I whispered back.

"That's not the only thing." He chuckled again, and I couldn't help but roll my eyes. I'd walked straight into that one. I would smack him, but...I kind of wanted him to keep doing that thing with his mouth.

He carried me across the floor and dropped me back onto the bed, gently cradling my head before it hit the mattress. Without another word, he climbed on top of me, and then braced his arms on either side of my head. My heart was a trembling mess, and my mind could barely lock onto a single lucid thought.

Was this really happening?

Should it be happening?

There were rules, and he wasn't even my mate, and sometimes he really did annoy me, and—

Oh my god.

In the blink of an eye, he'd ripped the pillowcase gown in half, exposing my very braless breasts. Cool air swept across my already peaked nipples, hardening them even more. With a wicked smile, he lowered his mouth to my right breast and dragged his tongue across my nipple.

I shuddered, my body bucking beneath him. Pleasure sparked in my gut, and deepened the aching knot between my thighs. Breath held tight in my throat, I gripped the bedsheets with my fisted hands, clinging on for dear life. I didn't think I could let go or I would get swept away.

"My god," he whispered as he ran his thumb along my stomach. "You are so beautiful."

My heart swelled. "No one has ever said that to me before."

His thumb slowed as he drew his gaze up to my face. Confusion rippled in his bonfire eyes. "Never? Not even by the other men you have been with?"

I bit my lip, flushed, and glanced away.

"Norah," he said softly, dangerously. "Have you been with a man before?"

I ground my teeth together. God, this was embarrassing. "No."

With a curse, he shifted away, leaving a gulf of cold

air in his wake. He blinked and shook his head, as if he were snapping himself out of a trance.

Cheeks flaming, I glanced down at where my breasts were still very much on display. Gingerly, I grasped the sheet and pulled it up to my chin.

"I'm sorry," he murmured. "I shouldn't have touched you like that, not when..."

"Not when I'm so horribly inexperienced?" I asked with an embarrassed laugh.

He caught my hand in his. Warmth flooded into my skin, as much as I tried to stop it. "No, Norah. Nothing of the sort." His palm flattened on my cheek, and he gently angled my head toward his so that I could look into his eyes. They churned with need and something more. "But I am not your mate. And even then...there are the rules."

"I thought you didn't care about the rules."

He chuckled. "I don't. Most of the time. But it seems you've brought something new out in me. I want to do right by you, and I'm afraid if I take you now I'll want to take you again. And again. And again a hundred times. But then it will have to end, and we'll both end up in pain."

My heart thumped. "But maybe you are my mate."

"Do you truly believe that?"

Instead of answering, I asked my own question. "Isn't there a part of you that thinks it could be the two of us? I feel...something." I didn't know how else to explain it. A spark, a tug, an undeniable urge to be with him sounded too strange to speak out loud.

"Lust?" He grinned and dragged his thumb across

my jaw. "Oh yes, I feel that, too. But no, Norah. There isn't a part of me that thinks you could be my mate. There has never been a Summer fae in the history of Otherworld who has been able to shift."

My heart dipped. "I don't think I like this mating business."

"Hell, I don't like it too much right now either."

"Magic is weird, right?"

"It is very weird."

"What else can Summer fae do, besides healing?"

He chuckled. "We are very good in bed."

I pushed up onto my elbows and glared down at him before smacking him in the arm—gently. "Well now that's just cruel."

His grin widened, and he waggled his brows. "The cruel truth."

"Oh, come on. You don't expect me to believe that one of the Summer fae's gift is the gift of...sex."

"I guess you'll never find out, now will you? It's a shame. You would have enjoyed screaming my name. Over and over and over…"

My mouth dropped open. "I think your gift is being a smug, egotistical—"

"Come here." He wrapped his arms around me and pulled me onto his chest, his muscles rippling beneath me.

My breath caught, and I stilled with my cheek plastered against his very taut pecs. "Um. I'm not going to complain, but I'm confused."

"The rules say nothing about cuddling, and I'll sleep far better if you're close."

My heart did a little flip-flop, and every cell in my body heated up a thousand degrees. *He* might be able to sleep, but I wasn't entirely sure I would. His body under mine was very...distracting.

Still, there was something oddly comforting about his touch. The heat of him was like a soft, familiar blanket. I had so many more questions I wanted to ask him, so many things I wanted to say. And there was a lot I wanted to *do*.

But it did not take long for sleep to drag me under. The last thing I heard as I drifted away was the steady thumping of his heart.

Dim sunlight streamed in through the tiny window overlooking the small Autumn village. I squinted as I opened my eyes, only to find Liam's face mere inches from mine. We were turned toward each other on the bed, our shoulders digging into the hard mattress. He no longer held me close to his chest. His heart no longer beat beneath my ear. Had he pulled away in the night?

With a sigh, I climbed out of bed and felt my clothes where I'd hung them up. Thankfully, they were dry, so I wouldn't have to ride all the way back to the Academy in this ridiculous pillowcase gown. That was ripped in half. From when Liam had almost claimed me as his...and then had pulled away, knowing that I wasn't his mate.

I changed before Liam could wake, but I swore when I turned around, one of his eyes was partially cracked.

"Morning, darling," he drawled with a slight smile. "You ready to get going?"

So he had been watching then.

"If we don't head back soon, we won't get back to the Academy tonight," I said slowly. A part of me wished we could stay here longer. Just another day or two. I was eager to get back to my lessons, but this time with Liam had revitalized me in a way I hadn't known I'd needed. I felt even more ready to take down the Redcaps than I had before.

And...I hadn't *hated* spending time with Liam, even if I knew it could never be more than what it had been when we'd fallen asleep cuddled up together. Another night spent like that...I couldn't say I'd mind it. Which was why I could have used another day or two like this. It might not be against the rules, but I doubted anything like that would ever happen behind Academy walls.

"Your wish is my command."

We were back on the road within the hour. Luckily, the return trip to the Academy was much more uneventful than the ride to Esari. No one tried to stop us, probably because they realized we were on our way out of the Autumn woods rather than trekking in from somewhere else. The sun was still shining in the sky when the horse trotted back onto the Academy grounds. Within moments, we were surrounded by five fae, and every single one of them was pointing a sword our way.

One of the swords belonged to Kael. I stiffened when I saw him. His cruel eyes, his thin curving lips. It was the first time I'd laid eyes on him since the night he'd abandoned me on the cliff to face the Redcap alone, and anger still very much burned in my veins. This fae before me, who had thrown me at the feet the very thing that had killed my friend, without any help from him…he was probably my mate. Instead of Liam.

I almost *hoped* he charged with his sword. That way, I'd have an excuse to fight him for all I was worth.

When he flicked his eyes across my face and then to Liam, he frowned and lowered his weapon, motioning for the others to do the same. They were all wearing leather armor and bracers made from steel. I'd seen some of them during Watch Duty, standing guard for the Academy.

"Liam, where the hell have you been? And why do you have Norah with you?" His voice was cold and edged in steel.

The muscles in Liam's back tightened. "She has the weekend off, no? I was just showing her around Otherworld."

Kael's glittering dark eyes narrowed. "Her roommate reported her missing. We thought she'd been taken. Or worse."

Whoops. I hadn't even thought about what Sophia might do when she found me missing. I'd been too swept away in the excitement of a quest.

And the idea of spending time with Liam.

"It's not like you to overreact, Kael," Liam said with a chuckle. "Students explore Otherworld all the time on the weekends. There was no reason to jump to conclusions."

"I wasn't jumping to conclusions." Kael frowned and glanced at the four guards who were watching the exchange with expressions ranging from irritation to anger to distrust. Kael raised his arm and waved at the looming Academy behind him. "Return to your posts."

As the four guards began to disperse, each heading toward a different watch tower, Liam dismounted the horse and held out a hand to help me do the same. This time, I only stumbled a little, though I did almost twist my ankle. I was improving?

"What's with the armed guards?" Liam asked, gesturing to the retreating fae. "Night doesn't fall for another few hours. We don't need to worry about creatures just yet."

"While you two were having your little joy ride, the Academy has been undergoing a series of attacks from the Redcaps," Kael said, his voice as icy as his eyes. "Last night, the student on Watch Duty in the northwestern tower was attacked and killed."

Horror pounded through me. I glanced from Kael to Liam, whose face reflected the same revulsion I felt. A strange buzzing filled my head. A student was dead. A changeling keeping watch in the northwestern tower. I swallowed hard.

"But that's Norah's tower," Liam said, fists clenching. "That's where she usually stands watch. She's spent five out of seven nights there since she came to Otherworld."

Kael gave a curt nod. "So, you can see that I wasn't jumping to conclusions, Liam. This cannot be a coincidence, especially after what happened in Manhattan. The Redcaps appear to want Norah dead. It's not safe for her to leave the Academy."

CHAPTER FIFTEEN

My life at the Academy went from strange-yet-*intriguing* to just plain terrible after that. Finn, Liam, Rourke, and Kael seemed convinced that my life was in danger at every turn, and I was forbidden from stepping outside of the Academy walls. That included restricting me from participating in Watch Duty, something they all thought would please me.

But I'd kind of enjoyed the task, as strange as it sounded. It was *doing something*, even if it was nothing more than just keeping out an eye for danger. It had been time outside, under the stars. Now, I could longer breathe in the fresh air of summer and smell the wildflowers that dotted the campus grounds.

Instead, Kael had taken it upon himself to add some in-depth one-on-one training to my curricula, which meant I was supposed to spend an extra four hours a day doing coursework. With him. In the library. He seemed to think it was the only way to keep me alive.

Not that he cared if I lived or died. Clearly.

When I showed up for my first extra lesson with him, I glared at him for awhile before plopping into the chair across the table from him. I waited, wondering if he'd bring up what had happened. He didn't.

Instead, he pushed a book across the table and told me to read about the various types of flowers found in the Winter Court's lands. Candlelight flickered in the quiet library as I dragged my eyes across the pages. Kael just sat there, watching. An hour later, he yanked the book away and told me to recite what I'd learned.

"There's the Winter Moonlight," I said, chin on fisted hand. "It's a white flower that turns to pink toward the end of winter."

"Wrong." He tapped a finger against the bandage on his arm, something he tried to hide under his sleeve but failed. "It's called the Winter Moonbeam. Come on, Norah. This isn't, as you humans say, rocket science. You can do better than this."

"I'm exhausted," I said, frowning at him. "And I don't see how this is at all relevant to fighting Redcaps."

He let out an irritated sigh. "Because you need to understand and know your world before you start swinging swords around."

"Why are you even helping me?" I fisted my hands and leaned forward. "You act like being in my presence is the most annoying thing in the world. Like you'd rather be anywhere else than training me."

"You're just not what I expected."

"Gee, thanks." I rolled my eyes. "You know what? Neither are you. But I guess we're stuck with each other, aren't we?"

"At least I am trying to prepare you to join my Court," he said with a dismissive wave of his hand. "You? You act as though you'd rather be frolicking around with Liam in the woods."

"Maybe that's because you left me for dead on a cliff with nothing but a bow and arrow I clearly can't handle." I crossed my arms over my chest and glared at him. "Of course, maybe that's what you wanted. That way you wouldn't be stuck with a mate you don't want. I bet you even hoped I'd get killed."

There it was. All the words I'd been dying to say since the moment he'd vanished into thin air, abandoning me to pretty much certain death. I knew I'd gotten lucky. It wasn't skill that had saved me that day. It was pure, unbridled fear zeroed in to determination.

"This is tedious." He pushed back his chair and stalked over to the window, peering out into the darkness of summer midnight. His whole body was tense, the back of his neck rippling beneath the soft glow of the library torches. Of all four of my instructors, Kael was the hardest to understand. He was so cold and distant, much more so than the other Winter fae who studied or instructed at the Academy. And it was as if he held all of it against me, in particular.

It seemed like it was more than just the fact I was a lot different than what he'd wanted.

Why else would he have left me for dead?

After a moment of strained silence, Kael let out a bitter sigh. "The reason I want you to study the plants is because knowing them may come in handy one day. Winter Moonbeam looks a lot like another flower, one that can heal a Redcap bite wound if used quickly enough." He looked over his shoulder and met my eye with a pained expression. "That one is called Winter Starlight, and it's very difficult to tell the difference between the two flowers unless they are studied very closely."

What?!

I swallowed hard, my head ringing at his words. "So, it could have saved Bree?"

"Perhaps." He pursed his lips. "Perhaps not. Some wounds are too deep and too fatal, but others are..."

He trailed off as he clenched his hands around the window ledge. The move almost looked...pained. That was strange. Had he lost someone to the Redcaps? Had he tried to save them but had been too late? They were questions I was dying to ask, but I never would. Not with him. He'd only brush me aside like an irritating fly that wouldn't stop buzzing around his head.

And as much as I hated myself for it, I felt a small piece of my heart soften toward him. But only a small one. Because he was still a jerk. One who didn't deserve my sympathy.

"Well, can you show me then, please?" I asked through clenched teeth, hating that I was asking. It felt like he'd won. "If there's something out there that can help save someone who gets attacked, I want to know what it is. Hell, I want to know everything I can about the Redcaps."

With a nod, he strode back over to the table and dropped into the chair. His dark eyes met mine, and for a moment, my breath caught. He no longer looked as though he couldn't stand the sight of me. He almost looked as if...as if the raw depths of his soul were yearning to make me see something no one else could. But then he blinked and sat back.

What the hell was that?

"As with everything, there's a lot you don't yet know about the Redcaps." He held up a hand when I began to ask what. "Don't worry. I'm going to fill you in, but there's a lot to learn. We're going to continue with the basics. How to fight them. Then, we'll get into exactly who and what they are, and why it's essential to prevent them from taking more lives. For the future of Otherworld."

I furrowed my brows. "So, that's that then."

He glanced up from the book. "What do you mean?"

"You're not going to apologize for leaving me to die."

"You didn't die, Norah. You're sitting right in front of me."

"But—"

"Aren't you?"

"That doesn't matter. I *could* have died."

"But you didn't."

"I don't see how that matters. Your intent was—"

"To prove to you that you aren't helpless."

My mouth dropped open, shock pummelling my gut. How had he known how much I worried about being helpless? He couldn't read minds. Could he?

"I'm going to start reading now, and I expect you to take down some notes." He pointed at the parchment before me, and then he began reading. I opened my mouth to try to turn the conversation back onto that horrible night, but he carried on as if he didn't notice.

Grumbling, I grabbed my pen. And then I took down his every word.

I took the books and my parchment of notes back to my quarters. Sophia's door was ajar, and her light snore drifted toward me while I tiptoed past the sofa and into my bedroom. Kael had taken me through plant after plant for the past hour, pointing out the various properties of each. I had to admit, my eyelids hadn't been as quite as heavy as they had been before, mostly because I finally understood the importance of what he was trying to teach me.

There was a plant out there that could cure a Redcap bite. A flower that could save someone's life.

I didn't understand the how or why of it, but a lot of things about Otherworld didn't make sense.

After changing into sweats and a tank top I'd borrowed from Lila, I settled into bed with the books, scanning the words until my eyelids finally drifted shut. I wasn't sure how long I sat there like that when a long, sharp screech whispered through my open window. Immediately, I was on my feet, eyes wild and heart pounding madly in my chest.

The curtains fluttered in the soft summer breeze, bringing with it the stench of sweat and blood. And then a long, sharp claw slid onto the window-frame, hooking around the wood.

I stumbled back, wildly searching for anything I could use as a weapon. A broom handle. A kitchen knife. Anything at all.

But I only had me.

Another claw hooked around the frame, and I watched in horror as a Redcap slid through the billowing curtains, landing heavily on the hardwood floor of my room. My heart thundered in my ears as the dark creature, covered in mounds of grimy black fur, cocked its head and stared at me.

Those eyes, I thought as I stumbled back another step. They were a rich, deep blue. So different than the black eyes of the Redcap I'd fought on the cliff. For a moment, I almost forgot I was facing off against the creature of my nightmares with nothing but my fists. There was something so familiar about those eyes. And they looked so horribly, horribly sad.

The creature began to shudder, its dark mangy fur trembling in the night air. For a moment, I thought it was a strange form of pre-attack, like it was readying itself to launch my way with its claws. But then something different began to happen. The fur transformed, the thick darkness of it melting away to reveal pale skin.

The fangs began to shorten, and the claws disappeared into long and slender fingers. I stumbled back, barely believing my eyes. For the first time since I'd arrived in Otherworld, I suddenly wondered if I was going crazy again. Because the beast was melting away to reveal a form that was very much human.

A human who looked a whole lot like...

A girl, one with long dark hair that was matted to a pixie face. The girl glanced up at me from where she heaved deep breaths, clutching the ground as her entire body trembled. Those deep blue eyes locked on my face, and everything within me exploded at the sight.

I stumbled back, eyes wide, my hands clutching frantically at my throat.

"Bree?" My voice was small and timid. My mind was unbelieving.

"Oh, Norah," she said with a sob. And when I heard my best friend's familiar voice, all I could do was fall to my knees and weep. I crawled toward her and took her dirt-painted face in my hands, searching those familiar eyes for the truth.

"Is it really you?" I asked as the tears streamed down my face. "I thought you were dead. That thing. It killed you. How are you here? How are you alive?"

And why did you look like one of the monsters two seconds ago?

She shuddered, her body soaked in sweat. In an instant, I ripped the sheet off my bed and draped it around her shoulders. Her body felt like ice. I stayed there silent next to her while her chest heaved, waiting until she felt as if she could speak.

Finally, she said, "When that thing attacked me, it turned me into one of them. I'm a Redcap now, Norah. That's how I'm here. And it's how I'm alive."

With a deep breath, I shook my head, even though I'd seen her transform right in front of my eyes. "That can't be right. It must be something else. Some kind of weird magic that makes you look like one."

"No," she breathed as she slowly lifted her eyes to meet mine. "And it's worse than you think."

"What do you mean?" My heart hammered hard. I couldn't even wrap my head around Bree being alive, much less the fact that she was now one of the very monsters I'd been training to fight. She was Bree. My best friend. My family. And now she was here. Alive and well, though a hell of a lot worse for wear. All I wanted to do was hug her tight and wipe away the tears, but there was a cloud of dread hanging over our reunion.

"I followed you through the Faerie Ring," she began, sniffling. "At first, I was going to try to talk to you, but you're constantly surrounded by those four fae who would kill me in a heartbeat if they saw me."

Frowning, I shook my head. "They wouldn't."

But that was a lie. They would. If Bree was right, if she truly was a Redcap, they would.

"Yes, they would," she said in a harsh voice, wrapping the sheet tighter around her shoulders. "To them, I'm a Redcap. A thing to be hunted and killed, even though *they* are the ones who created them in the first place."

Dread dripped down my spine. "That can't be right."

"Oh, it is," she said bitterly. "When I realized I couldn't get to you, I went in search of other answers. I ended up stumbling on a pack of Redcaps, ones who can still change back into humans like I can. Have they taught you where the wolves come from yet? Have they told you what happens to the human babies they steal?"

My heart jumped around in my chest. Because I knew without a doubt that I would not like whatever would come next. These had been questions I'd been asking. Questions that had been expertly dodged for days. The Academy didn't yet want us to know the truth about the human changelings, a fact that had been niggling at me since I'd arrived. And yet, I'd blindly accepted it. The vague answers. The dodges. The carefully changed conversations.

"Tell me, Bree."

She winced and placed a trembling hand on her neck. Deep red scars crisscrossed her skin. The place where the Redcap had slashed her with its massive claws.

"The pack of Redcaps told me that the humans who are brought to Otherworld are corrupted by the magic and the power here. Humans weren't built for this world. So, they change. Into something dark, something vicious. Something part-fae themselves. They become these monsters." She took a deep breath. "And then they're let loose in the human realm, spreading their disease with a swipe of their claws."

"No," I whispered, eyes full of burning tears. "They must have been wrong. The fae wouldn't do something like that."

Liam wouldn't do something like this. Finn wouldn't either.

Or would they? I'd only been here a couple of weeks and already I'd come face-to-face with how devious, dangerous, and dark they could be.

"It's part of their Tithe to the demon realm," Bree continued. "In exchange for the demons leaving Otherworld alone, the fae create sixteen Redcaps every year. On the Summer Solstice, they're sent to prey on humans."

With a shuddering breath, I stood from the floor and began to pace across the hardwood. As happy as I was to see Bree, the news she brought me was worse than anything I could have imagined on my own. To hear that the fae were behind this...

"But they have Hunters specifically trained to fight the Redcaps. Why would they—"

"The Tithe only says they have to return the monsters to the human realm. It doesn't say they can't kill them after they do. And don't forget that it's more than just the human changelings who get transformed. Any innocent who comes into contact with one, well...look at me. I got attacked, and now I'm one, too. And there are hundreds of us. Some have come back to Otherworld, like me."

"Hundreds," I repeated before I dropped to my knees in front of her. "But Bree, you seem so..."

"Normal?" She let out a bitter laugh. "I'm far from it. When I'm in my wolf form, all I can see and smell is blood. I haven't killed anyone though. Not yet anyway."

That last bit she muttered so softly that I almost didn't hear her.

Her hand snatched my wrist, and her fingernails sunk into my skin. So hard that my veins began to pulse. "Not all of them are able to control themselves as well as I can, Norah. They're more beast than human. I came here to warn you. You need to learn how to fight. One day, they're going to come for you."

"Me?" I whispered. "But why me?"

Soft footsteps thudded on the living room floor, and Bree's body went razor sharp. She stood, letting the sheet pool around her feet. Slowly, she backed up to the window, her eyes so wide that they reminded me of twin full moons.

"Norah?" Sophia called out. "Who are you talking to?"

"Go," I whispered furiously, my gaze locked on Bree's waxen face. "If you're right about all of this, you need to get out of here."

"You're not safe here, Norah," she hissed back.

"I'm safe enough." In two quick strides, I crossed the room and took Bree's arms tight in my hands. She was so solid, so real. And I had to make sure she stayed that way. "I don't know what they'll do if they find you in here, and I don't aim to find out. There are a few small villages near the edge of the Autumn woods. Go there. Hide. Steal food when you need it. I may be able to fix this, but I need some time."

A soft knock sounded on my door.

Bree swallowed hard and nodded. She backed up to the window and disappeared behind the billowing curtain just as Sophia cracked open my door. I stayed there, gazing outside with my back turned her way. My heart trembled, but I suddenly felt a clarity of mind that calmed the frantic beat in my chest.

Bree was alive. She might be in some serious trouble, but she was alive.

"Norah?" Sophia's voice held a frown. "What are you doing? Is someone out there?"

I took a moment to ready myself, but then I turned her way with an expression of intense weariness painted on my face. "Sorry, I didn't mean to wake you. Kael has me learning about some plants, and I have to recite a bunch of stuff out loud to him tomorrow. I was just practicing."

She scrunched up her face, her eyes flicking to the discarded bedsheet on the floor. "I could have sworn I heard another voice in here. A girl."

I laughed and shrugged. "Must have just been me talking to myself. I think I'm so tired I'm getting delirious."

"Okay." A pause. "You should get some sleep. We have History of Fae in the morning. It's so dull that you're going to nod off if you're this tired."

"You're right. I should get some sleep," I said with a

nod. "Probably a bad idea to burn out during my first month here."

With a smile, she moved back to the door but hesitated before she left my room. "Are you sure you're okay?"

"I'm fine."

And I was. For the first time since I'd arrived at Otherworld Academy, I felt as if I knew exactly what I needed to do. I would no longer flail around, seeking answers to questions I didn't even know I was asking. I would find a way to cure Bree, even if it meant lying to every single person here. It wasn't like they'd bothered to tell me the truth either. Not even Liam.

And if any Redcaps came at me? I'd be ready.

CHAPTER SIXTEEN

Finn taught History of Fae. Despite his upbeat personality, even he couldn't make the long, boring tales he shared sound interesting. It was a class we had every Tuesday and Thursday, yet it felt as if we'd covered no ground at all. Maybe because he was keeping the juicy parts of history to himself.

So, I decided to rectify that.

Halfway through class, I raised my hand and gave him a steely smile. I'd been waiting for this moment all day. Hell, I'd been waiting all night. After Bree had disappeared through my window, I hadn't been able to sleep, too worked up by the knowledge that my fae instructors had been lying to us.

They'd been lying to me.

Finn's sparkling green eyes caught mine. It was hard to imagine he could be behind something like this. Rourke, I could believe. Maybe even Kael, though his anger toward the Redcaps would seem to suggest otherwise. Liam? It certainly wouldn't be the first time he'd hidden something from someone, but I'd let him *kiss* me...and more.

But Finn?

"What is it, Norah?" Finn asked. "Do you have a question about the lineage of Sterk, the great fighter from the Age of the Moon?"

I didn't even know who he was talking about. I'd been so zoned out that I hadn't been listening to the long list of Sterk ancestors. None of us had.

"Sterk was clearly awesome and all," I began, shifting on my seat. "But I think I can speak for everyone when I say that what we'd all really like to know? The history of the changelings."

Several of the other first-years murmured in agreement.

Finn's brows winged upward. "I see. Unfortunately, that topic isn't on our syllabus for today."

"It's not on the syllabus at all," I countered, anger building in my chest. I knew. I'd looked in the middle of the night when I couldn't sleep. "Look, we all know you don't want to tell us, so it must be something pretty bad. But that isn't fair on us. These are our lives. We deserve to know the truth about where we came from and why we're exchanged with human babies. Not to mention, what happens to them after you send them back to the human realm?"

"Yeah," Griff spoke up from behind me. "What happens to the humans?"

Finn crossed his arms over his chest and scanned the room. "Do you all want to hear this then?"

Every single changeling in the room spoke with a resounding yes.

"Very well." His eyes flicked to mine, full of amusement but something else. Suspicion, almost, and disappointment. Fine with me. I didn't care. He and the other fae inside this godforsaken castle were transforming innocent humans into murderous beasts.

Still, he carried on. Most of what he told us, Bree had already explained to me. The Tithe. The human transformations. I was relieved to see that everyone was just as horrified as I'd been.

"Can't you do something to stop it?" Lila asked, her voice shaking.

Finn merely shook his head. "The Tithe cannot be broken. If it is, both the human and faerie realms will suffer. Yes, what happens to the human children is terrible. I hate it as much as you do, but we don't have any other choice."

I ground my teeth together. Surely there was always a choice.

Sam raised a hand, and Finn nodded to her. "What exactly is the Tithe? Is it sending sixteen changelings into the human realm or is it *taking* sixteen humans?"

"Ah." Finn's smile widened. "Clever girl. It is taking *and* returning sixteen humans each year. The fae changeling swap is merely a bi-product of that."

I furrowed my eyebrows. "Why swap at all?"

"Another good question," Finn said with a nod. "Our realms require balance. If we take sixteen souls, we must give sixteen. So, each year, when we take sixteen humans, we must give sixteen babes of our own. And when we return the humans, we are able to bring you back home. In fact, we *must* bring you back home, or else the balance of our realms is disrupted."

"Disrupted how?" Griff asked.

At that question, Finn merely gave a shrug. "We have never tested it, and we do not intend to. I think I can speak for all fae when I say that we will not do anything that would risk the safety of our people."

Five more hands shot into the air, but the distant clang of a bell interrupted our questions. Grumbling, everyone stood to gather their books and papers, readying themselves to head to the next lesson. It was the first time anyone had seemed even remotely reluctant to leave History of Fae, though I had a feeling we'd be bored stiff again soon enough. Finn had indulged us, but I had a feeling he wouldn't again.

"Norah?" he called out as I slung my bag over my shoulder. "Can you stay after class for a moment?"

Uh oh. I might very well be in trouble. I'd kind of taken control of the class and run with it, but I didn't regret it in the least. Now, everyone else knew the truth about the changelings, and I'd gotten more answers, though I still had so much I wanted to know.

The classroom emptied as I walked up to his grand oak desk. He perched on the edge, tossing an apple aimlessly in the air. He didn't even glance at it as it landed perfectly in his open palm.

"Interesting discussion today," he said.

"Yep. I thought so." I crossed my arms and met his steady gaze. "That's why I asked the questions."

"Indeed."

"You should have told me what the Redcaps really are," I said, narrowing my eyes. "It seems a little odd that you would keep it from us for so long."

"You've been here less than a month, Norah."

"And you should have told us from day one."

"Why?" He arched a brow, still tossing the apple. "So that you could begin your time here fearful and upset?"

"Oh, I'm not fearful," I said, edging toward him. "I'm angry. Innocent humans are dying, and you're doing nothing to stop it."

I glared at him, heart pumping hot blood through my veins.

"Do you know what would happen if we didn't commit to the Tithe?" he asked, bouncing the apple once more. And then he stopped. His fingers tightened around the red skin. "The Dark Fae would destroy every single one of us. We have no other choice, Norah. Hate us all you like, but we're not the ones who started this entire thing. The Dark Fae are."

A chill swept down my spine.

"But what I want to know is how you knew all of this already. Something tells me you didn't read it in a book."

Uh oh. Time for a diversion. I didn't want him to get any weird ideas in his head, or to wonder where I'd gotten my information. If he discovered that Bree had come to visit me—in Redcap form, no less—he might tell the others. And the others would insist on tracking her down.

I would *never* again let anything happen to Bree. I'd protect her with my own life if I had to.

"You know, I've been thinking a lot about what Court I might belong to," I said in a teasing, singsong kind of voice that sounded a lot like the way he spoke. Smiling coyly, I stepped closer to him until my hips brushed against his.

Amusement flickered through his eyes, and he raised his brows. "Is that so, Norah?"

"It just seems—to me, at least—that Winter and Autumn don't make sense." I shifted slightly closer. So close that the wild, fresh scent of him filled my head. "For one, I've never really been fond of the cold. And they're just so serious, you know?"

His green eyes sparkled. And, this time, he was the one who shifted closer. Now, his mouth was only an inch from mine. My heart raced through my chest.

"Something tells me that you're suggesting you might be mine," he said, his voice dropping an octave. "You know what they say about Spring mates, don't you?"

"No," I whispered.

He grinned. "When true Spring mates make love on the ground, flowers bloom all around them at the height of their pleasure."

I swallowed hard, and my cheeks blazed. Was he serious? I couldn't be certain.

"So, if you truly think you're my mate..." He slid his hand around the back of my neck and massaged my hot skin. With a gasp, I dropped back my head and stared up at the ceiling, my skin sparking from his touch. "I can throw you over my shoulder and carry you into the forest where we can test it for ourselves."

Oh my god.

He was still massaging my neck, something that felt so good I thought I might melt into a puddle on the floor. Not to mention the bit about him carrying me outside. I knew firsthand that he wouldn't hesitate to throw me over his shoulder. But would he really take things further than that?

My heart pounded against my ears.

I had a feeling that he most certainly would.

"Or," he said, dropping his hand away. Cool air whispered against my neck in its place. "You could be trying to distract me from the fact you knew about the changeling humans before you asked about them in class. Have you been talking to the older students?"

My brain was fuzzy, and my body begged for more of his touch. But I couldn't let him see how much he'd gotten to me, or the fact that I'd actually been considering letting him carry me outside…

"I guess you caught me," I said in a faux-abashed voice. "I got curious, so I asked around."

"Hmm, well I can't blame you, but I'd appreciate it if you didn't try to show me up in class like that." His eyes dropped to my chest where my nipples had hardened and were clearly poking through my shirt. *That* was how much an effect his little massage had on me. "Though, I have to say, it seems we've both enjoyed our after-class chat. Be sure to let me know when you want to take that little trip into the forest."

With a wink, he turned back to rifle through some

notes on his desk, and it took a very long time for my face to cool down. Was that just another joke? A tease? A way to throw me off my game?

Or had he meant it?

And why did I desperately want to find out?

When I strode into the library after dinner, Kael was glowering out the window, as per usual. I dropped my study books onto the table and crossed my arms over my chest, conjuring up a strength and confidence I'd never known I had until now.

"I want to ramp our training up a notch," I said. Voice firm. Eyes clear. I wasn't going to take no for an answer. "I want to know more about that plant, and I want to practice ways to fight the Redcaps. No more reading, Kael. I'm ready to learn how to fight."

I expected him to argue. He'd been dead set against physically training me so far, and I didn't expect that to change anytime soon. But when he turned from the window, his eyes held a hint of defeat.

"I know about Bree," he said.

My mouth opened, but no sound came out. This couldn't be happening. I hadn't told a soul about her visit, and I didn't know what I would do if he insisted on tracking her down. He might think she was a threat, but she wasn't. Bree was a lot of things, but she wasn't a killer. She wasn't anything close to that.

"Sit," Kael said. Even though I wanted to stand tall, I obeyed, practically falling into the chair.

He strode closer to me and braced his palms on the wood surface, leaning so close that his breath whispered across my cheek. "I assume she's spoken to you because you look like you're about to vomit."

Swallowing hard, I tore my gaze away. I wanted to look anywhere else than into his glittering eyes. Those eyes that always felt as if they could see through every barrier I tried to put up between us.

"Don't worry. I'm not going to send Hunters out to kill her," he said, still leaning close. "I won't tell the Head Instructor either. Or Finn, Rourke, or Liam, though I believe you'd find them more understanding than you think."

"What?" Heart in my throat, I glanced back at him. Nothing in his eyes suggested that this was all some sort of trick or a joke. In fact, Kael never joked. He was far too matter-of-fact for that. A trickster, he was not. So, when he said something, I felt as though I should believe it.

"You heard me." He pushed away from the table and stalked back toward the window, glaring through the thick panes. "Your friend is going through a torturous time right now, but there's no evidence to suggest she's fallen prey to the beast. As long as she keeps the blood off her hands, I'll make no move against her."

My heart thudded against my ribcage and I curled

my fingers against the edge of the table. "How do you know about her? What do you mean about the beast?"

He let out a heavy sigh. "Many humans who are attacked by Redcaps become one themselves. Unknowingly, they seek out Otherworld, since they belong here more than the human realm. Somewhere, deep down inside, they know this. When they do enter the faerie realm, one of two things usually happens. They either join the Wilde Fae and embrace the savage monster within. Or they fight it. Unfortunately, neither option ends well."

"Bree is fighting it," I said. "She's not going to become a savage beast."

"You're right," he said with a nod. "And she will likely die because of it."

I gripped the table tighter, so tight my knuckles went stark white. "But she's alive. I saw her. She came in through my window. Sure, she was in pretty bad shape, but she was alive."

He turned to me then, a deep sadness echoing in the hollow black of his eyes. "Her body cannot withstand the place between human and beast, as she is right now. She's infected. As long as she fights for her human self, her life is forfeit."

"No," I whispered. "You're wrong. She said there were others. Redcaps who were like her. Ones who are still human."

"There are." A pause. "And if they do not give into their transformation, they'll die, too."

Suddenly, I could no longer stay sitting. I stood from the table and pushed back my chair so hard that it toppled to the floor behind me. "But if she gives into the transformation..."

"Then, she'll become a beast permanently, like the one who attacked her in Manhattan, like the ones we hunt. She'll no longer be able to transform into a human, and there will be a savagery to her that isn't truly Bree. She'll be in there, but she'll be...twisted."

I shoved my hands into my hair and stormed away from Kael. This couldn't be happening. I'd just gotten Bree back, and now I was discovering that it had all been a twisted lie, one she didn't know the truth of herself. She wasn't going to survive this. And, if she did, she'd become something so wrong and so twisted that it would be even worse than death.

She would become the thing that had almost killed her.

"There has to be a way to stop this," I said. "There has to be a way to undo it. That plant. You said it could cure a Redcap's bite. What if we got some for her? Would it stop her from dying?"

His lips pressed into a thin line. "Think, Norah. I know you took the books back to your room with you."

Eyes wide, I nodded with realization. "Winter Starlight can cure a Redcap bite, but a fully-transformed Redcap cannot touch it without suffering from an intense, life-threatening fever."

"Correct." He gave a curt nod. "So, you can see the dilemma. If Bree is able to hold off the beast, then we may have time to give her the cure. But there's a risk. If her transformation is further along than we realize, it could very well end up killing her."

"I have to try," I said without any hesitation. Kael was right. It was a risk, but it was the only option we had. Either Bree would die from holding off the beast, or she would become one herself. If there was even a chance at all that we could save her, we had to do it.

CHAPTER SEVENTEEN

"We'll go tonight," Kael said after striding over to the window again. "Our absence will not be noticed if we go now."

"Go where?" I asked as he grabbed his black cloak from the back of his chair, along with a long, slender sword he slung across his back.

"We must go to the Winter Court, Norah. That's where you'll find the Winter Starlight."

"Right...but won't it take a long time to get there?"

He let out a low chuckle. It was the first time I'd heard him make any kind of noise resembling laughter. "You're forgetting that we can shift, Norah. Here. You'll need to wear this."

He passed me a cloak similar to his own, and I slung it around my shoulders. It was heavier than the Autumn cloak had been, and much, much softer. There were two deep pockets that were lined with something resembling fleece, and the hood was layered with the same, only twice as thick.

"Ready?" he asked after I'd patted the various pockets and linings of the cloak. "Just wrap your arms around my neck and close your eyes."

I blinked at him. "Do what now?"

"Don't look so scandalized," he said with a slight smile. "Until you've practiced shifting, this is the safest way to get you there. You don't know where we're going. You could end up halfway across the realm if you went alone."

But my feet felt frozen in place.

"There are rules, Norah," he said. "Instructors and recruits must have platonic relationships only, even if they know they're mates."

It was my turn to give him a slight smile. "Yeah, but something tells me that the little no-romance rule is rarely followed."

"Hmm." His smile faded. "It's a rule that should be followed. Otherwise, serious problems can arise, and I would never want to do anything to cause you pain. It's bad enough that you're likely stuck with me anyway. I certainly wouldn't want to be. So, you'll have no advances from me."

I cocked my head and frowned. What was that all about? He might be closed off and cold at times, but it wasn't like he was unappealing, just as long as he wasn't talking. Okay, so maybe he wasn't the nicest fae around, but that was his own damn fault. It was almost as if he was purposely trying to push people away.

Still, he was exceedingly attractive. With his dark hair curling over his ears and his broad, muscular chest, he was the very definition of tall, dark, and handsome. Of course, he'd abandoned me to face a Redcap alone, and he *still* hadn't apologized. It didn't matter how gorgeous he was. He was an ass.

Swallowing hard, I stepped in close and wrapped my arms around his neck. His body was tense against mine, and he was clearly uncomfortable with our closeness. But why? It wasn't just because of the rules. His strange little speech had told me that.

Darkness blurred around us, thick and heavy. Wind whooshed around my face. The temperature suddenly dropped, the thick heat of summer flickering away into a dying light. In its place, a bitter cold sunk into my bones, biting at my cheeks and my hands.

When I opened my eyes, I saw nothing but the heavy blanket of the night sky. Overhead, thousands of stars sparkled in the deep black. They were the only light for miles on every side, but they lit up the snowy mountainside, displaying a breathtaking view of towering pine trees that spread out on every side.

We were high up. Very high up. There was a steep drop to our left, though the right side sloped gently down to the edge of the snow-covered pines where a cave was carved into the side of the mountain. Up ahead, a thicket of winding brambles created a maze of bushes. Somewhere, deep within it, a small pale pink dot stood out from the blanket of white flowers. That would be the Winter Starlight. One was ready to be picked. The others were not.

I shivered and jammed my hands into the pockets of the cloak. "Let me guess. We need to get to that one pink flower in the middle of all of this. Why can't we just shift over there?"

"I'm afraid that this quest is yours alone from this point on, Norah." Kael's eyes were focused on something just behind me. He wouldn't meet my gaze, no matter how hard I frowned at him.

"That's not fair. You can't do this to me again. It's not right to just keep dumping me places when you haven't even bothered to give me any training."

His dark eyes flicked to my face, and then away again. "You're perfectly capable of climbing through the thicket yourself. It may take you an hour or so, but it's not particularly difficult or dangerous. I'll stand watch in case something in the forest gets curious."

I shivered, though this time, it wasn't for the cold. "You're actually going to make me go get the flower myself." I laughed and shook my head. "Okay, fine. If that's how you want to be, then so be it. It's not like I actually wanted your help anyway."

The only evidence he heard me was the flicker of his clenched jaw.

With a heavy sigh, I rolled my eyes and turned toward the thicket. The thick branches and waxy leaves weaved together like a net. This was going to take awhile. I ducked underneath the first branch, and leaves slapped me in the face for the effort. Gritting my teeth, I continued, ducking and twisting and shoving branches aside. My breath was heaving when I finally climbed over the last one. Before me, the sole pink flower fluttered in the winter breeze.

For a moment, all I could do was stand and stare at

it. This pretty little flower would either be Bree's destruction or her saving grace. But I didn't yet know which one.

A lion-like roar ripped through the quiet night. I froze with my hand halfway toward the flower, shivers of dread coursing down my spine. Eyes wild, I searched the night. The roar had come from where I'd left Kael. When I twisted his way, I had to grasp onto a branch to hold myself steady. A strange, terrifying creature was lurking toward him with a mouth full of sharp, jagged fangs.

My heart tumbled through my chest. The creature wasn't a Redcap. No, it was a lot worse than that. It was bigger, for one. Almost as big as a house. It made Kael—strong, muscular Kael—look like an ant in comparison. An ant that was cowering before a creature that was almost part-lion, part-dinosaur.

Kael bent his knees and raised his sword. "Grab the flower, Norah. Now!"

I didn't want to do anything of the sort. There was a massive creature two seconds away from attacking Kael, and I couldn't just stand here picking flowers as if I had zero cares in the world. But then Kael swung his sword at the creature, and I was no longer so desperately afraid for him.

He moved with a fluidity that defied logic. It was as if a dance had taken over his body, one with swords and violence, rather than one to the beat of the music, but it was a dance nonetheless. The blade rippled beneath the glittering stars above, and power sang as it sliced through the air.

Kael might be smaller than the creature, but I'd never seen anyone or anything look more powerful than he did in that moment. And so incredibly brave.

The awe of him made me temporarily forget what we'd come here for.

The blade sank into the creature's left leg, and a horrible gurgling noise echoed through the night. With a sharp gasp, I twisted away from the gory sight that followed. So much blood. Thick and pouring onto the ground. My fingers trembled as I focused on the flower and plucked it from the tangle of weeds.

When I turned back to the fight, Kael had managed to get another blow into the creature's right leg. The lion-like monster was thrashing and roaring, but it showed no signs of stopping anytime soon. Kael slashed his sword again and again, each time hitting the creature even harder than before. Soon, the monster began to stumble away, and I breathed a heavy sigh of relief.

But just before it turned away, it swatted its large, beefy claw at Kael's stomach. The world seemed to slow to a stop as I watched Kael's body launch through the air. His sword clattered to the ground, and his cloak flittered away on the frosty wind. The creature roared and pounded its fist at the ground, blood arcing through the air.

Kael landed heavily in the thicket with a thump.

With a sharp cry, I shoved the flower into the depths of my cloak pocket and began to pick my way through the thicket, desperate to reach his side. Kael. The mighty, powerful Kael. He couldn't be dead. Not when all he'd been trying to do was help me save my friend.

Before I could reach him, the creature's massive claws soared through the air and squeezed around my body. My heart went wild, and so did my legs and my arms. I kicked and squirmed and pushed to escape, but the rough paw held me tight before lifting me from the ground.

It dropped me just beside a puddle of its thick blood, and the stench that filled my nose made my throat close in tight. My god, it smelled rank, and its dozens of wounds were still oozing with more of that disgusting blood.

What was it doing? Was it trying to make me fight?

Out of the corner of my eye, the shimmer of Kael's sword caught my attention. Before the creature could notice, I dove to the side and grabbed the sword from the ground. It was a hell of a lot heavier than it looked, but I managed to hold it up before me just as the creature lunged my way.

I jumped to the side, swinging the sword wildly. Nothing good came of that. The creature merely stepped out of my range and watched me wave the weapon like a lunatic. And clearly like a person who had never handled this kind of blade before.

I needed to get control of myself and fast. My fear and desperation were charging through my veins, and I'd only get myself killed if I didn't calm down.

Quietly, I lowered the sword and took several deep breaths in through my nose, remembering how to keep the panic at bay. The creature's eyes narrowed as I settled my nerves. Sure, I was still terrified of this monstrous creature. It was huge. It had massive claws and fangs. And I didn't know what the hell I was doing.

On the other hand, it had some pretty deep wounds, and there was no way it could last much longer. All I had to do was fend it off for a little while. I didn't even need to wound it more. Its blood was everywhere, and it could barely walk. So, I took in my last deep breath and curled my hands tight around the hilt of the sword, holding it close to my chest. The blade was completely vertical, pointing straight up at the sky.

The creature lunged forward and roared, but I held my stance. It was trying to provoke me, trying to get me to waste my energy fighting a battle I couldn't win.

After several moments of this, the creature's heavy breathing began to sound labored. Its shoulders slumped forward, and its paws dragged along the ground. It gave me one last look before heaving a rattling breath, and then lumbered away from where I still stood, the blade shaking in my hands.

When it finally disappeared, I let out the longest, most shuddering breath I'd ever had. My whole body felt weak and spent, even though I'd merely stood still. I'd been running on adrenaline, and now that the creature was gone, all I wanted to do was collapse on the ground.

But I had to make sure Kael was okay.

I pushed back through the brush and dropped to where he'd fallen. His eyes were closed, and his face was ashen. Fear coursing through my gut, I placed a hand on his neck to feel his pulse. It was there, a slight tremor in his neck. But there was something else. Something much worse, something that made all the blood drain from my face.

His skin was as hot as the sun.

CHAPTER EIGHTEEN

"Kael." I shook his shoulder, but there was no response. His skin was on fire, as if he was burning up from the inside out. I couldn't help but think back to what he'd said. Redcaps were allergic to this plant. If they touched it, an intense fever would take over their body. A fever that could be fatal.

But Kael couldn't be a Redcap, could he? For one, he was very much fae. He wasn't animalistic or savage. Plus, there was that whole thing about being a magical wolf, and as far as I could tell, he was flesh and blood.

My eyes flicked to the bandaged wound on his hand. He'd had it since after the day he dropped me off on that cliff to face the Redcap. My mind began to piece together puzzle pieces that felt as though they should never, ever fit together. But they did. Kael's wound, his strange attitude about the Redcaps, the way he'd told me that the quest to get the flower was mine and mine alone.

Surely he wasn't...

Surely he couldn't be...

Regardless, he was burning up, and if I didn't get him out of this brush, he was only going to get worse. I'd spotted a cave around the corner. All I had to do was get him there and do my best to calm the fever.

Easier said than done.

With a deep breath, I grabbed his arms and tried to lift him from the ground. Only, he didn't go anywhere. Kael was heavy. Much heavier than he looked. He must have approximately zero body fat, which meant I was trying to lift pounds and pounds of pure muscle.

As horrible as it was, I would just have to drag him there. He would likely get scratched and bruised, but at least he would be alive.

Snow began to drift from the sky as I jerked on Kael's arms. He shifted slightly through the brush. It was only an inch or two, but it was something. Enough to solidify my determination. Grunting, I pulled and pulled. Each time, Kael barely budged, but I finally got him out of the brush where I plopped onto the ground, sweat streaming down my face.

The snow was coming down heavily now. I really needed to get Kael under some cover, or he was going to get soaked to the skin. And that would only make the fever worsen.

It was easier to slide him across the snow than drag him through thick branches, though my energy was fully spent by the time I got us into the cave. Once inside, I draped my cloak over his body and got to work on a fire. There were a few branches and old twigs scattered across the cave floor. Enough to get some flames going.

I wasn't entirely sure how I knew how to do this, but the motions came to me as if by second nature. Soon, a small fire began to take shape, and a soft warmth began to spread through the cave.

Sighing, I eased onto the ground beside Kael and felt his forehead. He was still impossibly warm. Truth was, there was nothing much I could do for him. We needed to get back to the Academy where the healing powers of the Summer fae could save him. Perhaps I could shift back to the grounds, like I'd done before.

It was worth a shot.

With a deep breath, I closed my eyes and focused my thoughts on the Academy. On the cold stone walls. On the soft glow of the candlelight in the Great Hall. The familiar sounds and scents of my new home rose up around me, and for a moment, I thought I'd done it.

But when I opened my eyes, the darkness met me instead. We were still very much inside that cave, miles and miles from the Academy's walls.

Pressing my hands to Kael's burning chest, I shook my head. "I'm so sorry, Kael. I don't know what to do for you. If only I could get you home, the Summer fae could heal you..."

A strange thought took shape in my mind, one that clearly made no logical sense in the least. I'd shifted before, when I'd been stranded on that cliff. Therefore, I was an Autumn or a Winter fae. But our Head Instructor had also said that it was easy to get it wrong in the beginning.

And, truth was, I did feel drawn to the ways of the Summer Court. I liked the heat. I liked the sun. I loved the way I could hear the chirping crickets as I drifted off to sleep every night. I didn't find the warmth stifling. Instead, it made me feel free.

And then there was Liam, the hotheaded, passionate Summer fae who I had to admit made me feel something. There was a strange connection between us, one that was next to impossible to ignore.

Maybe, just maybe, I wasn't a Winter or an Autumn at all. Maybe I was a Summer fae.

Maybe I could heal Kael.

No, that doesn't make any sense, Norah, a small, logical voice whispered into my ear. *You've felt a connection with Finn, too. And you're clearly not a Spring.*

"Not to mention that weird attraction to Rourke," I muttered to myself. As much as I hated to admit it, I'd felt a spark of something toward him, too.

And the fae before me. As I'd watched him face off against the creature, there'd been so much power flowing off his body that it was impossible not to notice. He was cold and distant, yes, but there was something more there, too. Something he kept hidden from everyone. Something I'd seen a hint of before.

I shook my head at myself. So what if I was attracted to all of them? Everyone else at the Academy probably was, too. They were gorgeous fae males with glistening skin, muscular bodies, and blinding smiles. I couldn't help it if I felt a connection with more than one of them. We weren't mates. Not yet.

Which meant I still didn't know the full truth

about my powers. Perhaps we'd all been wrong. It was worth a shot.

I took a deep breath in through my nose to steady my nerves. After lifting Kael's heavy cloak from his body, I slid my hands beneath his shirt. His skin was smooth and hot, and my fingertips played along the ridges of his abs. I swallowed hard and stared down at him. His fever must be catching because I'd never been hotter in my life.

But now was not the time to get carried away by how strong and muscular his body felt beneath my hands. I closed my eyes and focused on the fever radiating off of his body. I had no idea how Liam had healed me, but I mimicked what I'd seen him do. He'd touched my skin and closed his eyes. Within moments, the pain had gone.

Heal, I thought, directing all my thoughts and emotions to Kael's slack body. *Fight off the fever. You can do it, Kael.*

A strange sensation began to pool around my hands. Fire and light. The scent of frost fell away, replaced by a rush of wildflowers and summer rain. My entire body began to tremble, as if an unseen violent force was charging through me. Head spinning, I squeezed my eyes tighter, not certain if I should welcome the sensation or push it away.

But this was Kael's life. He'd put himself in danger to help me save Bree. So, I dropped back my head and opened myself up to the strange power that was taking over my body.

Pain exploded around my fingers, sharp and deep and raw.

And then it all vanished into nothing as unconsciousness consumed me.

A soft hand caressed my cheek, and the sharp, tangy scent of mint filled my nose. Groaning, I opened my eyes to find Kael leaning over me, his face blotting out the full moon in the sky. His eyes were pits of black, but the expression on his face was much softer than I'd ever seen from him before.

My heart twinged.

"Thank the forest," he said as he continued to brush my cheek with his thumb. Shivers danced along my skin. "For a moment there, I was worried you weren't coming back to me."

"I don't feel so great." My mouth felt as dry as the desert, and some kind of evil jackhammer was drilling into my skull. Even my vision was dizzy. Kael wasn't just Kael. I swore there were four of him bouncing around in front of me. Not really a bad thing though. It was a pretty nice sight.

I reached back to rub my neck, and my fingers came into contact with a leg. Kael's leg. I blinked, heartbeat flickering. It seemed my head was in his lap.

Oh my god. My head was in the gorgeous Winter fae's lap.

"You'll feel rough for a few hours," he said with a

tenderness in his voice. "You tried to heal me without understanding how the power works. It can knock out even the most experienced fae, and this was your first time doing it."

"And it worked," I said, realizing just how alive and well Kael was. In fact, the tables had turned. I was now the one flat on my ass. "You're okay? The fever is gone?"

At that, Kael's face clouded back over, transforming to his usual stoic expression. His jaw clenched, and the thumb caressing my cheek ceased to move. "Yes, the fever is gone. I suppose you have some questions, and you no doubt are thrilled to discover you're not a Winter fae now that you know the truth about me."

"Come on. That's not fair," I said with a frown. "Don't assume I'm going to judge you just because you're a...well, what *are* you, Kael? Because you certainly don't look like a Redcap to me."

"I'm not a Redcap. Not truly." He let out a heavy sigh. "Two years ago, I was infected when I was fighting against a group of Redcaps who had gone on a killing spree in Boston. They needed to be stopped, and I thought I could be the one to stop them. Instead, I got bitten."

Chills swept down my spine, but I kept my mouth shut. Kael seemed hesitant enough to tell his story. I didn't want to interrupt him with questions, for fear he'd change his mind about sharing this part of himself.

"Because I was already fae, my body was able to withstand the venom to a point, though I regret every single day that I didn't go straight in search of some Starlight." He curled his hands into fists and shook his head, jaw clenching tight. "The beast does not control me. I control it. But it is still inside of me, and every so often, my body must change into that creature or I'll go mad. That day on the cliff...I thought I had it under control. I was just trying to scare you into action. But instead...I'm so sorry, Norah. I'll never forgive myself for biting you."

A deep silence rained down upon us while I processed his words. After the fever, I'd had a hunch that it was something like this, though the pain in his voice was worse than I'd expected. He hated what he'd become, so much so that he let it control him. He didn't want anyone to get close to him, for fear they'd find out the truth and push him away.

All this time I'd been angry at him, convinced he'd left me for dead. But *he'd* been the one I'd faced off against. He'd thought he had the beast under control, but he hadn't.

"Is that why you think that no one would want to have you as a mate?" I finally asked.

His jaw rippled as he nodded. "No one wants a beast. I never planned to come to the Academy, but I had no other choice. My father forced me to come here. The only way I can inherit his lands is to bring home a changeling mate. Otherwise, I'm homeless and penniless. No Winter fae can survive without both. It is far too harsh and cold here."

I peered up at him, suddenly desperate to press my palm against his cheek. There was so much pain and anger in his voice. He was not the monster I'd thought he was. He was anything but.

"Well, I'll tell you what. Your father sounds about as terrible as my step-dad."

Kael arched an eyebrow. "That's what your focusing on? Not the fact I'm one of those monsters you hate and fear?"

With a soft smile, I reached up and touched his face. His skin was no longer on fire, but he felt just as strong and as real as ever. "You're not a monster, Kael. In fact, you're pretty much the opposite."

He caught my hand in his and pressed it tighter to his cheek, but then, his eyes darkened. "You're only saying that because you now know that you're not a Winter fae. If you were able to heal me the way you did, then it's impossible. You'll belong to Liam, the opposite of all that I am."

Confusion rippled through me. Not about my nature. I'd had the same questions. Did this make me a Summer fae? But what did that mean about my ability to shift? Disappointment and happiness were mixed together as one. I didn't know what was up and what was down.

"Liam's not so bad," I finally said, though the words didn't seem strong enough to convey exactly how I felt. "But...you're not so bad either."

He lifted his eyebrows. "Faint praise."

"I don't think I know how to explain how I feel." I glanced at where our hands were still interlocked, and I sighed. "To be honest, I'm confused. One minute, I think I want to be a Summer fae. The next minute, I want to be a Winter, especially when I realize that Winter fae are not as cold and unfeeling as they want everyone to think."

"I could kiss you right now," he said in a rough voice, his fingers tightening around mine. "No one has ever accepted me for what I am. And yet here you are...and I can never have you. One of the other changelings is my mate, but I can't imagine any of them by my side."

My heart thundered hard. I wanted him to kiss me, too. My hands were even shaking at the thought of it. "Maybe the healing thing was a fluke. Maybe we'll find out I really am a Winter fae."

"And do you want to be a Winter fae, Norah?" His eyes glittered in the darkness of the cave. "Do you want to be mine?"

Yes and no, I thought. I wanted to be his, and I wanted to be Liam's, but I didn't dare voice that thought aloud. Instead, I merely gave him a soft smile. "Yes."

With a growl, he pulled me into his arms and kissed me fiercely. His lips were hot on my skin, even without the fever. I moaned as his tongue speared my mouth, tense desperation churning between us. I laced my hands behind his neck, and my back arched instinctively. Need pulsed between my thighs.

His kiss deepening, he palmed my ass and pulled me closer. My legs spread on either side of his hips so that I straddled him. Between us, I felt the unmistakable hardening of his length, even through both my pants and his.

"Let me thank you for what you've done for me," he murmured against my lips.

I gasped, pulling back to stare into his eyes, my heart thumping so hard that it almost shook my entire body. "Thank me how?"

A dangerous smile curved his lips. "Lie back."

My heart squeezed tight. "I thought you cared about the rules."

"I do care about the rules." His gaze darkened; his thumb caressed the back of my neck. "I will not mate with you, Norah. But there are other things I can do. Lie back."

I wet my lips. I had no idea what had gotten into Kael, but my need for him was so great that I did not dare stop him. With trembling lungs, I slid off his lap and leaned back onto the chilly dirt floor of the cave. Instantly, he was above me, gazing down at me with a look of adoration that made my heart quake. His dark hair fell into his eyes as he smiled.

His lips found mine once again before they trailed down my throat. Sparks danced along my skin as his kisses went lower. He lifted my shirt and kissed my stomach, taking his time to draw his tongue above the band of my trousers. I trembled as desire coiled.

"You are so beautiful," he whispered against my skin as he slowly tugged my pants down my thighs, and then tossed them into the corner of the cave.

I trembled as the wintry breeze caressed my bare skin.

I couldn't believe that I was naked in a cave with Kael.

His mouth dropped onto my stomach once again, and my back arched as a new wave of desire stormed through me. Wetness pooled between my thighs as his tongue danced lower and lower down my body. My breath was heaving; my fingers were curled into the dirt. I could barely lie still, nor could I hear anything but the heavy thudding of my heart.

Suddenly, his hands gripped my thighs, and his fingers dug deep into my skin, as if he were claiming me. Need ripped through me, and I moaned, opening myself up to him, desperate for something more than his tongue on my belly. I needed him to do *something* and soon or else I might shatter beneath the weight of the ache.

But he did not take me there yet. He dragged his tongue up my stomach and then curled his tongue around my swollen nipple. My body bucked beneath his kiss. Stars danced in my eyes. His lips tugged against my nipple, teasing, sucking, driving me further toward the edge of a cliff I was desperate to leap right off of.

My fingernails jammed deeper into the dirt as his mouth moved to my other breast. His tongue drove me wild. I was an aching mess beneath him.

"Kael, please," I panted, spreading my thighs, so needy for him that I swore I'd painted the ground beneath me.

With a curving smile, he edged down my body. He lowered himself between my thighs and gazed up at me. Slowly, with his eyes locked on mine, he dragged his tongue across my aching core. I bucked beneath him as exquisite pleasure shot through me. His tongue slipped against me once more, and I cried out, my voice echoing through the silent cave.

Kael pulled back and licked his lips, smiling. "You taste like berries."

And then he dove between my thighs once more with such a feverish energy that it made my body quake. His tongue lapped against my core, sending wave after wave of pleasure storming over me. I couldn't think. I could barely even breathe. My core tightened beneath his mouth, and then a delicious *rip* went through me, as if glass shards surrounding my need exploded all at once. My body spasmed, throbbed. And then a delicious sense of bliss warmed my limbs.

With a shuddering sigh, I gazed down at him. He stared up at me, his mouth still only inches from my skin.

"Enjoy that?" he asked, looking a bit smug.

"What do you think?" I asked in a whisper.

Smiling, he leaned over me and dropped one last hot kiss on my mouth. "Thank you for saving my life."

"I mean, I'll happily save your life again if it means you'll do that."

His smile dimmed, and he brushed my hair away from my face. "If only you were my mate, I would do that every night for the rest of our lives."

My heart pounded as I gazed up at him. I was so screwed. I was never going to be able to figure out what I wanted.

How could I ever choose?

CHAPTER NINETEEN

When we returned to the Academy, Finn, Liam, and Rourke were waiting for us in the library. They looked...disgruntled, to say the least. Arms were crossed over chests, frowns were pulling down lips. They really had the whole disapproving teacher look down pat. I wondered how long they'd been standing here like this.

I also couldn't help but wonder if they could tell what had happened between Kael and I in the cave. And how they would react if they found out.

"Honestly, Kael." Rourke was the first to speak when we shifted back. "I could believe it of Liam, but you? You've got better sense than to take Norah away from here when a bunch of Redcaps have been stalking around just waiting for a chance to attack."

"She was fine," Kael said in a curt tone of voice. "We were far enough away from the Academy that Redcaps weren't an issue."

Redcaps weren't an issue, but...

Liam's face was lined in a scowl, and his bonfire eyes scanned me from head to toe, missing nothing. "Then, why is she ten shades paler than normal? Why is she shaking? What the hell have you done to her?"

Finn was by my side within an instant, sliding his arms around me before I went splat onto the floor. Because Liam was right. I was suddenly nauseous and dizzy, and I felt as though I could barely stand.

Finn huffed as I leaned heavily against him. "Look, Kael. I know she's probably your mate and all, but you can't do stuff like this."

"She's not my mate," Kael said softly, *painfully*.

"What?" Rourke frowned. "Are you finally conceding that shifting doesn't belong to you and you alone? I keep telling you she's an Autumn fae, and not Winter, but—"

"She's not yours either." Kael lifted a finger, pointing it straight at Liam. "She's his."

Every head in the room turned toward Liam, whose frown had morphed into an arrogant grin. He crossed his arms over his chest and shot me a wink. Even though I hated the direction this conversation was headed, my cheeks flamed anyway. It was annoying how easily the Summer fae could make me blush, especially since it did nothing but feed his massive ego.

"I knew she wasn't a cold season," he said. "You've been so stuck on the fact she shifted when she was terrified, but I always thought her fear had more to do with it than anything else."

"Now, wait a minute," Finn said, directing his

attention toward Kael. "Why do you suddenly think she's a Summer fae?"

"I had a little run-in with a Breking in the mountains," Kael said, his lips pressed tight together. "She wasn't able to shift us back, but she did heal me. That must be why she's so weak."

Liam gave me a wide grin. "Good going, darling."

"Spring fae are sometimes able to heal as well," Finn argued. "It isn't a gift that is *solely* the realm of Summers. My second cousin can heal others."

Rourke frowned. "Again, she was most likely afraid in that scenario. I don't think we can accurately call her a Summer fae until she's been at the Academy longer."

"I agree. She's clearly Spring."

"Guys," I said, holding up my hands and twisting my way out of Finn's warm embrace, despite how nice his arms felt around me. "Please stop. You're all giving me a headache in addition to the headache I already have from the healing thing I did."

The four of them fell silent and stared at me. I shifted on my feet. It was a little unnerving to have their undivided attention like this, but a part of me kind of liked it, as much as I hated to admit it. They were arguing over which Court I belonged to...which meant every single one of them must have felt the same connections I did.

Why did it have to be just one of them in the end?

"I'm tired," I finally said. "I'm going to go get some rest."

They all started talking over each other, arguing about who would escort me back to my room. With a roll of my eyes, I held up my hand again. "I can make it to my room by myself."

They didn't argue, but they did follow me out into the hallway to watch me walk away. And now that I had my back turned to them, I could let the massive smile widen across my face. Now this...this I could get used to.

As soon as the sun broke through the morning clouds, I slid out of my bedroom window and whispered across the lawn. I'd donned an Autumn golden cloak, and I managed to clamber onto the horse Liam and I had taken when we'd visited Esari. I needed to find Bree, give her the flower, and return to the Academy before anyone noticed I was gone.

It was strange going alone. While I'd spent most of my life in the presence of my own company, Otherworld Academy had been different. There was always someone around, except during the long stretches on Watch Duty. At first, I found it unnerving, but I'd grown used to the bustle of activity and the changelings who were beginning to feel like friends.

When I reached the edge of the Autumn woods, I slowed the horse and dropped to the ground. I'd told Bree to hide out somewhere nearby, but it was impossible to know exactly where she'd gone. I'd just have to explore every inch of the edge of the woods until I found her.

After at least two hours of walking, the crack of a branch sounded from behind me. I whirled on my feet, expecting to see Bree's relieved face under her mess of dark hair. Instead, several gold-cloaked fae stood before me, aiming arrows at my throat.

"Who are you and why are you here?" A silver-haired fae strode forward from the group, his golden eyes glittering like stars.

I held up my hands, heart pounding. "I'm one of the students at Otherworld Academy. I'm just here looking for my friend."

His eyes narrowed. "The Academy is hours away."

"I rode a horse," I said, hands still raised. "I left it back there at the edge of the woods while I searched for my friend."

"And why is your friend lost in our woods?" he asked in a steely voice. "As I said before, the Academy is hours away. It seems unlikely she would have wandered that far from home."

I didn't really have a good excuse for this, so I had to use the first thought that popped into my brain.

"She found out that she's an Autumn fae last week," I said. "She was curious about this place, so she decided to go off and explore. It's been a couple of days since she left, so I thought I'd come looking for her."

The fae didn't look convinced. "Then, why haven't the instructors sent a search party out for her? These woods are dangerous for a lone changeling female to be wandering around, especially at night. A new one, at that. There are creatures out here who could devour her whole."

"You're right," I said, biting my tongue. "I thought I could find her myself, but clearly I was wrong. I'll tell my instructors as soon as I get back to the Academy."

"What does your friend look like?" a female fae asked from where she stood clustered with the others. Her bow had slightly lowered, but the intensity of her stare kept my fear firmly in place.

"Long, dark hair," I said. "Really blue eyes. She's about my height, but she's a little thinner."

The fae male in front turned sharply to face the others behind him. They all exchanged measured glances, and my palms began to sweat. They knew something, though the expressions on their faces didn't make me think it was anything good. Had they seen Bree? Or had they seen the monstrous version of her?

After a long, torturous moment, he turned back to face me with a cruel mask painting his sharp and pointed features. "You made a mistake in coming here, changeling."

My heart galloped hard in my chest. If only I hadn't left my horse behind, I could get the hell out of here before the situation turned worse. They must have seen Bree, and they must have known she was a wolf. Had they hurt her? Had she managed to get away?

But as terrified as I was by their arrows aimed at my chest, I couldn't back down. Not now. Bree needed me. I wouldn't let her down again.

Taking a deep breath, I lifted my chin and met the

fae male's gaze head on. "Listen, I'm not lying. My friend is lost in these woods, and I'm trying to find her. Do you know where she is?"

The fae male's gaze flicked to my mother's necklace dangling from my neck. His eyes widened slightly, and his voice was softer when he asked, "Where did you get that necklace?"

"This?" I traced my finger along the edges of the pendant, my heart pulsing at the memory of my mom and what I'd left behind. "It was a gift from my mother."

The fae male was quiet for a moment. "Your friend is no longer here. She was chased out of here by Hunters."

"Where did she go?"

"Your friend is no longer your friend," he said as if I hadn't said a word. "You would be wise to cease your search for her. And the next time you trespass on another Court's lands, you should be careful not to lie. The next group you meet might not be as forgiving as we are."

I opened my mouth to argue, but he held up a hand to stop me.

"Leave now, changeling. Return to the safety of your Academy." He took one last glance at my necklace. "These woods are not safe for you."

I didn't waste any time getting the hell out of there. As soon as I found my horse, I gripped tight on the reins while he galloped back to the Academy. My plan for saving Bree was beginning to unravel, and I didn't know how to tie the strings back together again.

She'd been in the Autumn woods, but they'd forced her to go somewhere else. Had she returned to the free territory? Or had she tried to take sanctuary in one of the other seasons? If so, how would I ever find her? Kael had said she might not have much time. I needed to get this flower to her before it was too late to save her from the beast within.

When I returned to the stables on the Academy grounds, Liam was waiting for me beside the empty stall. His arms were crossed over his chest, and fire danced in his eyes. He was a picture of pure masculinity, but that fire and fury was aimed right at me. And I knew exactly why.

"Are you trying to get yourself killed?" The words exploded from his throat with an intensity that made me jump. The horse neighed beside me and pawed at the ground before backing up a few steps.

"You're scaring your horse," I said.

He snorted. "Of course Sapling's scared. You took her from the stables without asking me, when there are Redcaps roaming the forest every night."

"Oh, stop being so bossy. I'm not an idiot, even though you seem to think I am." I rolled my eyes. "I left at dawn. No Redcaps."

"It's still dangerous." He stalked toward me and wrapped his hand around my neck, forcing me to look into his orange eyes. My breath caught. "Don't you know what could have happened to you out there?"

My heart lurched in my chest, both at his words and at the look in his eyes. His hand was tight against me, but it was strangely gentle, almost as if he were afraid I would break. "You said it was safe during the day. You said I could go for a swim in the river if I wanted. Why is going for a horse ride any different?"

"And you just went for a horse ride?" he asked as he took a step closer, keeping a tight hold on my neck. "You didn't go searching for someone? Or something?"

My heart beat harder. Had Kael told Liam and the others about Bree? He'd said he wouldn't, but Liam, Finn, and Rourke had been in a state when we'd gotten back from our trip to the Winter Court. Maybe he'd ended up telling them everything.

"I don't know what you're talking about," I tried.

"Nope. I can tell by the flicker in your eyes that you're lying." He leaned down so that our eyes were in line, and a storm of summer rain and wildflowers filled my head. "Kael told me about Bree. I know you went to find her. You should have asked one of us to go with you. Don't you understand how worried I've been all day? It's been driving me out of my damn mind. There's a hole in the wall over there. Want to know what it's from? Me. Driven crazy thinking something had killed you."

"Liam," I whispered, shaking my head as I flicked

my eyes to the wall. There was in fact a massive hole, and the wood had splintered all over the floor.

"If something happened to you," he growled, "I don't know how I could handle it. It would destroy me, Norah. Don't you get that?"

His grip tightened on my neck, and he yanked me closer. Hungry lips pressed against mine, and his tongue dove into my mouth. Excitement and desire sparked through me. Heat spread through my gut. I pressed up onto my toes and wrapped my arms around his neck, pulling him closer.

He growled and hooked his arms underneath my legs, hoisting me from the ground. I almost moaned from how good it felt to have his lips on my skin. It was every bit as passionate and fiery as I'd imagined. Maybe even more so.

My back hit the wall when he slammed me into it. He braced his hands on either side of my head, pinning me in place. Growling, he leaned down nicked my neck with his teeth. I gasped, shuddering beneath him. Had he bitten me? And why had it felt so damn good?

"You shouldn't have run off without telling me, Norah," he growled into my ear, and then he nipped me again.

I moaned, eyes rolling into the back of my head. He grabbed my wrists in one hand and held them above my head, his fingernails digging into my skin. His fiery eyes flashed as he leaned in with a glimmering smile.

"What are you doing?" I whispered.

"I'm doing what I should have done several days ago. I'm claiming you as mine."

Chills swept down my spine just as need coiled tight in my core. I arched my back, tugging him closer with my thighs, which was about all I could do with the way he had me pinned so securely against the wall. My movement must have driven him as wild as he was driving me because a moan of need escaped from his throat.

He kept my wrists pinned in place as he shoved his trousers down to the floor. A moment later, he'd ripped mine off me in one fluid motion. I couldn't help but notice he was pretty fond of tearing clothing in half.

"I'm not going to have any clothes left by the time you're done with them," I whispered to him.

"Good." A delicious smile curved his lips as he angled closer, pressing his hard length against my core. "Frankly, I'd rather you never wear an ounce of clothing again."

"I don't think the Academy would approve."

"Fuck the Academy." He leaned closer and dragged his teeth along the delicate skin of my neck. I shuddered beneath him, warm wetness pooling between my thighs. His length still pressed against my leg, growing harder with every passing beat.

His lips trailed hot kisses up my neck and against my ear. I dug my fingernails into my palms, my arms trembling with the need to wrap myself around him. Squirming, I rubbed my core against his length, desperate for him to take that final step, to pierce my need, to fill me up until nothing else existed but the space where our bodies intertwined.

He tensed, his breath hot on my neck. "You really do like playing with fire. Don't you, darling?"

I nodded, unable to speak out loud.

"I want to fuck you, Norah." He pulled back then, gazing into my eyes. "But I know what that means. I know I'll be the first, and I know there's some confusion about whose mate you'll truly be. So, I will stop this. Right here, right now, and I'll walk away. If you tell me that's what you want."

"I don't want that," I breathed without a moment's hesitation. "I want you."

With a satisfied growl, he released his hold on my wrists and cupped my ass. My arms twisted around his neck, instinctively. I held on tight as he slowly pushed inside of me. Liam trembled with chaotic energy, but he took his time. He paused when I winced, waiting until I gave him a nod. When he pushed in deeper, it felt as thought I might be ripped wide open. Pain lanced through me, and I whimpered. Liam paused once again, his eyes locked on mine.

"Are you okay?" he whispered.

I bit my lip, and then nodded. "Please don't stop."

After a pause, he pushed in further until his shaft was fully inside of me. A delicious heat spread through me, building when he slowly rocked back, and then plunged inside me once more. It was a pleasure unlike any I'd ever felt. Our bodies collided, coming together until it felt as though we were one.

Timidly, I ground against him as his pace began to quicken. A low moan rumbled from his throat in response, and a thrill went through me at the sound. It made my own pace quicken until we were clinging on to each other, desperation and need pounding us together.

Pleasure built up like a storm desperate to break. Tension mounted. My ears rang with the sound of my own moans. For once, I didn't care who saw or who heard. All I cared about was Liam.

His breath was hot on my skin as my pleasure broke, hurtling through me like a bullet train. I shook in his arms, my core convulsing with a million quakes. Breathless, I clung on tight, feeling his shaft throb between my thighs. He shuddered and dropped his forehead against mine. Our gazes locked as we came together, and I swore I could see his soul in his eyes.

Liam dragged his thumb against my cheek. "Norah, I—"

A throat cleared from behind us, and Liam stiffened. I pulled away from him, breath heaving, stars dancing in my eyes. Someone had walked in on us, *like this*, and I had the sneaking suspicion that it might be one of my other instructors. Heat flooded my entire body. I wished the earth would swallow me whole.

"Liam, I thought you knew better than to get involved with a changeling student before her graduation." The Head Instructor's voice was sharp and cold, and dread slipped down my spine. Slowly, Liam eased me onto the ground. My knees were shaky underneath me, especially when I turned to face Alwyn. Her face reflected everything in her voice.

"Apologies." He gave her a curt nod, one that held

none of the warmth he'd just been showering on me. "But I have reason to believe that Norah is my mate."

"As far as I'm aware, Kael has much more reason to believe she's a Winter fae." She tsked, shaking her head. "There are reasons these rules exist, Liam. Go to my office. I'll be there shortly, and we'll have a chat about this situation."

"It was my fault," I blurted out. I had no idea why I said it. The words just popped out before I could stop them.

She raised her eyebrows. "I don't doubt you were involved in this, but I have something else I need to speak with you about. Bree Paine. I've received word from the Autumn Court that her wounds infected her, and she's quickly transforming into a full Redcap. And they believe you know where she is."

My heart hammered hard as I hastily gathered my pants into my arms. What was left of them. "I don't know what you mean."

"You know exactly what I mean." A pause. "Where is she, Norah?"

"Honestly, I have no idea," I said, hoping she could see the truth in my eyes. Because I didn't know where Bree was. She'd been run out of the Autumn Court, and there was no telling where she'd gone.

Alwyn narrowed her eyes and sniffed. "For your sake, I hope you're telling the truth. Because if she shows her Redcap face anywhere near this Academy, we won't hesitate to shoot her on the spot."

CHAPTER TWENTY

"Where have you been?" Sophia hissed when I took my seat next to her in our History of Fae class. "You keep disappearing all the time, and people keep asking me where you are. I don't want to get you in trouble, but there's only so long I can make up excuses."

"Sorry," I said with a wince. "There's been a lot going on. Kael and Liam have been giving me some extra training since I pretty much suck at everything. Guess they think I'll be useless if I don't get any help."

I hated lying to Sophia. She'd been nothing but kind to me since we'd met. She was always there to listen to me complain about my sleepless nights, she'd never judged me once for my terrible skills, and she didn't laugh when I fell flat on my face when I tried something new. And now I was repaying her by keeping secrets and lying to her. Truth was, I was just too scared to tell anyone what was going on. The entire Academy hated the Redcaps, and half the new changelings were hoping to join the Hunters when they graduated. If any of them knew I was trying to *help* one of the 'monsters'...well, I didn't think it would go down very well.

She frowned. "That's strange, since Liam was one of the people who was asking me where you'd gone."

"Right." A pause. "Well, he and Kael aren't great at letting each other know what's going on."

What a lame excuse. If I were her, I'd see straight through it.

Luckily, Finn saved me from having to come up with more nonsense to throw at her.

He strode to the front of the class, and his eyes met mine for a long moment. They sparked with something....dangerous almost. Frowning, I made a question-mark with my eyes, but his gaze merely intensified. What was going on?

When he reached the front of the class, he dropped a heavy book on the table where it fell with a thump so loud that it made the entire class fall into an eerie hush. And then he smiled that devilish smile of his before shoving the book straight into the wooden trash bin beside his desk.

"If you look at your syllabus, you'll see that we were scheduled to discuss the lineage of Gregor the Giant, but that's pure nonsense. We don't need to talk about that today." He flicked his eyes toward me, and then away again. "Instead, we're going to cover a topic that I believe many of you are very interested in. Marin, the Queen of Fae who was assassinated by the Autumn Court."

Every single changeling in the room sat up straighter, including me. I'd been begging to hear this story. I'd even searched the library for information on her. If there'd ever been any books about her reign, they'd been removed.

He smiled, and his perfect teeth sparkled beneath the candlelit glow of the chandelier. "That's what I thought. You see, Marin is cloaked in a bit of mystery here at the Academy. And elsewhere in Otherworld, if you're too young to have been there yourself. Luckily for all of you, I was alive during those times. I was even present at the event where she was assassinated."

I glanced at Sophia and raised my eyebrows. She looked just as intrigued as I felt.

Finn continued. "You see, each year there is a Royals Ball to celebrate the new political structure of Otherworld. Before Marin died, there were four Courts, but each of them was ruled by a Lord and a Lady. These Royals were able to make small decisions for their fae, but at the end of the day, Marin had the last word. The Autumn Court yearned for sovereignty. So, they took it."

I shook my head and leaned forward on my elbows just as Sophia raised her hand with a question. "Why did that give the Courts sovereignty? Surely if she died, her son or her daughter would take over instead? Or another family member? At least that's how it works in the human world."

"Indeed it does," Finn said with a nod. "But Marin had no sons or daughters. She had no brothers or sisters or nieces or nephews. She only had her harem, and they were assassinated as well. That left no living heir, which meant there was a vacuum of power. Something had to fill it, and the Autumn Court took the opportunity to present their version of what the Courts should look like instead. The highest ranking Lords and Ladies became Queens and Kings, and here we are."

Griff's hand shot up in the air. "Did you say harem? Like, as in an actual *harem*?"

Finn's eyes twinkled as he laughed. "Oh yes. Marin, the Queen of Fae had four husbands, one from each of the seasons. She was blessed with powers from Spring, Summer, Autumn, and Winter, and so she decided that she would never be happy without all of her men by her side."

My blood roared in my ears, and the entire classroom melted away. There was only Finn and me, and his words about Queen Marin. She'd had four mates. Four of them. One from each of the seasons. And no one had stopped her?

Four mates. Four husbands.

It sounded too good to be true.

"Norah, is there something wrong?" Finn's laughing voice broke through my thoughts. Everyone in the room was staring at me. I realized that I'd been sitting open-mouthed with my hand pressed to my boiling neck. My cheeks had filled with heat, which no doubt meant I was blushing up a storm.

All because I couldn't get the thought out of my head. Marin and her four mates.

"I guess I'm just surprised," I said in a voice that

sounded more like a squeak. "In the human realm, that kind of thing isn't really...ideal."

"Ideal?" Lila giggled. "Sounds pretty ideal to me. Can you imagine having four swoony men at your beck and call every day and night?"

Oh yes. I could imagine it very well. It seemed like the perfect fantasy come to life.

"Sounds awful to me," Griff said with a frown. "You'd have to share your girl with three other guys?"

I was looking at Griff when he said that, but I suddenly felt as though I was being watched. My breath caught, and I slid my gaze away, only to find Finn's sparkling eyes locked on my face.

"Oh, I wouldn't mind sharing," he said with a wink. "If another female fae just as brave, as caring, and as breathtaking as Queen Marin came along. In fact, I daresay there must be a woman out there who's even better."

My eyes nearly popped out of my head at that. Who did he mean? His gaze was locked on my face, but surely he didn't mean me. I was a first-year changeling who could barely dismount a horse without falling flat on her face. I'd had moments where I'd been able to protect myself, but I'd practically bumbled my way through them.

But I didn't get to find out because the bell clanged, signalling the end of our lesson. And Finn was out the door before the rest of us could budge an inch.

After everything that had happened, I wasn't entirely certain that Kael would be waiting for me in the library that night. He and I hadn't really had a chance to talk since our little trip to the cave, and I had no idea how he felt about what had happened between us. But when I pushed open the door, I found that not only was he there, as always, so were Liam, Finn, and Rourke.

At the sight of Liam, I couldn't keep my face from turning five darker shades of red. Memories flashed in my mind. Images of his body against mine.

"What are you all doing here?" I asked by way of greeting. I had a feeling I wasn't going to like their answer.

"We need to talk to you about Bree," Rourke said in a matter-of-fact tone that betrayed none of what they felt about the matter. Did they want me to stop looking for her? Did they want to hunt her down themselves? Liam had heard what the Head Instructor had said. Were they now tasked with trying to kill my friend before I'd had a chance to heal her?

"Speaking of that," I said, narrowing my eyes as I turned to Kael. "I can't believe you told them about Bree."

"You didn't leave me much of a choice after you ran off to find her by yourself," Kael said, his voice holding none of the warmth it had in that cave we'd shared that night. "I know you don't want to hear it, but it's for the best. These three are trustworthy. All they want to do is keep you safe."

With a heavy sigh, I dropped down into one of the chairs, all the fight draining out of me. "I know they're trustworthy. You all are. It doesn't matter though. I told Bree to hide out in the Autumn woods, but they chased her out of there several days ago. I have no idea where she is now. She could be anywhere in Otherworld."

Rourke pursed his lips. "Unlikely. If you were scared and on the run, where would you go?"

"Me?" I raised my eyebrows. "I'd...well, I'd probably go home. Or near home, anyway. I wouldn't want to be roaming around in a place I didn't know very well."

"Exactly," Rourke gave a nod. "Which means she's probably sticking close to the Academy. You're here, the only familiar thing in these strange lands. After the ball, we'll all go out to look for her. We can then take her someplace safe, and administer that cure."

"The ball?" I looked from Rourke to Finn. "What ball?"

"The annual Royals Ball," he said with a quirk of his lips. "I mentioned it today in class, or were you too distracted by all my talk of harems to pay attention to that part?"

My cheeks flamed. In fact, he was right. I *had* been too distracted to remember much else. My mind kept replaying the facts. At one time, a female fae had mated with four males. She'd had a connection with each of them, just like I did with my four instructors. If only I could have been in her position. If only I didn't have to end up with only one. Because now that I had the idea in my head, I truly wanted them all.

"You shouldn't have taught that today," Kael said with a sharp glance in Finn's direction. "When Alwyn finds out, she's going to be pretty angry. Queen Marin is not a topic we're supposed to be teaching. If the Autumn fae found out, they could make life difficult on us."

"She's an important topic," Finn countered. "What happened during her reign matters greatly to who and what we've become now."

"I still don't understand what's going on with this ball." I stood, interrupting their back-and-forth. They all sure liked to bicker a lot, though I could tell it was done in a lighthearted way. A brotherly sort of banter without the hard feelings of a true feud. "Why does it mean we can't try to find Bree now?"

"The Royals Ball is this weekend, Norah," Rourke said. "Which you'd know about if you weren't dashing off to the stables every day."

He cut Liam a look, who merely smirked in response. He must have told them what had happened. Great.

"Each Court sends representatives to attend the event. The Queens and Kings won't come, of course, but some lesser Royals will attend." Kael shook his head and grimaced. "That means there will be extra guards roaming the grounds. If any of them spotted a Redcap, they'd kill it in a heartbeat. We can't risk going for Bree while they're here."

I puffed out a frustrated sigh and sank back into the chair. I hated waiting. Bree needed my help, and the clock was ticking. This stupid ball was only going to delay what shouldn't be delayed any longer.

"Don't look so glum, Norah. We'll find Bree soon," Finn said, cocking his head to the side. "Besides, you'll enjoy the ball. It's your first chance to dance in Otherworld, and it'll be a dance like you've never danced before."

CHAPTER TWENTY-ONE

The Royals began to arrive the very next day. The Autumn fae were the first to join the celebration, striding down the hallways in their golden robes with hair the color of the setting sun. Liam found me on the sofa in my quarters, flipping through the book about the Starlight plant. I was yearning to find some hope within the old, weathered pages. I needed to know this would all turn out okay.

He didn't bother to knock on the door, and his body filled the doorway in a way that made it seem as if the entire room had been consumed by his fiery presence. And I *still* had yet to be alone with him since the stables. To say being near him made me nervous now? Well, that was just putting it lightly.

He wore a tight-fitting pair of black trousers, and a tunic that clung to his broad, muscular shoulders. His hair swept across his forehead, the fiery color matching the intensity of his eyes. My gaze tripped across his square jaw stubbled with just the hint of a shadow. He was one of the most gorgeous beings I had ever seen in my life.

"Norah, the Autumn Court has arrived," he said in a gruff voice that did little to mask his irritation at their presence in these halls.

I kept my eyes focused on the book. I figured if I didn't keep staring at him, I wouldn't feel that overwhelming desire to climb up him again. After his little chat with the Head Instructor, he probably didn't want me to anyway, and I had approximately zero desire to make an idiot out of myself.

"I saw them arrive earlier. It was kind of impossible to miss them, you know."

A pause. "Is there a reason you won't look at me?"

I swallowed hard. "Nope."

Liar, liar, liar.

Liam strode over to the sofa and sat without any invitation from me. "You need to be careful around them."

At that, I glanced up. My curiosity got the better of me. His orange eyes were swirling with an intensity that always took my breath away, and it was difficult to concentrate on what he'd said before, not when he was looking at me like that. Like...he wanted to eat me up.

"I thought they were just minor Royals here to have fun at our ball. Why do I need to be careful?"

He frowned and glanced at my roommate's cracked door. Sophia wasn't home right now, but she'd return at any moment. Was he really that worried about my roommate overhearing our conversation?

He dropped his voice to a whisper, which sounded strange coming from him. Liam never whispered. "Remember what we learned when we visited Esari?"

I nodded.

"Well, this ball is to celebrate the anniversary of Marin's assassination. I wouldn't be surprised if they thought it was poetic to plan another assassination on this date again."

Dread pooled in my stomach at his words. Surely they wouldn't. Not here. Not now.

"But this is an Academy. We're students. Who in the world would they want to assassinate here?"

Something flickered in his eyes, and he glanced at the cracked door again. "Have you told anyone else about how you were able to heal Kael?"

Alarmed, I shook my head. "No, I didn't really know how to explain it without giving away the fact I went to the Winter Court to find some Starlight for Bree."

"Good." He nodded. "What about your roommate? Did you tell her?"

"I…" I shook my head. It was awful. There had been so many times when I'd wanted to tell her. Keeping secrets from my closest friend at the Academy felt like the biggest betrayal of them all, but every time I opened my mouth, the words got stuck in my throat. Sometimes, it felt like I was living a double life. "I'm not really used to having friends. I was scared if she knew what I've been up to, she'd want to run far, far away."

"Well, that's ridiculous," he said in a low growl. "Anyone who isn't fond of you is an idiot, especially if they knew how pure your heart is."

I blinked at his words. I wouldn't exactly call my heart *pure*, especially when it was currently yearning for the affections of four different fae males. But I didn't dare say that out loud. Instead, I smiled, yearning to reach out and wrap my arms around his neck and—

Footsteps sounded in the hall outside, and Liam cocked his head with a frown. "She's back. Don't tell her about your gifts, Norah. Don't tell anyone."

That evening, we all dined together. The Summer Royals had arrived, along with the Spring fae contingent. Only the Winter fae had yet to walk through the Academy's front doors. Extra tables had been added to the expansive Great Hall, along with hundreds of flickering candles, and the buzz of conversation made the place feel electric and alive.

Everyone was excited about the upcoming ball. Changelings had taken it upon themselves to find dates, much to the Head Instructor's disapproval. Griff and Lila were going together while Sophia had been asked by one of the third-year students. The Instructors—a.k.a. our future mates—were strictly forbidden from participating in any sort of pairing up, so it seemed the changelings were just trying to make the best of the situation.

"I'm actually glad I'm going with Griff," Lila whispered into my ear. "I mean, is it horrible that I like him so much more than any of our potential mates? I mean, I figure I'm a Summer, right? Look at me. Flaming red hair. I love the sunshine. But Liam? I don't know. He just doesn't do it for me."

"He certainly does it for me," I muttered beneath my breath, remembering the way his tongue had driven me wild.

She cocked her head. "What?"

My cheeks flamed. Had I just said that out loud?

"Nothing," I said quickly.

"Sam said the same," she added. "She's pretty certain she's Autumn, and she doesn't have any interest in Rourke. And Sophia has barely looked at Finn. What about you? You're going to end up mated to Kael, right? I mean, he's just so cold and distant. I can't imagine him kissing anyone? It'd be like kissing a wet noodle."

"A wet noodle?" A flicker of irritation went through me. "Well, that's just rude. Sure, they can be kind of annoying at times, but they're the strongest men I've ever met in my life. I can't imagine how you could think anyone is better than them. Hell, I'd mate with all of them if I could."

The room had gone strangely silent, and my words echoed off the walls around me. My heart froze in my chest as I slowly turned to find that every single fae in the room was staring right at me. I swallowed hard, and my whole neck went white hot.

This was...embarrassing, to say the least.

Gripping the table, I turned toward the table at my left where the instructors were all dining together. Yep, sure enough, all four of them had heard me. They were staring at me, each wearing an expression that ranged from amusement to shock to intrigue. My god. If only the floor would open up and swallow me whole right now.

I'd clearly let that whole harem nonsense get into my head, and now the entire Academy knew about it.

The silence seemed to stretch on for ages. Just when I thought I could take no more, the glass window exploded behind me. Shards rained down on the stone floor, and Lila jumped up with a scream. I scrambled back just as another window crashed, the massive claws of a Redcap shooting through the hole left behind.

With a sharp gasp, I stumbled back. The windows at the other side of the Great Hall faced a similar fate, and two more Redcaps jumped through. They landed on every side of us, their sharp claws glinting off the light of the candles lining the walls. Changelings were screaming and racing toward the tall double doors that would lead to escape. But a Redcap jumped in front of them just in time, trapping every single soul in this place.

Finn and Rourke were by my side within an instant. One behind me, one in front, forming their arms in a circle to keep me protected from the creatures. I wanted to argue, to tell them to go help anyone else but me, but the terror in my heart had my mouth glued shut.

There were four Redcaps in the dining hall now, slowly circling the fae and changelings. I glanced around, desperately trying to find Sophia, Lila, and Sam. They were all huddled together, ducking low behind the table where we'd just been sitting. One of the creatures was bearing down on them. Its claws were only inches from their heads.

"Rourke," I whispered, my heart beating madly in my chest. "Help them. Please."

"I'm not leaving your side," he said through gritted teeth.

"Neither am I," Finn added. "Kael took Liam to get some weapons. He shifted away the second the first window broke."

Indeed, he and Liam reappeared within seconds. Both were wielding swords that matched the ones they'd held that day in New York, that night that now felt so very, very long ago. Kael whirled and tossed a second blade into the hands of our Head Instructor while Liam tossed a sword to one of the third year instructors. Together, the four of them converged on the nearest Redcap, their blades swinging through the fear-filled air.

I found myself clinging tight to Finn's arm as I watched Kael and Liam battle the creatures. My heart was in my throat, and my blood roared in my ears. They were so strong and so brave. Much braver than I was. Of course they were the two who had taken charge to save the day. They were the kind of fae to risk their lives for the sake of others, and I loved them for it.

When the first Redcap fell, it ignited a pure, unbridled anger in the others. They began to launch themselves at the cowering changelings. Claws swiped faces. Blood spilled. Rourke stepped in front of me to block my view of the carnage, wrapping his arms around me and pulling me so close that I could hear his frantic heartbeat in his chest.

The fight raged on. Screams filled the air as well as the gruesome sound of blades slicing into flesh. I wanted to do something. Anything other than stand here helpless, but Rourke kept a tight hold on my body, keeping me firmly out of harm's way.

When it was finally over, the sight that met my eyes made me fall to my knees. The Redcaps had been defeated, and their corpses littered the hall. With them, three fae had fallen, blood pouring from gaping wounds.

"Who is it?" I whispered to Finn, who had wrapped his arm around my waist to hold me steady.

"I'm so sorry, Norah. Sam didn't make it." His lips pressed into a tight line. "We also lost a third-year changeling, along with her mate. He jumped in front of her to protect her from the Redcap, but—"

He sagged against me, and I supported him as best I could.

"Alright everyone," our Head Instructor called out

as she moved to the center of the floor. She wiped sweat and dirt and blood from her forehead and dropped her sword to the ground where it clattered, a steely echo in the sudden quiet of the hall. "I think it's best if everyone returns to their rooms for the rest of the evening. You'll be escorted there by your instructors who will stand guard, just in case more of the creatures try to attack."

Frightened whispers shuddered through the crowd.

"We'll have extra guards patrol the grounds tonight, and all nights going forward, until we can be sure the threat is gone," she continued. "They had the element of surprise on their side tonight. They won't have that again. Unfortunately, I'm afraid this means we won't be able to go ahead with the ball tomorrow night."

"That's not an option." One of the Autumn Royals stepped up to our Head Instructor's side and gave her a sharp, pointed frown. There wasn't a speck of blood on her billowing golden cloak. "The Royals Ball is not an optional event. It is not just a celebration. It is a reminder of who our true rulers are. Queen Viola would take it as a major slight if you were to cancel the ball, and I think we're all very aware that it is never a good idea to slight our Queen."

Eyes wide, I glanced at Rourke. He shook his head in disgust, but he kept his thoughts private. I had come to realize that Rourke was no ordinary Autumn fae. He clearly didn't approve of much of what they did.

"You cannot possibly expect these students to celebrate after what's happened here tonight?" Head Instructor Alwyn asked, her mouth slightly parted in surprise. "After what's happened to their fellow students and friends?"

"We don't just expect it," the Autumn fae said with glittering yellow eyes. "We demand it."

CHAPTER TWENTY-TWO

The Great Hall had been transformed, but the ghosts of the attack still lingered behind. At some point during the night, the Autumn fae had cleared the room, disposing of the Redcap bodies in a bonfire on a distant hill. I knew because I'd seen the flames from my bedroom window, the spot I hadn't been able to vacate all night. I just kept imagining those claws. All that blood painting every surface of the hall.

And I couldn't stop thinking about Bree. She was somewhere out there. I had to hope the Redcaps hadn't come across her first. I had to hope I could get to her while she was still breathing.

Now, I stood in the hall-turned-ballroom, drinking in the strange eeriness of the celebration. Earlier in the day, someone had left a package just outside my door addressed to me. In it, I'd found the most beautiful dress I'd ever laid eyes on. It was midnight black with silver sleeves filled with starlight. With an open back, at first I'd felt a bit shy about wearing it. It revealed more skin than I was accustomed to showing, but when I tried it on, the silky fabric fit me like a glove. Like it had been made specifically for me. Even the bottom of the dress was the perfect length, and it spread out across the floor with more silver specks dotted across the fabric like a glorious painting of a clear night sky.

Sophia had shouted and exclaimed and clapped her hands, and she'd tried to convince me to wear my hair in an elaborate up-do that didn't suit me. Instead, I'd let my long locks fall in natural waves down my back. It made me feel free and alive. If it weren't for the cloud of pain and danger that hung heavily over this event, I might even feel strangely happy.

But after what had happened, no one seemed particularly comfortable to be here right now. Except for the Autumn Royals who were smugly moving about the room in long golden gowns, their cold, intelligent eyes keeping a close eye on everything we said and did.

Kael slid up behind me and gently placed his hand on my back. My heart skipped, and I tried not to let my face show just how much of an effect that slight touch had on me.

"You look very beautiful, Norah." A pause as his dark eyes searched mine. "Is it safe to say that you like my gift?"

I widened my eyes. "*Your* gift? You mean...this dress is from you?"

"Of course," he said with a slight smile. "I assumed the color would give it away, as well as the stars. I wanted to give you something that reminded me of that night you saved my life."

The night in the cave.

My knees wobbled. That was pretty much the most romantic thing anyone had ever said to me, but Kael took my reaction to mean something else entirely.

"You okay?" He gently took my arm and furrowed his eyebrows. "Do you need to sit? Is something ailing you?"

"I'm fine." I cleared my throat and smiled. "Just a little overwhelmed, I guess."

Get ahold of yourself, Norah. One sweet comment, and you're already swooning onto the floor.

He scowled and glanced at an Autumn Court fae who slowly passed us by, eyes locked on where Kael's hand rested on my back. "It's truly heartless to make all the changelings endure this ridiculous celebration after what happened last night."

"Careful, Kael," the Autumn fae said with a chilly smile. "I wouldn't want to have to report you to Viola."

"Don't lie, Redmond. It's not the Autumn fae way," Kael shot back. "We both know that you would *love* to report me to Viola."

"You're right." Redmond's smile was full of sharp and pointed teeth, like that fae I'd met in the Autumn tavern. "A monster like you shouldn't be allowed anywhere near our so-called precious changelings." He sniffed my way. "Does your *friend* know about your special issue?"

"I know all about it. Thanks for asking." I shot him a sarcastic smile as sweet folksy music filled the hall.

"Now, if you'll excuse me, I think I'd like to go do something more interesting than talk to a bigot. Kael, would you like to join me?"

Kael pursed his lips and tried to keep his chuckle under his breath, but I heard him. It was a deep, soothing sound. A sound I wished I could hear more of. Kael didn't laugh nearly enough. Somehow, I needed to rectify that.

He kept his hand on my back, and I had a feeling it was more in spite of Redmond than because he necessarily wanted it there. But I didn't mind. I liked the idea of seeing Redmond's smug smile fall right off his stupid face. So, Kael steered me toward the dance floor. At the moment, it was glaringly empty, but we walked past everyone on the outskirts until we were the only ones there.

"Care to dance?" He held out a hand and gave me a mock bow.

With a laugh, I took his outstretched palm into mine and curtsied back. He pulled me to his chest and wrapped his arms around my waist, swaying to the beat of the music. Delight and surprise made my stomach begin to flutter. This was unexpected. Of all the fae to ask me to dance, I wouldn't have guessed it would be Kael. Finn, most likely. Liam, if he was in the mood. Rourke and Kael? Never.

And yet here we were, the only two fae on the dance floor.

The upbeat song whirled around us, and I lost myself to the strange, delightful music of the fae. We spun and spun, our arms wrapped tight around each other. Light and sound all mixed together as one, and soon, the world felt as though it dropped away. The music was everything, along with the dance. It was loud and big and wild, and I'd never before felt so alive.

Kael's eyes were alight. Somehow, the deep darkness of them seemed as if they were filled with a thousand stars, and I knew, right then and there, that I could spend the rest of my life counting each and every one.

And then the song stopped. Kael's feet slowed, and I followed his lead. The world jerked back in around us. My breath was ragged, and my cheeks were warm. Kael's face had filled with color, too, and his eyes still shone with that strange cosmic light. All around us, others had begun to join us on the floor. And then the music started up again.

Our bodies took over as soon as the notes filled our ears. We spun and whirled and laughed, our limbs twisting and curling around each other. The hall transformed into a kaleidoscope of shifting colors. There were no solid walls. No tables. No one else but us. It was magic. Pure delicious magic. A kind of magic that filled every part of my soul. It had been hidden deep within me all these years, and now it was flowing out of me in a way that made me wonder how I'd never known it was there.

All because of Kael. And Finn, Rourke, and Liam. I'd spent my entire life asleep, and they'd woken me from a deep slumber I never again wished to have.

The music slowed. Usually, this would be my cue to take a break. I liked to spin and whirl and stomp rather than sway side to side, but this song...I couldn't walk away. My arms tightened around Kael's neck, and I pressed my face to his chest. His heartbeat matched the rhythm of our steps.

His hand began to caress my back. So gentle. So soft. He was nothing like the monster he claimed to be. I pulled back and tipped back my head to look up into his star-studded eyes. A light smile lifted his lips, and I reached up to trace my finger along the curve of them.

A part of me expected him to stiffen and pull away. Despite our connection, despite our moment together in the cave, I knew he was still wary of getting close to me. He still worried about the rules, about us not being mates. But he didn't tense, he didn't flinch, and he didn't pull away. Instead, his grip around my waist tightened, and a shuddering breath escaped from his lips.

"Thank you for the dress," I whispered to him. "I don't feel as though I deserve something so beautiful, but thank you."

"Don't talk like that," he murmured, dropping his forehead to mine. "You deserve something this beautiful and more. And the truth is, Norah, the dress is not what makes you beautiful. It's everything else. Your eyes. Your heart. Your fire. I've never met anyone else like you before, and I doubt I ever will."

He dropped his lips to mine, and my entire body sighed.

"Alright, you two. Break it up," a sharp voice cut through the moment, and two strong arms yanked me back. Blinking, I turned with a frown to find Redmond dragging me away from Kael, whose tortured expression made my heart break.

"Let go of her, Redmond," Kael said as his cold, steely mask fell over his face. "You can't manhandle the changelings like this."

Redmond's grip only tightened on my arms. "Oh, but I can. I have direct orders to do whatever is necessary here. That includes taking this miscreant to be questioned about her actions."

Kael's face clouded over. "What are you talking about? She's not a miscreant."

"I have it on good authority that she's been harboring a murderous Redcap." Redmond's gold eyes glittered as he pointed across the room to where Sophia stood staring at me with a mixture of horror and guilt. "Her roommate informed me that she had one in her room and that she's been sneaking out to meet it wherever it's been hiding."

"What?" I felt as if I'd been punched in the gut. "Sophia? Is this true?"

She clenched her jaw and glanced away as if she couldn't stand the sight of me, but her voice trembled when she spoke. "I'm sorry, Norah. I covered for you as long as I could. But you saw what happened last night. Sam *died*. You can't keep protecting your friend. Not when she's capable of killing us all."

Redmond dragged me down a flight of curving stone stairs I'd never seen before. When we reached the bottom, I quickly understood why. Cells lined both walls. Thin, tiny rooms that held nothing but a single hard mattress each. He yanked opened the nearest one, threw me inside, and slammed the gate in my face.

Shivering, I crossed my arms over my chest and stared at the Autumn fae. "This isn't fair. You can't just put me in a dungeon because you think I'm trying to help my friend."

He raised his eyebrows, and his golden eyes practically glowed against the light of the torches. "But aren't you helping your friend? I realize that much of Otherworld is new to you, but you must realize that it's a crime to harbor a murderer, just as it is in your precious human realm."

"For one, I'm not *harboring* her. And two, she's not a murderer. Stop saying that." I strode forward and gripped the iron bars. Pain immediately shot through my gut, and I stumbled back.

The fae let out a low chuckle and shook his head. "Silly girl. You cannot touch iron, not even here."

"This is ridiculous. Let me out of here. Bree's not a murderer. Yes, she got infected with the Redcap virus, but she's fighting against it." Taking a deep breath, I stepped up to the bars again. This time, I was careful not to touch them. "You have to believe me. She's not a threat to anyone. I've been trying to help her, by undoing the whole thing. I wanted to give her Winter Starlight."

He barked out a harsh laugh. "You actually believe that you can save a beast. Be careful. The last fae who spouted that kind of nonsense got herself killed."

At the question-mark in my eyes, he continued. "Queen Marin, the ruler who was assassinated by our Court eighteen years ago. Good riddance, I say. She too believed that Redcaps were intelligent beings who could be reasoned with, but you saw the destruction they can cause. They're monsters and nothing more. And every single one of them should be kept under tight control."

I fisted my hands by my sides and glared at Redmond. "Did you ever stop to think that maybe this is all *your* fault? The Redcaps don't just come from nowhere. You create them. And then it spreads and spreads and spreads. Because maybe, just maybe, what you're doing is wrong."

He stepped closer and sneered. "Maybe you're not so much like Marin after all. She was a big lover of all you changelings, including the Redcaps. Said you were a gift from the gods. But what she didn't realize is that *we're* the gods. And the time of the changelings is over."

My heart thumped hard, and all the blood drained from my face. "What does that mean?"

"Oh, you'll see." His grin stretched across the entire width of his face. "But first, you're going to stay down in this cage."

CHAPTER TWENTY-THREE

I didn't sleep. At least a day passed where all I could do was sit glumly in my gorgeous gown, glaring at the flickering torches in the hallway of the dungeons. I tried shifting, but it was no use. Whatever magic I'd used when I shifted before was gone from me now.

My mind tripped over Redmond's words as I desperately tried to figure out what he'd meant by them. The time of the changelings was over? Surely he didn't mean what it sounded like. Did he truly want to get rid of us all? And, if so, why?

Footsteps echoed down the corridor. I stood from the hard mattress and backed up against the wall furthest from the iron bars. I didn't want to be a coward, but I also didn't know what the hell was coming for me. And I wasn't about to make anything easy on whoever it was. If they wanted to get to me, they'd have to open that gate and come inside the cell themselves.

And maybe, just maybe...I could get out into the hallway before they could.

I might not have a sword, but I had fists.

Firelight flickered on the walls, and a male in a deep golden cloak strode into view. For a moment, I could barely breathe as he strolled up to the iron bars, his face hidden in the shadows of his hood. But then he lifted his chin, and his bright golden eyes met mine. It was Rourke. All the tension in my body whooshed out of me, and I rushed up to the bars, hope and relief pouring through me.

He held up a set of keys and jangled them in the air. "Time to get you out of here, Norah. Apologies it took so long."

A grin split my face. "Are you kidding me? I'm just happy to see you. How did you get down here? Does Redmond know you're doing this? I thought he locked me in here to ask me questions about Bree, but he hasn't been back. Do you know what's going on?"

He let out a light laugh and shook his head. "One question at a time. I'll explain everything as soon as I get you out of here."

He slid the key into the lock and twisted, using a gloved hand to pull open the gates. I rushed into the hallway and threw my arms around him. He let out an oof of surprise, and his entire body went tense. After a moment, he softened and rubbed his hand across the small of my back. Shivers coursed across my skin from where he touched me. Rourke might be an Autumn fae like the ones who were making our lives so miserable, and the ones who might very well be trying to end us all, but he was nothing like them.

"I'm sorry about what my brethren did to you," he muttered against my hair. "But I'm afraid it's even worse than you think."

I pulled back and looked up at him with a frown. "What do you mean?"

He let out a heavy sigh and shook his head. "I'm afraid it's a long story. Let's get you upstairs so you can have some food and a bath. Then, we'll explain everything."

As glad as I was to have a chance to take a bath, I hated to change out of my gorgeous ball-gown that Kael had given me. The soft, sleek material felt so nice on my skin, and the sparkling sleeves made true darkness feel like an impossibility. But Rourke insisted I change into some training clothes, so I donned a pair of black pants, a black t-shirt, and my trusty boots for good measure.

Afterwards, he led me into a dusty, lofted room where students were busy practicing hand-to-hand combat with the instructors. I slowed to a stop and raised my eyebrows. The first-years were here, too. Sophia was pounding away at a punching bag, her fists wrapped tight in a splotchy gauze. It was the first time our instructors had taken us from theory to practice, and I had a horrible sinking feeling in my gut because of it.

I wanted to learn how to fight. Desperately so. But the timing could only mean one thing. Trouble was brewing.

Liam, Finn, and Kael all abandoned their posts, striding over to wrap their arms tight around me in turn. My heart swelled as Liam crushed me tight against him, as Kael whispered soft words into my ears, and even as Finn threw me over his shoulder for good measure. Even though Redmond had told them he hadn't harmed a hair on my head, they'd still been worried for my safety. They'd even argued over who would release me from my cage.

After our reunion, the three of them dispersed, taking up their posts with the other changelings.

"Usually," Rourke began as he led me to an empty punching bag near the rear of the room, "we hold off on this kind of training with first-years, and for good reason. Otherworld is new and confusing for you, you don't yet know the true power of your gifts, and you have no idea what you're capable of. If we let you loose with swords, you could end up doing far more damage than you realize. One time, a first-year Summer changeling ended up burning down an entire wing of the Academy when he got into a fistfight with one of the third-year Summers."

"And yet they're all in here training now." I arched an eyebrow. "Why? And where are all the Royals?"

He pursed his lips. "After Redmond stole you away, the other Autumn Royals staged an assassination attempt on Alwyn. We were able to stop them, but one of them escaped, along with Redmond. We're guessing they've gone straight home to report what happened. The Summer and Spring Royals have returned to their own Courts, too afraid for their lives to stick around here. The Autumn fae will undoubtedly send others to finish the job. So, the only thing we can do now is prepare."

My mouth dropped open as I stared at him. "They tried to kill our Head Instructor? But why would they want to do that?"

"The answer to that question is what none of us knows. It seems they intend to take down the Academy," he said with a frown. "Anyway, that is why it took so long for us to get to you. Redmond locked the door that led into the cells below, and he hid the keys. It took me some time to determine where he hid them. It turned out they were in your room, something I should have known as soon as I realized what he'd done. He has always been a fan of irony."

"Why couldn't Kael just shift into the cell to get me out?"

"What good are dungeons if Winter fae can escape them?" he asked.

"Good point," I said with a nod. So maybe my inability to shift out of the cell didn't mean I'd lost my grasp on the Winter fae magic after all.

"So what now?" I asked as I glanced around the room at all my fellow changelings throwing their hands and legs against the punching bags. They were trying, I'd give them that, but they looked about as skilled as I was. Which was to say, not very skilled at all. Their punches were wild. Their kicks awkward and messy. But they were trying. They were learning. Our instructors were finally teaching us how to fight.

Rourke's lips twisted into a strange smile, and he patted the punching bag that dangled from the ceiling. "You're finally going to get what you've been asking for, Norah. If the Autumn fae come back, I want you all to be ready for them. We're not going to allow them to pick you off one by one. Ready to learn how to fight like a fae?"

A grin lit up my face. "Oh, hell yes."

"Good." His golden eyes dropped to my chest. "Now, take off your necklace."

Frowning, I reached up to curl my fingers around the pendant I'd worn every single minute of every single day. It was the only thing keeping me anchored to who I'd been before. "My mom gave me this."

"It's very pretty. However, it can be a serious liability when you fight."

I hesitated. My mother had given me this necklace in a moment of desperation. She'd been afraid for me, and I'd been afraid for her. She'd asked me to wear it always, so wear it I had. Taking it off felt like a betrayal, even though I was certain she'd understand if she were here now, as difficult as it might be for her to wrap her head around the whole changeling fae thing. How would she feel if she knew I wasn't truly her daughter? My heart hurt just thinking about it and remembering how stuck she was with that horrible man.

Did she worry about where I'd gone? Did she even know that I was missing?

"I don't think you understand what this necklace means to me," I finally said. "My mother...it's all she could give me when I ran from that horrible monster she married."

His golden eyes flickered. "I do understand. We watched you from afar for months. You can wear the necklace at any other time, but when you're training and fighting? It needs to come off, and I think your mother would agree. The enemy could use it to choke you."

To choke me. So, maybe he had a good point.

"Right, okay." With a heavy sigh, I reached up and undid the clasp on the necklace for the first time since I'd arrived at the Academy. Immediately, it felt as if a massive load had been taken off my shoulders. I felt lighter, which was strange. The necklace wasn't particularly heavy.

"Good." He nodded. "Now, show me your best punch."

I bent my knees and narrowed my eyes, zeroing all my focus in on the punching bag before me. I imagined that it was the face of all my enemies. My step-father who had emotionally abused me for years. The Redcap who had turned Bree into the tortured beast. Redmond, who had attacked my new home. They all formed one massive target on the bag, the sole focus of the anger and sadness that had been growing within me.

I pulled back my fist and punched.

The blow landed with a loud crack, and the bag jerked against its chains as the force of my fist lurched it sideways. I'd hit it so hard that it managed to swing up and hit the ceiling. The whole room went deathly silent as every single student turned my way.

Liam met my eyes from across the room, and his eyes sparkled with pride and approval. Kael rubbed his jaw, and Finn let out a low chuckle.

"Well, that was certainly interesting," Rourke murmured from beside me.

"I guess I'm a little bit pissed off?" I said, hiking the end of my statement into a question. How the hell had I been able to do that? I'd been the worst first-year of the bunch so far. I'd expected my punch to land me flat on my ass, not to almost take the punching bag off its chains.

"Good going, darling," Liam said with a wink. "Keep it up."

The other students slowly returned to their own training while Rourke steadied the whirling punching bag. His expression had become strange and intense as he kept flicking his golden eyes my way. It took him a long, long while to steady the punching bag, and I had a sneaking suspicion he was trying to bide his time.

Finally, I propped my fists on my hips and gave him a look. "You're stalling. What's wrong? Aren't you happy I'm actually able to do something?"

"I'm more pleased than you can imagine," he simply said.

"Then, what's the problem?"

"How would you feel about attempting to shoot the bow and arrow again?"

I blinked. "Are you kidding me? I'm more likely to end up shooting *you* than hit the actual target."

"We'll see," he said, his face a blank slate. "You clearly have your punch down pat. Why don't we attempt to ramp your training up another notch?"

"I mean, if you really think it's a good idea..."

"I do," he said, before I could finish the thought.

We didn't go outside for this one. No one said why, though I had a sneaking suspicion everyone thought we would be attacked the second we stepped outside the walls of the Academy. Instead, Rourke rustled up a target to set up inside the library, while the others continued practicing in the training room.

He handed me the bow and arrow without comment, but I couldn't help but note that he did take ten large steps away from me. This whole thing had been his idea, but he was clearly still worried I might take out his eye.

Not that I could blame him.

With a deep breath, I lifted the bow and stared hard at the wooden target at the other end of the library. Again, every enemy's face was plastered on the target in my mind's eye. They had stalked me. They had hurt my friends. They had tried to destroy this Academy. I took a deep breath in through my nose and loosed the arrow.

It soared across the library in a perfect arc, the sharp end hurtling straight into the center of the target. With wide eyes, I dropped the bow to the floor and stumbled back.

"Wait a minute," I mumbled. "That can't be possible."

Rourke moved up behind me and handed me another arrow. His eyes were flickering as he searched my face, and my stomach flipped over a thousand times. Leaning forward, he dropped his gaze to my chest again and breathed deeply through his nose.

"Do you know what you smell like, Norah?" he asked in a voice that was almost a growl.

Shivers coursed along my skin as I stood there frozen in place, every single part of me sparking with a delicious need that made it difficult to think about anything else. All I could do was whisper in response, "No."

"You smell like fire and rain, but also like frost and starlight." He leaned in closer, pressing his nose to my hair. It took all my self-control not to shudder against him. "Like wildflowers and crackling leaves and the damp earth after rain. I didn't notice it until now, but you smell like every season in this realm."

"I don't understand," I whispered, still frozen to the spot. "What does that mean?"

"It means you're different. And it means that something has been hiding the truth from all of us." He held up the necklace and closed his fingers around the pendant. "You won't be wearing this ever again."

CHAPTER TWENTY-FOUR

"What's this all supposed to mean?" I asked as I perched on the library table. After my little demonstration with the bow and arrow, Rourke had rounded up the others. He'd filled them in on what had happened, and every single one of them was now looking at me with expressions of pure awe.

Which...I didn't really understand. All I'd done was shoot an arrow into a target, something many of the other students had already done.

"What did your mother say to you when she gave you that necklace?" Kael asked quietly as he rubbed his jaw.

Frowning, I thought back to that moment. It was difficult to remember her exact words. My emotions had been running high, and my step-dad had just slammed his fist into the wall beside my head. I'd been a lot more focused on getting the hell out of there than on my mother's words about the necklace.

"She said something about wearing it always," I said with a shrug. "I assumed she just meant that it would be her way of always being with me, even if not in person. Why? What's the big deal about my necklace?"

Kael exchanged a look with Rourke, who dangled the necklace just in front of his squinted eyes.

"Autumn fae possess a particular set of skills," Rourke murmured as he spun the necklace this way and that. "One of them is imbuing objects—and even living beings—with our will. If, for example, a fae wished to keep your true power hidden beneath an illusion of incompetence, a necklace that you wore around your neck might be one way to do it."

I narrowed my eyes. "Incompetence?"

Finn let out a lighthearted chuckle. "Let's just say that it could make it seem as though you had trouble with some basic fae skills. Like the ability to dismount a horse without tumbling into a heap."

At his words, I shot daggers at Liam with my eyes. "You told him how clumsy I was on the horse."

Liam laughed, holding up his hands and shaking his head. "Darling, he didn't need to be told. Your two left feet are pretty much infamous by now."

"Wait a minute." I frowned. "I don't have two left feet. Have you ever seen me dance? I'm actually pretty good at it, and my balance has always been spot on. It's something I've worked on my entire life."

Finn arched his eyebrows. "That's actually a really good point. We *have* seen you dance, and you're more than good at it. So, then isn't it strange you aren't able to do anything fae-like without stumbling around everywhere?"

He had a point, one I'd never considered until now. I'd never been clumsy. In fact, I'd been the opposite. Dancing had given me a strong core and serious flexibility. There was no reason why I should be tripping on my feet every time I tried to take on a fae challenge.

"So, what are you saying? That *necklace* made me terrible at being a fae?"

"It's the only thing that makes sense." Rourke dropped the necklace onto the table as if it had a disease he might catch if he stood close to it for too long.

"She was able to heal Kael," Finn argued. "And don't forget she shifted off of that cliff."

"Both of those things happened when she was terrified," Rourke replied. "Her strong emotions must have temporarily overcome the power of the illusion."

I held up my hands, glancing from Rourke to Finn to Kael and then to Liam. "Okay, guys. It's a good theory, but my mother gave me this necklace. My very human mother who knows nothing about any of this."

"Maybe she knows more than you thought," Rourke said quietly. "Regardless, the necklace has clearly been masking your true powers. I think everyone will agree that it's best if one of us keeps ahold of it for now."

"But why would anyone want to mask my powers?" I asked, crossing my arms over my chest. "That's the part I don't get."

Rourke and Kael exchanged a glance again, and a

silent conversation passed between them. I opened my mouth to demand an explanation, but we were interrupted by the loudest boom I'd ever heard. Frowning, we all glanced up at the ceiling as the overhead lights began to flicker. Another boom quickly followed, along with the heavy patter of rain, so loud that it sounded like a roar.

"Sounds like a storm has arrived," Liam said with a growl. "Summer didn't get any of this bullshit until the Courts divided, and now it sounds like the whole sky is being torn in half."

They strode over to the windows to stare at the dark sky. Thick, angry clouds were rolling over the Academy, and the sharp crackle of lightning split through the night, so bright that it was almost blinding. Rain poured from the pregnant clouds, slanting sideways from the heavy wind that howled through the Academy grounds.

Shivering, I hugged my arms to my chest and backed away from the windows. Something about the storm felt wrong and unnatural, almost as if it were a prelude to battle.

"Are you alright?" Rourke asked, his hand whispering against my back before it fell heavily to his side. "I realize this is a lot to take in."

"I just don't understand what any of this means," I said. "Why would my mom have a necklace to hide my fae abilities?"

"Maybe she knew what you were all this time," he said quietly, shifting closer to speak into my ear, his breath soft against my neck. "Maybe she didn't want you to return to Otherworld."

I turned toward him, searching his golden eyes with my own, hoping I could see the truth in his gaze. "Do you really think that's it?"

His eyes flickered, and he glanced away. "I'm not sure. There are...other things to take into consideration. Either way, I hope that you will accept my apologies on the behalf of the Autumn fae. We are not all like Redmond."

"I know." I gave him a soft, timid smile. "Because there's you."

I swore his chest puffed up at least a little.

I continued, "But I've met some other Autumn fae who were...well, I wouldn't call them friendly, but they seemed as if they were actually concerned about my safety, too. In fact, they warned me not to have run-ins with other Autumn fae."

"There are some rebels amongst the Autumns," he said, his face clouding over. "They do not agree with Viola's reign, or her assassination on Marin. They are wanted fugitives, who prowl near the edge of the woods between the Autumn lands and the free territory."

"Oh." My eyes widened. "Do you think that's who I met that day in the woods?"

"Could be," he murmured.

Another boom shook through the sky, and Liam hurried over to my side.

"There's something out there," he said in a low voice. "We need to make sure all the changelings are in the training room. It's the safest place for them. No windows."

"Something is out there?" I asked, my heart thumping hard against my ribcage. "What is it?"

His mouth was a grim line. "It looks like more Redcaps. They're prowling back and forth just beyond the watch towers, which are currently empty. We thought it would be safest for everyone to hole up in the main building, but that means we have no one outside to hold them off."

I glanced at the windows, remembering the horror that had taken place in the Great Hall. "They'll just crash through the windows. There's nothing to stop them from getting inside."

"That's right." Rourke's jaw flickered as he clenched his teeth. "Which is why we must get everyone into the training room. *Now*."

CHAPTER TWENTY-FIVE

Torches flickered as we all scurried into the 'safety' of the training room. My instructors were right. It was probably the safest place in the Academy, but it almost felt as though we were trapping ourselves inside with no hope of an escape. There was just the one set of double doors, now blocked by a growing mound of chairs. There were no windows. No escape hatches. One way in, and only one way out.

Head Instructor Alwyn stood at the front of our worried huddled group, a sword clutched tight in her right hand. "Listen up. Now, I know you all are scared, but there's no reason for worry or concern. Some Redcaps have been spotted on the grounds, but they won't be able to get to you in here. All we have to do is sit tight until morning, and then we can go back to our regularly-scheduled lessons."

Griff stood from the back of the room, his hands

curled into tight fists. "Shouldn't we be out there fighting them instead of hiding in here like a bunch of cowards?"

"I agree." A third-year girl with short dark hair moved to Griff's side, crossing her arms over her chest. "I know the first-years are just starting to learn how to fight, but us third-years have been practicing for months."

"Your safety is paramount," Alwyn said. "No changeling will engage in fighting these creatures. We have a team of guards stationed just outside this door. Even they won't be going out into the storm to face these beasts."

"This is ridiculous," Griff said with a scowl. "First, we let the Autumn fae attack us and now this."

Alwyn's eyes flashed. "We have reason to believe the Autumn fae are the ones controlling these beasts. They're using them to attack our Academy."

Gasps rang out through the gathered changelings. I whirled toward Rourke, who didn't look the least bit surprised. He gave me a nod and dropped his voice to a whisper. "I wondered as much. It's unusual for the Redcaps to be so interested in our Academy. I thought something else might be at play here, and clearly Alwyn believes the same."

A heavy thud sounded outside of the barred doors, and the room immediately fell into a tense and uneasy silence. The thudding continued down the hall until it sounded so close that it might as well have been coming from within the training room.

Steel sang through the silence, and roars rose up in

response. My heart began to hammer as all I could do was stand there and listen to the violent sounds of battle. I held my breath and backed up so that I was pressed tightly against Liam's chest. I didn't care if Alwyn saw. I didn't care if she scolded the both of us until the ends of our days. I needed to feel his strength against me. I wanted to feel his warmth when every cell in my body felt brutally cold.

Screams and shouts and roars and whines sounded over and over and over again. There must have been at least five Redcaps outside the door, and it sounded as though our fae guards were no match for the brutality of the beasts. Liam curled his fingers around my arms, and his soft breath whispered against my neck. If I closed my eyes, I could disappear into his embrace and block out the horror of the night.

But I didn't want to block it out. Our guards were out there dying. And we were in here doing nothing to stop it.

Slowly, timidly, I pulled away from Liam's comforting embrace and strode to the front of the room where Alwyn was staring at the door with pure horror plastered on her usually stoic face. He didn't try to stop me. Instead, he gave me a nod, his eyes shining with something akin to respect.

"We should do something," I said, clearing my throat so that everyone could hear me over the roar of the battle. "They're dying out there."

Alwyn glanced over her shoulder, frowning back at me. "What do you expect to do, Norah? You're incompetent. Your failed challenges have been evidence enough of that."

Wincing, I forced myself to keep my eyes locked on her face. She'd put voice to everything I'd always feared about myself. Incompetent. Helpless. Worthless. But if there was one thing I'd learned in these past weeks, it was that those fears were unfounded.

I fisted my hands. "I'm actually not. I may not have had much formal training yet, but I have raw power. We all do. Not to mention the second and third years who have had some training. All of us together could easily fight these Redcaps."

"Like you did in the Great Hall?" She shook her head and let out a heavy sigh. "I appreciate your willingness to help your fellow fae, Norah, but the safest place for all of you is in here."

"Yeah, I don't think so," I continued. I wasn't going to give up that easily. "If the Redcaps kill our guards, then they'll aim all their strength at those doors next. After seeing them in action, I don't think that will hold them off for very long. They had the element of surprise in the Great Hall. None of us were ready to fight then. We know they're here now, and we've got enough weapons to go around."

"I agree with Norah," Sophia said, striding up to stand by my side. For a moment, all I could do was stare at her in alarm. She hadn't spoken to me since she'd told Redmond about Bree. A part of me wanted to hate her, but another part of me understood why she did what she did. In her eyes, all Redcaps were murderous creatures who had killed her friends. She didn't know Bree was different. How could she?

"Same." Griff joined us, along with Lila and several of the third-year students. Soon, every single changeling had moved to stand beside me, along with my four instructors who looked torn between giving me a high-five and hiding me away in a corner somewhere.

Alwyn ground her teeth and glanced at each of us in turn. "I shouldn't go along with this, but something tells me I won't be able to stop you even if I say no. Just…be smart. Don't do anything stupid. And let us instructors take the lead."

As the battle raged on outside, the changelings worked together to move the chairs away from the door as quickly as possible. When we'd finally moved the last barrier out of the way, Alwyn unlocked the door and threw it open.

The first thing I saw was blood. Lots of blood. The sight of it clogged my throat. A fae guard's body flew through the air and landed before us all with a heavy thud. We gasped and stumbled back, and a large mangy paw edged around the door. Liam threw himself in front of me as the Redcap slowly strode into the training room. It took one long sniff around the room before opening up its massive jaws and roaring in rage.

Everyone sprang into action. At least a dozen changelings and instructors launched themselves at the creature, swords and daggers swirling through the air. Many of the blades made contact, and soon enough, the creature had fallen to the floor. Those fierce beady eyes slid shut, and its last breath whooshed from its lungs.

We all stood staring at the creature. No one was certain what to do next.

"Is that it?" asked Griff.

His answer came soon enough. Four more beasts hurtled into the training room, each one storming toward a different cluster of changelings. Everything turned to chaos in that moment.

Liam pressed a sword into my hand, and as soon as my finger curled around the hilt, it was as if the weapon became an extension of my hand. I whirled through the air, slicing the blade at the creature I fought. There were five of us on one. Me and my four males against the Redcap. Liam's roar was as loud as the beast's, and Rourke moved with a speed and grace that matched the most glorious of ballets.

My sword found its mark several times, and after what felt like hours, the beast finally fell.

I whirled on my feet to face the next creature. It rose up before me, its brilliant blue eyes latching onto mine.

Blue eyes. Not black or red, but blue.

My heart shook, and I stumbled back.

No. It couldn't be. Bree would never do such a thing.

Alwyn's words rang in my ears. The Autumn fae were using the Redcaps, controlling them as a way to launch violent attacks on the Academy. Somehow, they'd found my friend, and they'd sent her here to kill me.

She hesitated, the deafening roar in her throat dying away. Out of the corner of my eye, I saw Griff charging toward her. Before I could think, I jumped in the way, holding up my hands as his sword swung toward me.

"No!" I shouted. "Stop!"

His sword froze in mid-air, only inches from slicing right into my neck. Griff frowned, stumbling back, his eyes locked on Bree's monstrous form behind me.

"Get out of the way, Norah," he said, voice harsh and full of furious emotion. "That's the last Redcap here. It needs to be killed."

"No," I said, more quietly now. "This isn't a Redcap. It's Bree, my oldest friend from home. She doesn't deserve to die."

Griff shook his head, letting out a harsh laugh as he gestured at the carnage in the hallway. "She helped kill all those guards, Norah. I get that you think she's still the human girl you knew back home, but she isn't. She's a monster now, one who is attacking us. Now, move out of the way."

"No. She didn't do this." My heartbeat was so loud in my ears that I could barely hear my own voice. "The Autumn fae are controlling her, just like Alwyn said. She would never attack anyone. Not on her own."

"You're talking about a Redcap, Norah. *A Redcap.*"

With tears in my eyes, I turned my back on Griff to look up into my friend's beastly face. Those eyes. They were so sad, so tortured. Bree was in there, somewhere deep inside the Redcap's monstrous body. She didn't want to be doing this, and I knew exactly how I could make this all okay.

"I've got a plant that can heal you, Bree," I whispered to her, reaching up to press my shaking hands against her rough fur. "You don't have to be like this anymore. Just...turn back into your real form so that they can see what you really are. Human."

"Norah," Kael said quietly as he inched up behind me. "I don't think you're going to get through to her, not when she's like this."

But I could only ignore him. "Bree? Come on, I know you can do it. I've seen you change back before. Remember?"

Tension filled the room as I faced off against the beast. We stood in the center of the training room, her sorrow-filled eyes locked on my face. She shuddered beneath my hand, and for a moment, I thought I'd made her realize what she needed to do.

But then her body stiffened, and she jerked her head toward a distant sound that none of us could hear but her. And then she was off, charging down the hallway. Griff let out an exclamation of surprise. He rose his sword and took off behind her.

"No!" I screamed, but it was too late. More changelings joined him in the chase. At least a dozen of them took off to hunt down my friend.

With a heavy sigh, I fell to my knees and pressed my hands flat on the cold floor. Bree was in there somewhere. I knew it. Even after everything that had happened, I couldn't give up on her. She'd certainly never given up on me. But I didn't know how to get through to her. Not when the Autumn fae were controlling her mind, and not when my fellow changelings were desperate to shove their swords into her throat.

There was nothing I could do now. As hard as I'd tried, I'd lost.

CHAPTER TWENTY-SIX

The thunder continued to rage outside while the changelings returned to their rooms. Several of the instructors had taken off to track down Griff and the others. They'd likely chased Bree out into the storm, and no one should be running around in the thunder and lightning, least of all right now when the threat of the Autumn Court was so fresh and so real.

And me? Well, all I wanted to do was plop face-first onto my bed and stay there for hours. I'd been trying so desperately hard to undo what had happened to Bree that horrible night in Manhattan. The attack on her had been my fault. I'd attracted the Redcap, and it had turned its ferocity on Bree because of that.

But it felt as if I'd only made things worse. I'd brought Bree to the attention of the Autumn fae, and they'd sought her out. To control her, to make her do things Bree would never do.

I would never get a chance to heal her now. Her mind and soul would be lost to the beast.

There was a soft knock on my bedroom door, and I merely groaned in response, my face still smashed onto my pillow. I didn't need to look up to see who it was. When the fae eased onto the bed beside me, the scent of frost and mist filled my nose. A delicious scent, but one that reminded me of what I'd been trying to do.

And how horribly I'd failed.

"Bree was still in there, Norah," Kael said quietly, rubbing his palm gently across my back. "I could sense it."

"So could I," I muttered into the pillow. "That's why I tried to stop Griff from attacking her."

"He won't get to her," he said. "In beast form, she's far too fast."

With a sigh, I rolled over to stare up into Kael's darkly handsome face. "I know. But that doesn't change anything. It's impossible for me to cure her now. She's gone. Right back into the hands of the Autumn Court."

Kael reached out and traced a soft thumb against the curve of my neck. Despite everything that had happened, despite the sorrow that was building up inside of me, his touch soothed me in away that nothing else could. Fire sparked in my gut, and everything within me sighed. I breathed in the wintry scent of him.

"There's one thing I know about you, Norah," he said, voice gruff, eyes shining with something I didn't quite understand. "And it's that you're a fighter. I've said it from the beginning, and it's why I thought you might turn out to be a Summer fae. You have a fire within you. Don't let what's happened to Bree douse that in any way. Instead, let it feed your flames."

With a sigh, I reached up and weaved my fingers through his. "I don't see how fighting can change anything."

"Don't you?" He arched his brows. "Here's a little training lesson for you. Suppose there is an enemy, one who has decided his mission is to destroy your home and everyone within it. He keeps launching attacks, and he has taken something of great value to you. What do you do in response?"

"Honestly? I don't know." I shook my head and glanced around the room, spinning through the various possibilities in my head. But I wasn't a strategy genius. I didn't know about fights, about wars, about battles. All I knew was my despair, my anger, and my desperation to save my friend. "Punch him in the face?"

Kael chuckled. "And what else would you do?"

Frowning, I pushed up from the bed so that we were now sitting face-to-face. Our hands were still locked together, and I swore it felt as though our hearts were beating in sync. "I mean, in an ideal world, I'd track him down, take back what's mine, and make sure he can never attack me again."

"Well." He smiled. "Wouldn't that be something?"

With a heavy sigh, I flopped back onto the pillows. "Yes, it would be something. It's too bad that's impossible."

"And why is it impossible, Norah?" he asked.

At the tone of his voice, I sat upright once again. "Because I'm assuming that attacking the Autumn Court is pretty much *not* syllabus-approved. And also against the laws of this realm."

"You're correct." He leaned forward now, dropping his voice to a low growl. "Do you know what else is against the laws of our realm? Planning assassinations. Attacking our Academy. And controlling the beasts. They've wronged us. They've hurt us. They have tried to take the most important thing in the world from me, and for that, we *will* be retaliating."

My heart lurched, and I sucked a sharp breath in through my parted lips. His words made my head spin, not to mention the fierce expression on his face. Kael was usually so calm and collected, so in control of his emotions, but something had set him off, revealing the true depths of his soul.

"What have they tried to take from you?" I barely whispered.

With a growl, he said, "You."

My breath caught in my throat, and I leaned forward to wrap my arms around his neck. His lips were soft and gentle, but his kiss was full of hunger. There was something so fierce about him underneath that cool exterior, and it made every cell in my body come alive.

Our kiss deepened as he pulled me onto his lap. My legs spread wide, encircling his waist. His thumb caressed my neck and a thousand tiny sparks lit up my skin, much like the stars that I once saw dance in his eyes.

I wanted nothing more than to stay here like this and to feel his mouth explore every inch of my skin. But there was something whispering in the back of my mind, a voice I couldn't hush even if I wanted to. With a heavy sigh, I pulled away from him, my entire body shaking with the yearning I felt deep within my gut.

"We can't," I whispered. "Not right now. Not when Bree is out there. All I keep thinking about is how scared and alone she must feel. I want you to do what you said, Kael. Retaliate. Force an attack on the Autumn Court. And I want to come with you."

CHAPTER TWENTY-SEVEN

As soon as there was a break in the clouds, we set off to the Autumn Court. Alwyn had insisted the first-years stay behind, but she'd allowed me to tag along after a strange whispered conversation with my four instructors. She had cast me curious glances after that. Not for the first time, it felt as though they were hiding something from me. Something that had to do with my powers and the necklace and maybe something more.

So, our rag-tag group consisted of eight instructors—three had stayed behind to keep an eye on the first-years—as well as Alwyn, me, and thirty second and third years. It was pretty much the entire Academy, and we were marching straight toward the Autumn tree line. Half the changelings and instructors had swords while the other half had bows and arrows.

Ironically enough, I was one of the rangers. It was the only way my four fae males would allow me to come along. I was to stay on my horse in the back, and

I was not to dismount under any circumstance. Rourke would stay by my side, since he was also strong with the bow. The others would go in with their swords, a fact that made me more than a little uneasy.

If any of them fell in this battle, I'd never be able to forgive myself. While I knew they were forging forward in this fight in order to save the Academy, I was here to save Bree.

When we finally reached the tree line, the heady warmth of summer fell away. It was replaced by an eerie chill, one that sunk deep into my bones. The leaves rattled in the wind, and trees creaked as they bent. We had truly entered Autumn now. There was no turning back.

And, I couldn't help but notice, we were being watched. I could *feel* several pair of eyes on me.

"Rourke," I said in a whisper, almost too low to hear over the heavy thud of the horses' hooves. "I think we've been seen."

"Oh yes," he said. "We were seen awhile ago. No one enters or leaves the Autumn woods without it being noted, and they would have seen us coming down the path, even though we were technically still in the free territory. The real question is, *who* saw us? A rebel? One of the villagers? Or was it one of the Court's scouts? If it's the latter, we will end up fighting very soon."

I shivered. I was ready for this. Or, at least I thought I was. Still, that didn't mean I wasn't nervous and maybe a little bit afraid. We had no way of knowing what we were walking into. We had no idea how many Redcaps they currently had in their control. And, we didn't know how big their army was.

Autumn fae were notoriously secretive. They'd kept the total number of their Hunters a private matter over the years. They could have hundreds. Or even thousands.

We could be walking straight into a trap.

A horn sounded in the near distance, and our little changeling army slowed to a stop at the edge of a forest clearing. Rourke motioned to Kael, who was near the front. He shook his head, a signal that we should move no further.

"Does it bother you that you're about to fight your own Court?" I asked.

"I suppose it doesn't matter now if everyone knows, not after what we're about to do this day." Rourke gripped the reins tighter in his hands. "I've always been against Marin's assassination. For several years, I joined the rebels. I left when I realized they were making no true difference to the fate of the Courts. I thought I could perhaps make more of an impact at the Academy instead. Make things better. Like they used to be."

"You? A rebel? But you're so..."

"Yes?" He arched an eyebrow. "What is it that I am, Norah?"

"Well, you seem like the kind of person who's a stickler for the rules."

"I am when it counts."

In the distance came the sound of galloping hooves. Kael let out a low whistle and flicked his hand in a series of signals that he'd drilled into our heads before we'd left the Academy. We were supposed to spread out now, archers hiding behind the trees in the back while the swords in the front formed a line the Autumn fae would not be able to cross.

With a shaky breath, I nocked my arrow and did my best to hold it steady before me. At any minute, Autumn fae would charge into the clearing, and I'd loose my first shot. It was a battle that might very well be the first of many to come. We were starting something here. Something that could lead to war, but there was no escaping it. Not if we wanted to survive.

Three horses charged into the clearing and slowed. Redmond, who had escaped during the assassination attempt against Alwyn, sat in the middle with a mangy-haired fae hidden just behind him. The other two horses were manned by fae soldiers, their golden eyes blank and emotionless.

"Good afternoon, changeling warriors," he called out. "I assume you're wondering why I've ridden out to meet you instead of charging into battle against your pitiful army."

Frowning, I glanced at Rourke. His eyebrows were furrowed as his focus intensified on Redmond. The Autumn fae was up to something, and I had a feeling we weren't going to like whatever it was.

"Just spit it out, Redmond," Alwyn said coolly from where she stood at the front of the pack.

He turned her way and shook his head. "It truly is a shame that an Autumn fae such as yourself would be so bold as to attack your own kind."

"That's pretty rich coming from you," she countered. "If I'm remembering correctly—and I am—you were the one who attempted to assassinate me in my own home."

"My apologies." He gave a sarcastic half-bow. "Merely a means to an end."

"What do you want, Redmond?"

He snapped his fingers at the fae warrior to his right. "I'm here to make a trade. A simple transaction. If you agree, then we will cease all attacks on your Academy."

Rourke stiffened. He leaned forward and whispered something into his horse's ear. And then his horse slowly began to edge in front of me.

The movement caught Redmond's eyes. His gaze flicked through the red-and-orange brush until it zeroed right in on me. "Ah. There she is."

Alwyn twisted her head to see who he was talking about. Alarm flittered across her golden features. "No, Redmond. I'm not giving you one of my changelings, no matter what you offer in return."

"You won't give me one of your changelings?" He arched an eyebrow and pointed a long and slender finger at me. "Or you won't give me *that* one?"

I frowned.

What the hell is going on?

Was he really that angry that he hadn't gotten the chance to question me about Bree? That didn't make any sense. He'd gotten her, after all. He no longer needed me to tell him where she was, so why was his focus on me?

"You're not getting *any* of them," Alwyn said. "And that includes Norah."

"Just think," he said as he slid to the ground. The mangy fae who had been hiding behind him still had her back turned our way, and one of the fae warriors began to help her down from the horse. "If you hand Norah over to us, none of your other changelings will have to die. There are how many of them here? Roughly thirty? Think about it, Alwyn. You're an intelligent fae. What is one life compared to thirty?"

"We need to get you out of here," Rourke hissed into my ear. He leaned over to grab my reins, but my eyes had locked onto the mangy fae. She'd half-turned as she'd dismounted, and her profile was achingly familiar. Pixie features, sharp tiny nose. Her dark hair was matted and dirty, but it was hers.

"He has Bree," I said, making no attempt to keep my voice low. I swatted away Rourke's hands. "Redmond has Bree."

A cruel smile spread across Redmond's face. "That's right, my dear. I have your precious Redcap friend."

Suddenly, Redmond had a dagger in his hands and his arm around Bree's throat. He pulled her to his chest, and he slid the dagger against the pale skin of her neck. My heart flipped as I stared at her, my whole body clenching with anger and pain. Her eyes were so hollow, and a deep purple was etched into her face. She looked terrible, as if she'd spent the past year stuck inside a tiny prison with nothing to eat but dirt.

"Norah," Rourke said in warning.

"You have your chance to save your friend," Redmond said. "That's what you wanted, isn't it? Come with me, and I'll give her over to your mate, though I honestly can't tell which one that is anymore. On the other hand, if you refuse, I will slice her neck. A quick death, though I hear it's painful."

I didn't even have to think about it. Without a moment's hesitation, I swung my leg over the side of the horse and dropped onto the hard-packed dirt. Rourke let out a shout and tried to grab my arms to pull me back. I jumped out of the way, giving him a sad smile.

"I'm sorry, Rourke."

And then I shifted away from him, disappearing into darkness. When I reappeared, I stood only inches from where Redmond held Bree captive. The look of delight in his eyes when he saw what I'd done made me want to punch the living daylights out of him. But I needed to bide my time. I wasn't planning to go down without a fight, but he still had his blade pressed against Bree's neck.

"Well. Looks like you made the right choice." His smile was razor sharp and cruel.

"Norah, what the hell have you done?" That was Kael's anguished cry, a sound that broke my heart in two. I couldn't bear to look at him, to see those star-studded eyes doused by the pain of what I'd done.

"I swear to god I'm going to kill him." That was Liam, and he'd begun to stalk across the clearing, the veins in his neck rippling with fury.

"Ah ah," Redmond said. He dug the blade deeper

into Bree's neck. "Your mates need to stay right where they are."

"Liam, stop," I said, eyes wild, heart pounding in horror when blood pooled on Bree's skin. "He'll kill her."

Liam came to a sudden stop, though I could tell it took all his self-control to stay where he was. His entire body shook, and his fists were turning the color of blood. At the edge of the clearing, Kael had fallen to his knees. Rourke was staring right at Redmond, his arrow nocked and ready to be released. Finn was nowhere to be seen, a fact that unnerved me. If he tried to stop this…I didn't doubt that Redmond would follow through on his threat.

"Okay." I held up my hands and shot Redmond a strained smile. "Look, here I am. Time to let Bree go. Time to let all of them go."

"Take her," Redmond shot over his shoulder at the other fae warrior.

The male jumped down from his horse, his golden cloak billowing behind him. In an instant, his arms were around me, pinning my wrists together behind my back. Irritation flickered through me at his rough handling, but I stayed still and steady. I didn't want to give Redmond any reason to believe that I wasn't going to go through with my promise.

"Got her," the warrior said.

But Redmond still held his blade against Bree.

"Happy now?" I said to him. "You've got me. Let go of Bree."

I was beginning to have a bad feeling about this.

My enemy was a master of deception with a heart filled with cruel, cold rage. I'd made the ultimate sacrifice, but as those glittering eyes pierced my soul, I feared that none of us would survive.

His lips twisted into a strange smile. "Is that really the best idea? I mean, she *is* a Redcap. Didn't she kill some Academy guards?"

My heart began to beat wildly in my chest. "You said you would let her go if I came with you. An exchange. Me for her. That's what you said."

He lifted his shoulder in a shrug. "Perhaps that was a mistake. I can't very well release a monster, especially not in the midst of our precious changelings. What would our Queen think if she knew I'd allowed them to get attacked?"

I narrowed my eyes, and my breath began to expel through my nose in rapid bursts. My entire body shook, and I could barely think straight as the realization of what I'd done washed over me. Redmond had never intended on letting Bree go. He was going to kill her, right in front of me. And then he'd probably move on to me next.

"Let. Her. Go!" I squirmed against the warrior's tight grip. He was strong, but a strange kind of power had begun to sing in my veins, one that made me feel almost invincible. I just needed a little more time…

Another set of footsteps crunched through the dead leaves. Another Autumn fae warrior came up behind us, and he had—

He had Finn. An unconscious Finn who had a bruise the size of the sun on his face.

"Found this one lurking around back there. What do you want me to do with him?"

"We'll kill him, too," Redmond said. "It will be a good training lesson for the changelings here. Don't rebel against the Courts, or else there will be serious consequences."

I'd had enough. I couldn't stand here trapped while Redmond threatened everyone I knew and loved. The power boiled inside of me, and a furious fire consumed my soul.

"Let them go!" My voice was so loud that the ground beneath our feet began to shake.

And with those words, the strange, wild power of my soul spilled out into the forest clearing. A harsh and bitter wind whipped around me, and the intensity of my command made me fall to my knees. A sharp, splitting pain ripped my skull in two, but I gritted my teeth against the force of it.

I wanted to free Bree. I wanted to free Finn. And I wanted these Autumn fae to go down.

Everything exploded into chaos. Bree vanished into thin air, followed quickly by Finn. The horses began to buck and kick, slamming their massive hooves into each of the Autumn fae warriors. Redmond screamed and stumbled back. His horse knocked him sideways where he fell into a heap on the ground.

I had to glance away when the hooves began to pound into his body. Bones snapped. Blood painted the orange leaves. The sound of it would haunt me to my grave.

Squeezing my eyes as tight as I could, I dug my

hands into the dirt and clung on to the earth. The wind that whipped around me had become a tornado of leaves and magic and pain, and I could no longer hear anything but the heavy roar of my blood.

Suddenly, the wind died. The leaves fluttered to the forest floor, and my heavy breathing was the only sound in the world.

I looked up. Bree knelt before me, her eyes shining beneath a face caked in dirt. She took my shaking hand in hers and squeezed.

"You saved me, Norah." Her voice caught, and the tears in her eyes began to spill down her cheeks. "You saved us all."

CHAPTER TWENTY-EIGHT

I felt as though I'd been run over by a bullet train. Soon after Bree had come to me in the forest, I'd passed out. When I woke up, I was in the infirmary again, back at the Academy. The early morning light streamed in through the open window, and my four fae instructors were dotted around the room, each and every one of them fast asleep.

I cleared my throat.

Immediately, Liam was on his feet, glaring at every shadow in the room as if he were in search of an enemy to fight. I let out a laugh and coughed, rubbing at my throat. Even my vocal cords felt as if they'd been tossed through a blender.

"Take it easy." Kael pulled his chair closer to my bed and took my hand in his. "You're going to have some pain for a little while."

"Where's Bree?" I asked. "Is she okay? Did you get her away from the Autumn Court?"

"Bree is fine," he said gently. "We brought her back to the Academy and administered the Winter Starlight. She's recovering well. We think she'll pull through this thing."

Relief whooshed out of me, so intense that it felt as though my entire body was spent.

"I don't even understand what happened." I glanced up at Rourke, who hovered behind Kael. "I'm sorry I shifted away from you like that."

His jaw clenched. "You scared the shit out of me. Try not to do it again."

"But what exactly was *it*, anyway?" I turned my gaze toward Finn. He was perching on the edge of the bed, perfectly balanced. "Where did you disappear to? I didn't know you could shift."

"I *can't* shift," he said with a light laugh. "You did that, Norah. First, you shifted Bree out of there, and then you did it for me. We ended up right next to Rourke."

My mouth dropped open. "But..."

"And then," Rourke added, "you turned the horses on their masters. They, ah...well, no need to go into the gory details. Let's just say that Redmond will no longer be a problem for us."

My face blanched. "Honestly, I don't think that was me. I didn't want them stampede to him to death. Besides, I barely even know how to ride a horse properly, let alone how to control them. *With my mind.*"

"And that's why you have the hangover from hell, darling," Liam said with a grin. "You used some seriously powerful gifts that you've never practiced before. It's going to leave you feeling like shit until you master them. Just...how about you not volunteer yourself to get killed next time you want to try them out?"

My head still felt muddled, like I was missing an important piece of the puzzle. "So, shifting belongs to Autumn fae and Winter fae. And the whole horse control thing is also Autumn. Does that mean I've been Autumn all this time?"

Kael and Rourke exchanged that weighted glance again, the one that said far more than words.

"Come on, guys. You clearly have a theory. I think it's only fair to tell me after I saved all your asses."

Liam barked out a laugh. "That's my girl."

"Don't encourage her," Rourke said before nodding at my Winter instructor. "Want to take this one, Kael?"

Kael sighed and rubbed his chin. "We have reason to believe that you have not one but four seasonal gifts. You seem to possess traits and abilities of the Summer fae, but the same can be said for Winter, Spring, and Autumn as well."

I blinked. "Is that a thing?"

"Not usually," Finn said in a singsong voice. "It's very rare. In fact, Marin was the last fae to possess the power of all four seasons. Some might find you a threat, which is why I believe you were given that necklace. It was meant to protect you from harm. Hide the powers, save the girl."

"Some fae would find it imperative to take you out of the equation," Kael said in a growl. "In fact, it seems as though Redmond had a pretty good idea of what you are somehow. I'm not sure what he intended to do with you, but it wouldn't have been good."

Chills swept down my spine. "So, you're saying that I, the girl who couldn't shoot a bow and arrow on her first day, can actually wield powers of all four seasons? You guys are playing a trick on me, aren't you? You thought it would be funny to mess with me after I completely ignored everything you told me to do during the battle."

Finn chuckled. "Only a Spring would think we were playing a joke on you."

"And only a Summer would get so boiling mad that she made a tornado out of thin air," Liam added.

"Only an Autumn would be devious enough to trick Redmond into thinking you were going to go along with him." When I opened my mouth to argue, Rourke smiled. "Don't try to play it otherwise. You were never going to go down without a fight."

"And only a Winter," Kael said, chiming in last, "would find enough strength in the darkness to shift two others out of that forest clearing without even touching them with her hands."

"You're not just one type of fae, Norah," Liam said. "You're all of them. And the four of us pledge to stand by your side no matter what."

"Because the storms have only just begun," Rourke said. "We may have won this fight with the Autumn Court, but there will be many more to come."

The saga continues in...
A Song of Shadows
(Otherworld Academy, Book Two)
Available Now

Also by Jenna Wolfhart

Otherworld Academy

(Reverse Harem Fantasy Romance)

A Dance with Darkness

A Song of Shadows

A Touch of Starlight

A Cage of Moonlight

A Heart of Midnight

A Throne of Illusions

Order of the Fallen

(Reverse Harem Fantasy Romance)

Ruinous

Nebulous

Protectors of Magic

(Reverse Harem Fantasy Romance, completed series)

Wings of Stone

Carved in Stone

Bound by Stone

Shadows of Stone

Demons After Dark: Temptation

(Paranormal Romance, completed series)

Sinful Touch

Darkest Fate

Hellish Night

Demons After Dark: Covenant

(Paranormal Romance, completed series)

Devilish Deal

Infernal Games

Wicked Oath

The Fallen Fae

(Epic Fantasy Romance, completed series)

Court of Ruins

Kingdom in Exile

Keeper of Storms

Tower of Thorns

Realm of Ashes

Prince of Shadows (A Novella)

The Paranormal PI Files

(Urban Fantasy/Paranormal Romance, completed series)

Live Fae or Die Trying

Dead Fae Walking

Bad Fae Rising

One Fae in the Grave

Innocent Until Proven Fae

All's Fae in Love and War

The Supernatural Spy Files

(Paranormal Romance, completed series)

Confessions of a Dangerous Fae

Confessions of a Wicked Fae

The Bone Coven Chronicles

(Urban Fantasy, completed series)

Witch's Curse

Witch's Storm

Witch's Blade

Witch's Fury

About the Author

Jenna Wolfhart spends her days tucked away in her writing studio in the countryside. When she's not writing, she loves to deadlift, rewatch Game of Thrones, and drink copious amounts of coffee.

Born and raised in America, Jenna now lives in England with her husband and her two dogs, Nero and Vesta.

www.jennawolfhart.com
jenna@jennawolfhart.com
tiktok.com/@jennawolfhart

Printed in Great Britain
by Amazon